# Solace in Scandal

## KIMBERLY DEAN

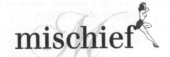

mischief

*Mischief*
An imprint of HarperCollins*Publishers*
77–85 Fulham Palace Road,
Hammersmith, London W6 8JB

www.mischiefbooks.com

A Paperback Original 2013

First published in Great Britain in ebook format by
HarperCollins*Publishers* 2012

Copyright © Kimberly Dean 2013

Kimberly Dean asserts the moral right to
be identified as the author of this work

A catalogue record for this book is
available from the British Library

ISBN-13: 9780007553457

# CONTENTS

| | |
|---|---|
| Chapter One | 1 |
| Chapter Two | 22 |
| Chapter Three | 45 |
| Chapter Four | 65 |
| Chapter Five | 90 |
| Chapter Six | 120 |
| Chapter Seven | 140 |
| Chapter Eight | 160 |
| Chapter Nine | 182 |
| Chapter Ten | 212 |
| Chapter Eleven | 234 |
| Chapter Twelve | 250 |
| Chapter Thirteen | 275 |
| Chapter Fourteen | 296 |
| Chapter Fifteen | 319 |
| Chapter Sixteen | 341 |
| Chapter Seventeen | 359 |

# Chapter One

Peace and calm.

Elena concentrated on her breathing as she tried to quiet her mind. She'd thought she'd been making progress towards that goal, but she'd worked too long on her dissertation today without taking a break and the effects were showing. She should know better by now.

Focusing on the tall trees across the lake, she inhaled fresh air through her nose and felt her lungs expand. It was that mystical part of the day when the sun sat fat on the horizon behind her and the night waited impatiently to move in. The beauty of nature surrounded her: a dense forest, a secluded private lake and aromatic earth. Tranquillity was practically reaching out to her, if only she could let it in.

Exhaling, she bent at the waist and planted her hands flat on the dock in front of her. The position lifted her hips and she felt tightness in her hamstrings. The disquiet in her mind was seeping its way into her body. She lifted her hips higher, pushing carefully against the tension, before dropping flat and arching up in the Cobra pose. The position opened her chest and released a kink in her back.

'Mm,' she sighed.

The leaves were heavy on those trees, she noticed, changing colour but not yet ready to fall to the ground. Some looked as if they were hanging on for dear life.

She knew how that felt.

*Serenity.*

From the prone position, she swung back up into Downward Dog. She blew the air in her lungs out through her mouth until her chest ached. The need for oxygen brought her concentration back and she relaxed her shoulders. She couldn't let herself get worked up like this. She was safe here, hidden and protected. She'd come here to find answers to all the questions running around inside her head, but she'd found something she hadn't expected. A haven.

In this, the unlikeliest of places.

Twisting into Warrior pose, she looked up to the house. It sat perched atop the hill behind her. The trees around it had been cleared, making sure there were no distractions from what was important. Wolfe Manor.

The sun was level with it now, making it almost glow, but it was impressive no matter the lighting. Built in the late 1800s, the residence was a testament to human ingenuity and grit. Thick limestone walls stood four storeys high, with a stair tower taking precedence out front. Turrets overlooked the corners, while two larger-than-life wolf statues guarded the main entrance. It was a mansion that made a statement.

Although that statement was being questioned after recent events.

Elena stretched her arms high overhead and felt the knot in her shoulder pop. It was ironic how she felt here, on this property. By all rights, she should feel anger and distrust. Outrage. The Wolfe family represented everything that the 99 per cent hated – greed, opulence, excess and unscrupulous entitlement. Yet while the manor stood proud and stately, its owners' house of cards had finally fallen down. Deservedly so.

Although their deception had nearly pulled her down, too.

She shivered in the cooling breeze. She didn't understand that kind of ruthlessness. What made some people think they were better than others? That they could push the less fortunate down and not allow them to breathe? She never would have come here if she hadn't been in dire straits, but Leonard had offered her refuge. The Wolfes wouldn't be needing the residence for some time, and the lake house had been empty before she'd moved in. Only the staff and groundskeepers remained.

Dear, sweet Leonard. Out of everyone, he understood

the position she was in and how powerless she felt. He'd come to her rescue when she'd needed him most, and she didn't know how she'd ever repay him.

She could start by taking better care of herself.

She focused on the lake again as a breeze stirred her hair and was surprised to see a thousand diamonds glittering back at her. The sun was glinting off the water now, making it appear as if lights were dancing on its surface. The beauty was undeniable. Pure, spiritual and unexpected.

Yet that wasn't what made her breath catch. 'What?'

The air. It had just changed.

It felt heavier ... pricklier ... It was subtle, but the hair at the back of her neck rose. It was the sensation one got in a quiet old house when a floorboard squeaked and nobody else was supposed to be home.

She was being watched.

The awareness destroyed her rhythm and the inner peace she'd fought so hard to obtain. Her first thought was 'predator'. She scanned the area around the lake and the rocky beach behind the dock. What roamed these woods? Coyotes? Red foxes? Deer? She couldn't think of anything dangerous, yet the feeling remained.

She finished the sequence she was going through, but turned reflexively when she felt the air behind her snap. 'Ah!'

A man.

Looking up, she spotted the source of the disquiet.

Suddenly, the benefits of the yoga disappeared. She recognised him on sight. Alex Wolfe. In the flesh. The most dangerous predator of all.

'Oh, dear God.' *What was he doing here?*

Their gazes connected and she felt a jolt. Even with him hundreds of yards away and up the hill, she felt his attention and it was solely on her.

Her stomach tightened and, for the first time, she felt the chill of the evening. With the sun going down, it was getting brisk. Too brisk to be wearing a skimpy sports bra and thin pants. She pressed her hand against her bare stomach, but was surprised to find her skin hot. Tingly.

Sweet heavens, he was something.

His hair was shorter than it had been in the last newspaper picture she'd seen of him. So short, it was almost spiky. His face wasn't as clean-shaven, either. He had that rough stubble that only male models and movie stars could seem to pull off.

And, apparently, billionaire felons.

His expensive shirt and pants fit him impeccably, yet the power radiating from him wasn't only the power associated with wealth and status. The disgraced entrepreneur was lean and chiselled. He'd done more on the inside than read books.

Warning signs flared in Elena's head, and she knelt to pick up her yoga pad. She'd learned to listen to her gut. The exercise usually sped up her pulse, but right now it was racing. He shouldn't be here – or she shouldn't. Her hands felt clumsy as she rolled up the springy foam. When she looked up again, he was still staring. Energy crackled in the air between them. She could feel the charge all the way down to her bare feet, and her toes curled against the sensation.

Sex. The man practically radiated it.

Goosebumps rose on her skin.

She didn't know him. She'd never even met him, but she wasn't stupid or naïve. Men found her attractive, and she recognised lust when she saw it. From the way he braced his hands against the marble railing and leaned towards her, the wolf seemed ready to pounce. When he uncoiled and folded his arms across his chest, her stomach sucked in even further.

'Mm,' she whimpered. She also recognised when the feeling was mutual.

Her response was inappropriate – unthinkable – yet she couldn't stop staring at him. Her nipples tightened, and she held her yoga mat against her chest to hide her reaction. The sun was gone, and its trailing streaks of light were dimming fast. The noises coming from the woods were getting louder. The chirps of crickets … the hoots of owls … A hot shiver went down her spine, and she started moving to the lake house.

She'd come here to retreat, but had she just ended up in the wolf's den?

One last time, she cast a glance up towards the main

house. Her ponytail swung over her shoulder with the movement and she felt the caress of a hot look slide down her bare back. He was still there. Watching. Wanting.

Quickly she moved inside and locked the door.

\* \* \*

*Two hours earlier*

The sun was glaring as the man walked out of the nondescript concrete building. The rays bounced off the grey walls and matching parking lot, piercing his polarised sunglasses. For some reason, the sun was brighter outside the walls than inside the complex where he'd spent the last eighteen months. Brighter, warmer and more intrusive. He headed straight into the blinding light, his Salvatore Ferragamo wingtips clipping a steady beat that was soon drowned out by the crowd outside the fence.

A commotion arose when they saw him. People called out his name and shifted to get better views. Cameras clicked and microphones were thrust through the holes in the chain-link fence.

'Mr Wolfe, what are your plans?'

'Do you feel remorse?'

'Where is your grandfather?'

Moving efficiently, his driver opened the back door to the Bentley and blocked their view. 'It's good to see you, Mr Wolfe.'

'Thank you, James.' He slid onto the supple leather seat, but the click of the closing door made his muscles tense. He didn't like that sound any more.

He placed the stack of spiral-bound notebooks on the seat beside him and stretched his legs as the Bentley headed for the opening gate. Into the mouth of the lion … The crowd swarmed the car, shouting and fighting for the perfect angle. The sun's rays bored through the tinted windows into the back seat. The man-made glass couldn't stop Mother Nature, but it obstructed the flash-bulbs of the cameras that tried to pry into his private space.

The paparazzi couldn't see him, but he settled his hand protectively over the stack of notebooks as the Bentley kept a slow and steady pace through the horde. There were more important things to think about, like the buttery softness of the leather seat, the brightness of that big yellow sun and the loud clank of the gate as it closed behind the moving car.

*Freedom.*

Awareness and caution coiled inside him like a snake. After eighteen months, he was finally a free man, but he wouldn't unwind any time soon. In fact, he doubted he'd ever totally relax again.

'Don't you worry about this, sir,' the driver said from behind the wheel. 'I'll get us through.'

'I have no doubt.' His voice was raspy from lack of

use. As much as he wanted to barrel through the crowd of gnats, he kept himself contained. Patience. He had it in buckets, although the snake inside him was lashing out.

At last, self-preservation forced the photographers in front of the car to give ground and James was able to pull through and escape. Once free, he dropped the hammer on the gas and the car gracefully picked up speed.

The Bentley probably hadn't been the most inconspicuous choice in the Wolfe garage, but the vultures from the press would have found Alex if he'd left in a city cab. If he was coming back out in the world, he wanted to do it in style and in comfort. He had nothing to apologise for.

The chauffeur turned onto an on-ramp for I-84 heading east. 'You relax now, sir. I put some newspapers and your laptop back there for you. It's only about an hour and a half's drive until we'll be there.'

Alex's gaze snapped to the carrying case on the floor. A computer with the Internet, a connection to everything he'd been denied while he'd been detained. He didn't have to settle for grade-school notebooks any more, but he kept the ones he had secure at his side.

Getting online was tempting, but he remained gazing through the window. There would be time enough for that soon. Right now he concentrated on the passing scenery, fully aware that the Federal Correctional Institution at Otisville was at his back.

He wouldn't think of it any more. It was the future on which he was focused now. Firmly. With steel-like focus. It was time to take back what was his.

\* \* \*

The sun was hovering just above the horizon when, an hour and forty minutes later, the car arrived at Wolfe Manor. Just outside the affluent town of Bedford, New York, the family home was situated on a hundred acres of prime virgin real estate. The gates that closed behind the Bentley as it pulled onto the property were as big and strong as those in Otisville, but the wrought iron here was styled in a pattern of winding ivy and leaves.

More importantly, Ax could control them.

Tall trees crowded the long drive, grouping closer as the Bentley left the main road. The forest soaked up the light, making it seem darker than it really was. At long last, all those trees opened up again in a man-made clearing and the main house rose before them.

'Here we are.' James stopped along the circle of the drive, got out and rounded the car to open the back door. 'Home sweet home.'

Ax looked at the wolves guarding the house's front door and the snake in his stomach curled into a tighter knot. There was nothing sweet about the place. Never had been, never would be.

But the land … He glanced at the grounds, from the manicured lawns and gardens to the woods that stood just beyond.

The front door of the house opened, silent for its size. A silver-haired man in a crisp dark suit bowed in respect. 'Master Wolfe.'

'Leonard.' Ignoring propriety, Ax reached out and shook the older man's hand. The grip was tight and went a moment past what was necessary. 'I see you've kept up the place while I've been gone.'

'Yes, sir.' The butler cleared his throat. 'We've done our best.'

With a nod, Leonard dismissed the driver and closed the front door.

It blocked out the piercing sun, but Alex was ready this time for the inevitable click. He breathed slowly and set the laptop and the notebooks on a side table. Glancing up, he took in the staircase as it loomed above him. He could gain access to anywhere he wanted here, whenever he wanted. Hell, he could sleep out on the balcony if he got the urge.

His shoes clipped along the polished hardwood flooring as he made his way into the main room. Everything was so familiar, from the heavy mahogany furniture to the ornate wall fixtures to the delicate vases with fresh flowers. Familiar, yet foreign. Loved, yet hated.

And right now he hated it with a passion that burned white hot.

11

The snake inside him leaped, attacking with a sudden surge. He swept up a black onyx wolf figurine from the sofa table, turned and hurled it at the wall. It cracked against the fireplace and shattered into pieces as it hit the ground.

Leonard wisely disappeared from the room.

Alex stood with his hands opening and fisting at his sides. He looked at the ceramic shards that littered the floor. 'Damn it.'

Tugging at his tie, he loosened his collar. That would not do.

Looking out of the panoramic window, he stared hard at the lake. Wolfe Lake. Deep and dark. Mysterious and beckoning. He shrugged out of his Savile Row jacket and tossed it over the back of an overstuffed chair. Opening the glass door off the main room, he stepped out onto the balcony.

It was quiet out here. He braced his hands on the balustrade and soaked up the silence until a noise caught his attention. He looked towards the trees. For the first time in months, he heard birds twittering and squirrels chattering. The lake was alive, too. With the sun low on the horizon behind him, the water reflected the rays like countless golden jewels.

A sanctuary. That's what these grounds were. He rolled his head on his neck and felt the fire inside his chest bank just a little.

But then he noticed movement and his chin came up. He looked again towards the water. This time it wasn't a bird or a squirrel.

It was a woman.

On his dock.

On private Wolfe property.

His spine snapped ramrod straight and his fingers dug into the limestone railing. 'What the hell?'

His gaze focused with laser-like intensity on the lone figure. Out there, over the water, a young woman stretched her arms high over her head. She looked like a siren, straight out of Greek mythology. Her loose low-slung white pants fluttered in a soft breeze that also captured the strands of her long dark ponytail. She stood motionless, breathing rhythmically, before gracefully stepping back and twisting at the waist.

She was doing yoga.

Alex stared on in disbelief. She moved fluidly from pose to pose, her body seeming long and lean, even though she was a petite thing. She controlled each movement, each breath and each position. She seemed so calm and peaceful as he stood fuming, enraged by the intrusion of her very presence.

He was about to call out to her, to order her off the property, when she folded in half and planted her hands flat on the dock in front of her. The position lifted her hips in a way that brought to mind only one thing and lust slammed into his body with all the delicacy of a battering ram.

Pure, white-hot and dangerous.

The words died on his lips and his mouth went dry as a bone. He felt like a voyeur, but he couldn't stop watching as she flexed and contorted, the water glittering all around her.

His fingers turned numb around the railing. He hadn't seen a woman in what seemed like for ever. Hadn't talked to one. Hadn't touched one and certainly hadn't made love to one.

Yet this beauty was no ordinary woman.

Hunger swirled around inside him, combining with the anger for a treacherous blend. He didn't know who she was and didn't like that she was here, but he was a red-blooded man. She was a sensual woman and he wanted her underneath him, naked and straining. He wanted to slide into her hot, tight heat.

Most of all, though, he wanted her gone.

He straightened, pulling back his shoulders as irritation won out – but then she relaxed from her exercise and looked over her shoulder. Their gazes connected and he nearly vaulted off the balcony to go claim her.

The air pulsed as their gazes locked. Each breath Alex sucked into his lungs was hot and jagged until she finally broke the connection. She seemed timid then, a scared little rabbit needing safety. She darted to the lake house, and he watched as the lights came on and the shades were pulled.

'Run, little siren,' he murmured. 'You run good and far.'

Turning away from the night, he stalked back into the house. 'Leonard?' he roared.

The ceramic shards in front of the fireplace were gone as if they'd never been. The decorative pieces on the sofa table had been rearranged so no gaps appeared. His manservant floated around this house like a ghost, but he heard things and knew more than anyone suspected.

Anyone but Alex.

'Yes, Master Wolfe?'

The butler appeared from the hallway behind him, making Ax turn. His eyes narrowed. He'd become sensitive to having people at his back. 'When did we start renting out the lake house?'

'We haven't, sir.'

He let one eyebrow lift. 'There's a woman staying down there. She was just doing yoga out on the dock.'

The butler glanced at the watch on his wrist and nodded. 'Yes, that is her routine. She finds the exercise challenging to the body and soothing to the mind.'

Alex cocked his head. 'You seem to know her very well.'

'We're friendly.'

Friendly. It wasn't the first word that came to mind when Alex looked at her.

He reached up to rub his stiff neck. He trusted Leonard, but the man was being deliberately evasive. 'Who is she?'

'Her name is Elena.'

Elena. He rolled it around on his tongue. It fit her. Elegant yet exotic. 'I gave you specific instructions to protect the house during my absence. By whose authority is she here?'

The Feds and the Securities and Exchange Commission regulators were still on his ass. They wanted access to his home, his businesses, his charities and his financial dealings. He'd already given them a pound of flesh, but the hungry zombies wanted more. He'd be damned if he'd give it to them.

Leonard cleared his throat. 'By my authority, sir.'

That gave Ax pause. 'Is she family?'

'Not quite, sir. She's the daughter of a previous employer. Miss Elena arrived needing shelter and a place where she could work on her studies. I didn't realise you would be returning so soon. Your ... timeframe ... was moved up so quickly.'

So quickly? A year and a half? Alex felt frustration bubbling up inside him. Apparently not even his butler was immune to a pretty face and a shapely ass. What did they really know about this woman? She used an old connection and they just let her inside the gates? She could be a reporter working undercover. She could be a wronged investor looking for revenge. Hell, she could be a gold-digging tramp who'd set herself up at the right time and place, hoping to latch onto the family's remaining fortune in a time of weakness.

He dragged a hand through his hair. 'Get her out of here. Tomorrow at the latest. I want the woman gone.'

'But Master Wolfe, I –'

'In the morning, Leonard. That's all the time I'll give her.'

The butler schooled his face and bowed stiffly from the waist. 'As you wish. I'll deliver the message to Ms Bardot personally.'

He was practically out of the room before the words sank in. Alex turned on his heel, away from the window. 'Bardot?'

He moved towards the kitchen when Leonard didn't return and they nearly collided in the hallway. 'Did you say "*Bardot*"?'

The butler gave a concise nod. 'Yes, sir. She's Randolph Bardot's daughter.'

Alex rocked back on his heels. Randolph Bardot, his grandfather's business partner. Son of a bitch.

He quickly backtracked. 'That can't be. I've met his wife and kids. They're only teenagers.'

And that seductress down the hill was a woman in every sense of the word.

'That would be his second wife, I believe. I was employed by Mr Bardot when Miss Elena was a young girl, before your grandfather hired me away.'

Alex stepped back to look through the picture window. The lake house was still locked up tight, but light glowed, warm and inviting. He wandered closer. Randolph Bardot's daughter. If he needed any more reasons to stay away from her, that one went to the top of the list. How much did she know?

Leonard followed quietly at his side. 'She's had a difficult time of it, too, since … the event. When she came asking for help, I couldn't turn her away. I thought you'd understand.'

Oh, Alex understood all right.

It was hell when you discovered the depths to which the people closest to you could sink, and her father and his grandfather had been hand in hand on their way into the gutter. He thought of her sweet face and her delicate form.

He scanned the lake again. The glittering jewels were gone, and the surface had turned dark and impenetrable. 'It's not good that she's here, Leonard,' he said quietly.

'I realise that now, sir.'

'I'll need to look into this.'

'Of course, but in the meantime?'

Ax didn't waver, but he decided to give an inch.

'She can stay.' Until he figured her out, she could stay.

\* \* \*

Elena's breaths were short as she braced her hand flat

18

above the lock on the door. Darkness peeked through the window panes and she yanked the short curtains into place. She backed away until she found herself in the bedroom. She tossed the yoga mat into the corner and began to pace about the room.

Alex Wolfe. The Ax. He was back. He was here. How could that be?

She dove for the bed, opened her laptop and quickly fired it up. It didn't take long to find the story. It was the lead on every news site she opened. 'Alex Wolfe Freed' read the headline.

'Good behaviour?' she coughed. '*Good behaviour?*'

The man had been at the heart of the biggest Ponzi scheme in the past century. He and his grandfather – and her father – had lied to people, wiped out life savings and driven businesses into the ground. Hundreds of millions of dollars were gone. She pushed the laptop aside so hard it slid across the bed. She dove to catch it before it could tip over the edge.

'That's all you need,' she reprimanded herself. That laptop held all the work for her dissertation, the doctoral degree that would help her support herself and her mother and get them out of this mess. Neither of them had the funds to buy a new one now.

She rolled off the bed and began pacing again but finally stopped and leaned against the doorjamb. She wasn't a pacer; she did her best thinking when all was still. She needed to slow down and consider what this change in her situation meant.

Alex Wolfe had been released early from prison. He'd done his time and served his sentence. He was a free man, back on his own property. She stroked the door's oak trim. This was his property.

She couldn't stay here. There was no way.

But where would she go?

Another shiver went through her, significantly cooler than the one she'd felt outside under his watchful gaze. There was nowhere else she could find the peace to do her work. It had become impossible back in the city. Once her classmates at NYU had figured out who her father was, the attacks had been relentless. The harsh accusations, the scathing stares, the stalking by the press …

She moved to the living room, wrapped herself in the afghan on the sofa and huddled into its cushions. The leather was Wolfe property; the afghan was hers.

She never would have come here if she'd thought she'd cross paths with the man. He was supposed to be behind bars for another six months, and she'd thought *that* sentence was too lenient. Most people had agreed with her.

'Damn overcrowding,' she hissed. How could the prisons be overcrowded when people who should be locked up were still roaming around free? People like his grandfather Bartholomew.

Angry with herself for going down that path, Elena

tugged the ponytail holder out of her hair and ran her hands through the long strands. She was scared, she had to admit it. What was she going to do? She wasn't ready to go back outside that wrought-iron gate, back into the real world. It had chewed her up and spit her out. She'd come here looking for answers.

But she didn't have them yet.

She glanced around the cottage. She'd grown accustomed to the quiet little place in the month she'd been here. The house was nicer than the one she'd grown up in, but that's how the Wolfe family thought of it ... as a bungalow. Yet it fit her needs. It had given her the seclusion she'd needed to lick her wounds and concentrate on her studies. Leonard had even given her free access to the library in the main house. She'd only ventured out to Bedford a few times for groceries or to the post office. She'd grown comfortable here.

She didn't feel so comfortable any more.

She pulled the afghan higher around her shoulders. God, the man was something. Enigmatic and provocative. She hated to think what he'd be like up close. All that danger and power and mercilessness rolled into one.

She shifted on the sofa, rubbing her thighs together unconsciously. She knew she should run, but the way he'd looked at her ...

What was she going to do?

This changed everything.

# Chapter Two

Elena slid another box into the trunk of her old-model Malibu and wondered for the hundredth time if everything would fit. She'd been up most of the night worrying and packing. It was amazing how deeply she'd settled into the lake house in such a short time. She hadn't collected much stuff, but it had expanded somehow. It was certainly strewn about. She was still finding NYU mugs in the kitchen and peppermint lipgloss in the bathroom.

She wedged the box tighter against one that was already stowed. The space was going to be needed. She hadn't packed up the second bedroom yet, the one she'd used as her office.

Her heart dipped.

She hated the thought of leaving before she was done. She'd made so much progress here. Things were organised the way she wanted, and the solitude allowed her to concentrate. That might not sound like much, but putting together a dissertation was a major undertaking.

22

Getting rid of distractions had helped, especially the kind she'd been facing.

She hoped another move wouldn't set her back.

She rubbed her hand over the ache in her chest. She might be leaving, but she didn't know yet where she was going. She couldn't return to her apartment in the city. She'd broken the lease there when she'd left to escape the paparazzi. It was going to take time to find another place she could afford where she could have some semblance of privacy. If she didn't finish her work on time, her PhD would be in jeopardy. That would affect her job offers and her ability to pay off her student loans.

She blew out a long breath. It was circular thoughts like this that had kept her up all night. She scowled towards the main house. And that was *his* fault. Her life was in turmoil again, all because an over-indulged rich man had charmed the legal system into going easy on him.

She found nothing charming about the situation whatsoever.

Wiping her hands, she turned back towards the lake house. She flinched when she heard someone coming down the hard-packed dirt drive. The footsteps were clipped and precise and heading straight for her. With the lid of the trunk lifted, she couldn't see who was approaching but she had a good guess.

She braced herself.

'Ms Elena?'

Her spine relaxed. 'Leonard.'

The butler came to an abrupt stop near the taillights of the car. A frown settled on his face when he saw her half-filled trunk, and the expression deepened the age lines around his mouth. 'You're leaving?'

She gave him a sad look. 'It's time. I appreciate the hospitality you've shown me these past few weeks, but I can't be a burden any longer.'

'You aren't a burden.' He folded his hands together primly, but she could see how tightly he held them. 'There's no need for you to go.'

'We both know there is.' She nodded towards the second-floor balcony of the manor. It was empty now. It had been empty every time she'd checked it since she'd caught his intimidating boss watching her from that perch.

He followed her wary look. 'Yes, Master Wolfe is home, but that doesn't mean you have to leave. He gave his permission yesterday eve for you to be on the property.'

Elena regarded her old friend. She was sure that permission had come at a cost, but had it been for him? Or would she be paying? 'That's a kind gesture, but I can't accept.'

She wouldn't take charity from a Wolfe. She couldn't stomach it, and she couldn't trust it.

'At least stay until your studies are complete. It would

be a shame to throw everything into a tizzy when you're so close to getting your degree.'

A tizzy.

Elena nearly laughed. Wasn't everything in a tizzy already? Alex Wolfe had shown up on his doorstep when she'd expected him to be in a prison cell for another six months. She'd never dreamed he'd be walking around a free man. Or that he'd be watching her … 'I'm not comfortable here any more, Leonard. You've got to understand.'

'I do understand, dear, but I think it would be more uncomfortable for you outside the manor's gates.' Those hands that he kept so tightly clenched together finally separated, and one waved up the road. 'They're already here, Elena.'

They. She didn't need more description than that.

The media.

Her head whipped around. From her vantage point down by the lake, she couldn't see any difference. She wouldn't have been able to tell anything was amiss from the manor either. The drive from the main gate was a good quarter of a mile long and lined by trees, yet she could picture the news vans parked along the shoulder of the main road. She envisioned their antennas lifted and all the reporters milling about. She was well acquainted with the scene, because the same thing had happened outside her apartment in New York.

'You're safer here,' Leonard insisted. 'The gate will hold them out and their cameras won't be of any use with the woods blocking their view.'

But they would try. Tension grabbed the muscles between her shoulder blades. Like hungry rats, the news outlets would swarm the place. They'd scurry around looking for openings and bits of tasty info.

'That won't stop them,' she said.

'If they trespass, the Bedford police will respond. They've already been notified.'

So the police would drop everything to respond to a call from an ex-con, but they hadn't done anything when she'd called them for help. Her hands clenched into fists at her sides. At its worst, she hadn't been able to set foot outside her building without reporters and cameramen harassing her. One had even grabbed her in the stairwell, putting his hands on her and trying to stop her for an interview. Who knew that a pothead on the third floor would be more helpful than the NYPD?

The tension between her shoulder blades crawled up her neck. She didn't want to go back to living like that. After that incident, she hadn't been able to leave her apartment without fear. She'd been trapped inside, as much a prisoner as Alex Wolfe, only he'd had a trial.

'How many are out there?' she asked. Maybe she could just zip through.

'Too many. The sheriff is already having to deal with

the congestion. They've set up outside the main gate and down the road. You'd have to drive right through them.'

Elena looked at her white Malibu. It was nondescript, but on Wolfe property that made it stick out like a sore thumb. Even if she put on a scarf and sunglasses, they'd track down her licence plates before she made it to Bedford.

The thought made her queasy. They couldn't catch her here. Not with *him*.

The tension swept outwards through her entire body. The tabloids would explode if they caught wind that she'd been a guest. The Bardot and Wolfe names were already twined in a sick, unbreakable knot. If they somehow put her and the younger Wolfe together?

She braced her hand against her car. *Oh, God.*

'They don't know you're here. At least, not yet.' Even Leonard's hands were twisting together now, all semblance of composure gone. 'It's a big place. The grounds and the house are such that you wouldn't have to interact with Master Wolfe if you don't want to, although I think the two of you should commiserate. The press have villainised him even more than they have you.'

That's because the man *was* a villain. Her only failing was genetic. She'd been born the daughter of a man without a conscience.

She turned towards the lake. No jewels gleamed from its surface today. If anything, the view was haunting. A morning fog clung to the low-lying regions. The mist hovered over the water like vapour rising off a cup of hot coffee, while trails of it wove through the trees.

It was as if even the grounds knew that the darkness had returned.

She let out a tight breath.

Would the situation outside the gates be even worse? It would be harsher, she knew. Inside the gates, there was quiet. Seclusion, even if it was in the belly of the monster.

'Maybe I can leave late tonight,' she murmured, fighting the decision she knew she had to make.

'They'll be here around the clock until they get what they want. You know that, and those individuals assigned to late-night hours will be even hungrier.'

Hungry for the illusive big 'get', only she had nothing to tell them. She hadn't been involved. She didn't know where the money had gone. She looked at those leaves still clinging to the trees, trying to withstand the weight of the dew that had settled on them.

'All right, I'll stay,' she said quietly. She had no other choice. 'But only until things settle down.'

Leonard's shoulders relaxed and his hands loosened into their customary position. 'Wonderful. You don't know what a relief that is to me.'

He stepped up to the trunk. 'Let me help you unload.'

'That's all right. I can do it.'

She didn't want to make more work for him.

'Nonsense.' He'd already lifted the heaviest of the boxes from the trunk, and she stepped aside to let him pass.

Elena wasn't sure she'd made the right decision. The manor looked as vacant as it had for the past month, but she could feel the new presence. The aura of the place had changed. The sleeping giant had awakened. She could feel it in the air; she could sense it in the ground beneath her feet.

Alex Wolfe wasn't a person who could be ignored, but she was going to do her best to avoid him. She needed to avoid them all.

Movement caught the corner of her eye, and her head snapped around. A curtain in a far window of the mansion swayed before settling back into place.

A shiver ran through her, and she grabbed a box from the trunk. The weight pulled heavily at the muscles in her arms, but she lugged the clothing back into the cottage and set it on the floor near the door. 'Over here is fine, Leonard.'

His white eyebrows pulled together. 'Do you want Marta to help you unpack?'

'No need.' She nudged the box closer to the wall with her foot. Unpacking wasn't part of her newly formed plan. She wanted to be ready to go, in case she needed to leave fast.

The butler finally bowed at the waist. 'Then I'll send her down with some hot chocolate for you.'

Elena did her best to work up a smile, allowing him that much. She knew he only wanted to help. Hot chocolate had been the treat he'd given her when she'd been young and in his care. 'That would be lovely. Thank you so much, Leonard, for everything.'

By the time she'd lugged in everything from her car, Marta was on her doorstep with a warm mug of cocoa. Elena accepted it gratefully. It had always managed to soothe her, but fixing her current problems would be a challenge. She sipped at the sweetness as she looked out of the window to the lake. All was still out there. No breezes disturbed the haze, and the water looked like black glass. Deep and endless.

It gave off the oddest looming sensation.

She wandered over to the side window and peered up at the manor. He'd been watching her again. She'd felt it. The back of her neck had prickled, yet a warm spark had run through her veins.

A warm, pulsing spark.

She shook her head. This was wrong. All wrong. She couldn't stay here, yet she couldn't leave. She was locked in the wolves' den, trusting the alpha male to protect her from the danger outside the lair.

It was insane. How had she gotten herself into this mess? What was she supposed to do now?

Jerking away from the window, she walked about the house. The mug cooled in her hands as she considered her options. There weren't many. She found herself in the doorway to her office. Piles of paper were strewn about, notes were taped to the walls, and her laptop waited for power. She was so close to making a breakthrough, she could feel it.

Yet it was all so close to slipping through her fingers.

She rolled her tight neck. Alex Wolfe had ruined everything.

She slammed the mug down on the coffee table, pivoted on her heel and headed to the door. She'd found a sanctuary, but all she wanted to do right now was run.

'Damn that man,' she hissed.

Why did some people have it so easy, while others had to plod and fight?

Moving past the dock, she headed for the trail that rounded the far side of the lake. She'd taken it several times over the past few weeks. The silence and the remoteness might help calm her down, especially the remoteness.

She couldn't shake the feel of him watching her.

The air was thick as she settled into a brisk hiking pace. There really was no air stirring today. The leaves weren't rustling and the lake wasn't lapping against the shore. It created an odd combination of serenity and foreboding. The mist in the air gathered around her, and it was only then that she realised she'd forgotten to put on a jacket. She wrapped her arms around herself and kept on going. The trees had closed in behind her and she could no longer see the manor bearing over her. Its overwhelming presence had disappeared.

With it, some of the tension left her shoulders.

Leaves crackled under her feet as she walked along the well-worn path, but even that noise was muted. The dampness coated the undergrowth, too. Lifting her chin, Elena inhaled the moist coolness. It was like a different world out here, and all of it was Wolfe property.

Maybe they really could avoid each other. The plot of land was huge, even for the wealthy who lived in this part of the state. Celebrities and politicians, writers and music-makers were all neighbours in this upscale New York county.

What must it be like to have that kind of wealth? To be able to live in a place that pushed the rest of the world away?

Who would risk all of this to take more?

She shook her head. Maybe she could hide away here for a little longer, at least until she had some answers and finished her dissertation. In the end, that was what was most important, her education. Her life plan. She doubted she'd ever be wealthy like this, but she needed to be able to support herself.

She ran a hand through her hair and found it heavy with dew. Out here, things seemed clearer. Calmer. Yes, she could do it. She needed to hunker down anyway. She'd dive into her work and ignore whoever or whatever was happening up at the main house. It didn't concern her anyway.

At least, that was what she kept telling the reporters.

Movement suddenly caught her eye, cutting her thoughts short. She stopped in her tracks, all her attention focusing on her surroundings.

Had that been a deer?

She peered through the openings in the trees. The leaves that still clung to the bushes made it difficult to see. With the dreary day, everything was blending. After a few hopeful moments, she decided she'd missed the sighting and continued.

That was when she heard the rustling on the path ahead of her.

Or was it further up the hill?

She stopped again and tried to quiet her breaths. One thing was for certain, she wasn't alone in the forest.

Listening hard, she picked up the gentle crunch of leaves and twigs against the softened earth. Her gazed darted around the area until she saw a figure moving through the trees. It wasn't a deer. It was walking upright along what must be another path, higher on the hill. A man.

Her breath caught in her throat.

Someone was stalking around the property and, from the way he moved, he was up to no good. For a moment, he stepped into a space where the branches were bare

33

and she could see him more clearly. He wore a fleece jacket with the hood pulled up over his head. His feet were swift and sure as he moved along the path with hardly any sound.

Elena took a step back.

Someone was trespassing. A photographer? A journalist? Something worse?

Her heart began racing.

Quickly, she evaluated her options. He hadn't seen her yet, or at least she didn't think so. She looked down at herself. At least she wasn't wearing bright colours. She rubbed her hands over her arms. Goosebumps dotted every patch of exposed skin, and a shiver ran down her spine. She glanced back along the path. She could go back the way she'd come, but she was on the main hiking trail around the lake. If others were sneaking around in these woods, she might run into them.

Her teeth worried her lower lip. There was a fishing spot down on the shore not far from where she was. From there, another trail ran along the edge of the lake. She could move quickly there. It was the shortest path back to the cabin.

She watched the figure and the silent way it moved until the grey sweatshirt blended in again with the fog. Keeping her steps quiet and her breaths quieter, she took the fork in the path that would take her away from him. Only the way was slick. She slipped once and had to catch a sapling to keep from falling. By the time she made it to the clearing along the lake, her legs were quivering.

She stepped over a fallen log and bent at the waist to take a steadying breath.

It choked off in her throat when she realised she wasn't alone.

The man with the hood stood lakeside with his back to her. As she watched, he side-armed a rock over the surface. It skipped three times before sinking into the dark depths.

Elena took a cautious step back and then another. She'd just about made her escape into the trees when the heel of her boot knocked against the fallen log. She tensed as the man turned.

And she found herself looking into Alex Wolfe's silver-grey eyes.

She sucked in a surprised 'Oh!' but then her mouth snapped shut. Fight or flight? The question struck her like a blow on the chest, but she found she could do neither. Instead, her heart beat like a drum-roll as she stared into the face of the man she'd sworn to avoid.

She waited for him to say something, but he watched her as warily as she watched him. He was taller and bigger than her, by nearly a foot and way too many pounds, all of them muscle. He had the fleece zipped close, and it emphasised the lean mass of his body.

Elena's mouth went dry. He was an impressive figure, yet nothing could have prepared her for the astuteness in those silver-grey eyes. It was like looking into the eyes of an actual wolf.

A hungry, sexual wolf.

Her entire body gave one delicious pulse. There was so much to see in those eyes. Hunger, anger, determination and desperation – but the emotions were there for only a moment. He blinked and, when he looked at her again, it was as if shutters had come down over his soul.

Only the hunger remained.

That was the one thing he couldn't hide, and a muscle in his jaw ticked. He wasn't happy to see her or he wasn't happy that she'd seen him.

It was difficult to tell which.

She pressed her lips together, unsure of what to say. 'Hello' would just sound stupid. 'I'm sorry' was better, but she refused to say the words to a man who had more to apologise for than anyone she knew. In the end, she just nodded. She started to turn away, but he moved then, pushing off his hood.

His hair was mussed. Without the hood, the shadow of his dusty beard seemed darker. Those silver eyes were still bright, and that face … It was a face that had graced magazine covers from *Fortune* to *Business Week* to *GQ*, but if he photographed well, he was even more beautiful in person.

Her stomach squeezed, but this time the sensation was deeper and more resounding.

God, why did he have to turn her into mush? Why couldn't he be smelly and hideous? It felt like a betrayal to be so attracted to him.

She wanted to step forward. She made herself take a step back down the trail instead.

'Wait.'

Her gaze snapped up to his face. The word had been soft, but the authority made her even more aware of him.

He reached for the zipper on his fleece. 'You're cold.'

He shrugged the hoodie off his shoulders before she knew what he intended to do. Stepping forward, he held it out to her. She looked at the offering. It was such a simple gesture. Nothing flashy or inappropriate, but, like her attraction to him, she didn't want it.

Yet looking at the jacket made her unbearably aware of the chill that had seeped right down to her bones. The low-hanging fog had coated everything – her clothes, her skin, her hair. Unlike him, she hadn't dressed for a hike. Her boots were flats, but more for fashion than for traipsing along the underbrush. They were zipped over her skinny jeans, and her lightweight sweater didn't provide much warmth. It clung, but its three-quarter sleeves didn't fully cover her arms. She shivered as she looked at the fleece he was holding out to her. Her wrists ached and her fingers felt numb.

'You can give it back to Leonard when you're done with it.'

He watched her, those entrancing eyes becoming more guarded. Who was the wild beast being tamed here?

Elena was proud, but she wasn't rude. She was freezing, and they both knew it.

'Thank you.' She took the final step forward that put her in reach. She stayed there only long enough to take the jacket. He was watching, so she sorted out the hood and the arms. Swinging it around her shoulders, she pushed her hands into the sleeves.

A fierce shudder went through her when she felt the warmth.

The heavy sweatshirt material felt soft and substantial. That alone would have been enough, but it still held his body heat. Her hands began shaking more as she realised just how cold she was. Her fingers were clumsy as she tried to catch the zipper. The two of them stood uncomfortably, feet apart, as she tried to start the metal tab. He'd just moved towards her when it caught. Shying away, she yanked the zipper all the way up to her chest.

It was only then that she realised another tell-tale sign she'd been giving off. Her face flared. Her nipples were hard. Their outline was clear against the light blue sweater she was wearing. The dampness made the material even more clingy, and the chill didn't help her condition. The hard peaks were still obvious with the bulky sweatshirt covering her.

Her chin snapped up, but his head came up much more slowly.

He'd seen. Obviously, he'd seen.

When he finally dragged his gaze to her face, the heat was back. It smacked into her like the air coming out of an oven on a cold winter's day.

Elena wanted to be angry and offended, but then she saw how he looked in his hiking boots, jeans and grey T-shirt. He didn't look like any billionaire she'd ever seen before. He looked like lust felt. Helplessly, her gaze scraped over him. The T-shirt was the soft kind that took the shape of whatever it was draped across, and there were all kinds of arcs and valleys she wanted to explore more. His biceps were thick, and his shoulders were wide. His chest was powerful, tapering down to a narrow waist. As she watched, the dampness in the air seeped into that dry material and the delineation of his muscles and tendons became more defined.

As did his masculine nipples.

Her mouth watered, and she jerked her gaze away. The heat in her cheeks was now a raging fire. It was time to go. With a nod, she dipped her head and turned. She didn't look back as she walked shakily down the path that ran along the lake.

The chill coming off the water was worse, even though the air stood like bated breath. She tugged the hood up over her head and pulled her hands into the sleeves. The hoodie was way too big for her, yet the extra material was appreciated. It hung down to her thighs and bundled her up.

She shuddered again, the warmth almost hurting.

Giving in, she glanced over her shoulder. She was disappointed to find he'd turned away. Another stone went skipping along the surface of the lake. He'd forgotten her as quickly as he'd noticed her.

The ball of heat building in her belly turned hard. That was the Wolfe she expected.

Tucking her chin against her chest, she watched her steps as she hurried back to the cabin. The time it took to get back was less than half what it had taken to round the lake to the fishing spot, but it seemed like for ever. Stepping inside, she quickly closed the door behind her so the heat couldn't escape.

'Darn it,' she hissed.

Her shivers were constant now, and she stomped her feet. She walked over to the thermostat and turned the heat up another five degrees. The hoodie might have warmed her core, but her feet were cold. She pulled off her boots, but her jeans were damp, too. With fumbling fingers, she unzipped them and pushed them to the floor.

Her shivers were becoming shudders that had her teeth clacking. She scurried to the bed, jumped in and pulled the covers up to her nose. The cocoon felt cosy and safe. Burrowing deeper, she waited for the warmth to come. Even her insides were trembling.

Problem was, she didn't know if it was from the cold or from running into *him*.

'What was he doing out there?' She'd thought she'd been safe that far out on the property, but she'd somehow managed to run into the very person she was trying to get away from.

She'd dreamed about that encounter every day for practically the past two years. It was what had kept her up last night, worrying and obsessing, but once it had been upon her, none of it had gone the way she'd imagined. She'd thought there'd be angry words. Tears and more lies.

Not *that*.

The cold knot in her stomach gave way to confusion.

All she could think about was the heat that had been in his eyes. Her eyelids drooped as she remembered those fascinating eyes, that gorgeous face and all those emotions that had quickly been shut off. A pretty exterior for such a flawed soul.

Another shiver went through her and she rubbed her legs together, trying to generate heat. She got more than she expected when the borrowed hoodie chafed high on her thighs. A gasp escaped her lips, and she went stock still. It only made her more aware of the garment that held her body, wrapping around it like a lover.

She took a shaky breath and smelled a musky cologne, faint yet powerful. His scent.

Rolling onto her back, she stared at the ceiling. He was a callous man; she couldn't forget that. Look at how many investors he'd betrayed. Look at the way he'd just turned his back on her. Her nostrils flared as she took another potent drag. Her hips rolled ever so slightly, testing the sensation again.

'Mmm,' she hummed helplessly.

The ribbed material at the hem created the sexiest of caresses, and her fingers clenched inside the sleeves of the fleece.

She knew he was dangerous, yet he'd given her the very shirt off his back.

How was she supposed to process that?

Her teeth sank into her lower lip. The heater cranked steadily, creating a soothing purr. Fatigue was pulling at her. That, and something else. The tension that she'd sustained all night was shifting into something just as powerful and maybe more profound.

Her body relaxed deeper into the softness of the bed. Warmth was finally settling over the room. Instead of the bite of a chill, she now felt the softness of the sweatshirt against her bare arms. The hood kissed the side of her neck, making it arch. The teasing was gentle, but it surrounded her, especially down low.

The friction against her thighs was hot, the ribbed material almost abrasive. She couldn't help the rocking motion of her hips. When the cool zipper dragged over the front of her panties, she moaned. The sensation was so shocking, her hand dove between her legs to stop it.

Or to keep it.

Her fingers stalled when she found wetness. The nylon of her panties was damp all the way through. She explored carefully, her thighs falling open as she delved deeper. Her entire body gave a shudder that had nothing to do with a chill when she touched the most sensitive part of herself.

'No,' she whispered into the slowly overheating room.

It shouldn't be like this. Not with him. Not with the scandal heating up all over again.

But she couldn't help herself as her hand skimmed away from her core, only to come back again, this time under her panties. She let out a whimper. Her flesh was plump and warm. Sensitive. Her heels dug into the mattress as her body bowed. The sweatshirt was all around her, not letting go.

She explored herself with just the pads of her fingers. The butterfly touches were creating zaps of energy that filled her whole body. Her breasts felt heavy and full and her nipples beaded tightly. She could feel the weight of the fleece upon them. With her breaths at a pant, she circled her tender opening. Even knowing it was coming, her hips surged when she pressed a finger inside.

'Heaven help me,' she whispered.

It wasn't heaven that was going to give her what she needed. From that point on, everything became a blur.

Her feelings, the complications, the public fascination, the slippage of time ... One finger became two, and her hips were lunging as she remembered the hunger on the wolf's face. The intensity of his sexual gaze. Perspiration broke out on her forehead, and cries of pleasure left her lips.

This was impossible. Dangerous.

Yet when the teeth of the hoodie's zipper raked across her sensitive nub, she arched off the bed, caught in a scorching orgasm. The sensation clutched her, dragging on as the fleece brushed insistently against her bottom. It let her go in degrees until she sagged onto the bed, her body limp.

The blur of her consciousness slid directly into fatigue. The little sleep she'd gotten the night before combined with the orgasm's drugging release. Her head rolled on the pillow and, once again, she smelled that sexy cologne. The hum of the heater lulled her.

Despite her worries and fears, she was soon asleep, with Alex Wolfe's sweatshirt wrapped around her, holding her tight.

# Chapter Three

'I'm fine, Mom. Really.' Elena stepped out of the lake house and tucked the key into her pocket. The ever-changing fall weather had swung around. The sky was a brilliant blue, although the temperature still had a bite to it. That slippery slope into autumn was getting steeper and steeper.

'But you're trapped there.'

'On a gazillion acres of beautiful private property,' she teased. Still, she gave a shudder to shake off the feeling of cabin fever. Her mother knew her too well. The fact that she couldn't leave – not without serious repercussions – was straining her nerves. She looked over the trees and the rippling water. It was a beautiful trap, but a trap nonetheless.

'Those darn bottom feeders,' her mother muttered. 'Please, honey. Just brazen through them and come out here to stay with me in San Diego.'

Elena sighed. 'You know I can't do that.'

She'd already tried running away once. The paparazzi had tracked her down here, although they didn't know it. There was nothing that would keep them from finding her at her mother's condo, and this place offered much more protection, unconventional as it was. Besides, a plane ticket would set her back financially and she couldn't afford the time it would take to pack up and move across the country.

'But you're stuck there with that reprobate.'

The edge in her mother's normally dulcet tone sounded harsh against Elena's ear, and her gaze swept along the balcony of the manor. It was empty and she saw no movement behind the windows. The 'reprobate' must be out on one of his walks again.

'He sticks to his house and I stay in mine.'

'So you haven't had to interact with him?'

Interact.

Well, that was a difficult word to define. The only time they'd spoken was the day they'd run into each other at the fishing spot, but there had been a lot more going on between them than words. Her fingers froze over the zipper she was toying with and she pulled her hand away as if she'd just touched fire. She needed to remember to drop the hoodie off with Leonard on her way back.

'We've bumped into each other a few times.' On the trails, but that was something her mother didn't need

46

to know. Alone in the remote, dense woods ... away from any other human souls ... It had happened twice more since that first encounter. Both times, that prickly awareness had returned.

Both times she'd scurried home to safety.

And hot, uncomfortable thoughts.

'You've talked to him?' Yvonne gasped. 'What did he say to you?'

'Nothing,' Elena said quickly. She looked to the sky and sighed. She hadn't wanted to worry her mom about this. 'We don't speak.'

No, they didn't speak. They watched each other, sensed each other, and circled. 'We don't have anything to say to each other.'

'You be careful of him. Elena, nobody knows the full story yet. Nobody knows what happened to his grandfather, and you're there all alone with him.'

'I'm not alone, I have Leonard.'

Yvonne let out a frustrated sound, but it cut off on a downward note. When Leonard had first made the offer of shelter, she'd encouraged it.

'I spend all my time in the lake house,' Elena said soothingly. 'I've got a lot of work to do. Remember? My PhD is our goal.'

Her mother blew out a breath. 'Fine, you're right, but I don't like it.'

'Neither do I, but that can't be helped right now.'

47

'If your father had just –'

'But he didn't.' He hadn't ever lived up to their expectations, and they both knew it. They both fell quiet for a long moment.

'We need to talk more about this, but I have to get to work. Thea didn't tell me she was running short on pastry bags,' her mom finally muttered. 'You call me if you need anything.'

'I will.' There wasn't anything her mother could do about the situation, the reporters or especially Alex Wolfe, but talking to her always made things better. 'Have a good day.'

'You, too, honey.'

'Bye.' Elena tucked the phone into her pocket and inhaled the fresh air. She'd been cooped up for so long she couldn't stand it any more. She needed to move around. She had to think about things other than supply, demand, stock evaluation and market volatility. She loved her studies, but sometimes they sucked her under.

Instead of going round the lake, she headed up the garden path. It was quiet, pretty and ruthlessly manicured. She hadn't seen her manor mate on this part of the grounds. He kept mainly to the lake and the untamed woods, sometimes exploring for hours. She'd started to keep track of him from the window in her office, when she managed to spot him. He was like his namesake in the way he moved around, silent and elusive.

The muscles in her thighs fired as she walked up the limestone steps on the steeper part of the hill. She was beginning to understand why he spent so much time outside. She'd only been sequestered in the lake house for a week. He'd been in prison for a year and a half. She couldn't imagine what that would do to a person's mind, especially a Type A, determined, forceful man like him.

Not that she was feeling sorry for him.

Her spine snapped straight when she realised where her thoughts were wandering. He had brought this punishment upon himself; he was the reason the reporters were here. She hadn't done anything to deserve any of this.

But she had to find a way to deal with it.

The back of her fingers brushed against something soft. Looking down she saw a blood red rose. Opening her hand, she cupped the heavy blossom. It was full and lush. Her thumb brushed over a velvety petal. Beautiful, yet hearty. It was thriving, even with the erratic temperatures and cold dew. Something inside her softened.

'A lesson in resiliency.'

Lifting her chin, she looked about. The fall garden was waning, but it was still a riot of colours and textures. The Wolfe Gardens could compete with any public garden that charged entry fees. Then again, their private benefactor probably spent more money on them, and the wear and tear was less.

She began travelling through the wandering maze,

appreciating the discoveries at every turn. The gardens ran all the way up beside the manor. Beyond that, there was a sweeping, expansive lawn, but then the trees started up again. They were thick all the way up to the main road.

An idea started clicking inside her head. She hadn't seen the reporters for herself. What if the situation wasn't as bad as Leonard had made it seem?

She was deep in thought when she turned into the English tea garden. So deep, she nearly barrelled in on the one man she was trying to avoid.

The Wolfe was in the garden.

Her breath caught and she quickly hid behind a white pergola laced with vines and roses. What was he doing here? Was he following her? She bit her lip, considering what to do. By rights, she should turn around, go back down the hill and lock herself in the lake house.

But the road was in the other direction.

She peeked around the corner. He was still heading away from her. Unlike her, he was a true pacer. She watched the way he stalked down the little path, his broad shoulders narrowing to a taut waist and even nicer butt. Her tongue ran over her lips.

Oh, damn. He was wearing the jeans again.

She ducked back into hiding when he pivoted. For a brief moment, she saw a muscled chest and bulging biceps. Yet she'd also seen the mussed hair and the shadows underneath his eyes. Something had him worked up.

She heard a curious tapping noise. When she risked another peek, she found that he'd stopped at the table. For the first time, she became aware of the patio furniture that had been set up in the centre square. It was white wicker with deep green cushions. What caught her attention, though, was the computer sitting on the table.

She frowned. What was he doing? Reading news articles about himself? Getting caught up on The Wolfe Pack's bottom line? Emailing cohorts who still agreed to associate with him?

She watched as he typed then pulled back to reference something. It looked like a grade-school notebook. For a moment, the red colour threw her. Even though he was dressed so casually, she would have expected his notebook to be leather-bound with a Mont Blanc pen within reach.

He followed along in the notebook, tracing a line, before looking back at his laptop. That, at the other end of the spectrum, was top grade. His fingers flew as he typed, but then he stood upright. Lacing his hands behind his neck, he stared at the screen. Finally, he swore and turned. His foot lashed out at an outdoor ottoman, and it went clattering along the flat stone patio before abruptly coming to a stop.

Elena jumped at the violence of the movement, but more so at the anger that lay underneath. It was gritty and fierce, palpable from where she stood. Almost immediately, though, it was tamped. With iron-like mettle, the man before her reined it all in. The anger sank back below the surface – or, more likely, was shoved. Standing with his fingers still wrapped together behind his neck, he let out another curse and looked towards the sky. The word was low and breathy, but it was enough to make her realise she needed to be moving along.

She headed into the garden maze, intending to take a path further away from the house.

'I wouldn't do that if I were you.'

She looked around quickly. Was there someone else around that she hadn't seen?

He sighed. 'Stay away from the front gate, Elena.'

That brought her straight upright. Her breath caught when she found him staring straight at her. His grey eyes were piercing and all too knowing.

How had he sensed her? More so, how had he figured out her plans? 'I ... I just thought I'd see if the reporters are still out there.'

'Trust me. They're dug in like ticks.' His attention returned to his computer screen. 'Ready to draw blood.'

Apparently they were talking now. Or were they?

He planted a foot on the chair in front of him and braced his forearm across his knee as he leaned forward. The position emphasised the long muscles in his back. Whatever he was working on had his attention more than she did.

Although he'd somehow spotted her when she'd made little to no noise.

She edged backwards. 'I'll stay hidden in the treeline.'

'Did you watch TMZ last night? They were trying out a thermal camera.' He tapped a few more keys on the keyboard. 'They managed to spot one of the rabbits that run around the place.'

His gaze was on her again in that second. '*My* rabbit.'

She froze under his stare.

'There's no telling how rabid they'll get if they spot a person.' That grey gaze slowly trailed down her body. 'Especially if it's female.'

There it was again, the crackling in the air. Self-consciousness overcame Elena as she stood before him – or was that just awareness? Awareness of her body, acknowledgment of their differences, him male, her female? He missed nothing with that gaze, and she felt the way her breasts filled out her knit top. She sensed the lift in the heels of her boots and the resulting tilt of her hips. Even with the extra three inches, she barely came up to his chin.

The hoodie's zipper bit into the palm of her hand.

His hoodie.

The one she was wearing and hadn't returned.

Her immediate impulse was to give it back, but the bulkiness hid her shape. In that moment, she could no more take it off than she could walk down a stripper runway. 'I suppose I shouldn't do that then.'

'Leonard will let you know when it's clear.'

She nodded. All right. That sounded like a dismissal. It rubbed wrong, but this was his land. He hadn't invited her here. 'Thank you,' she forced herself to say.

The sooner she got out of here, the better.

She turned on her heel, this time back towards the lake. His voice stopped her again.

'You haven't been doing yoga in the evenings.'

Oh, yes. He knew exactly what her body looked like underneath his fleece jacket.

Awareness ran like an electrical charge down her spine. When she looked over her shoulder, she found him still watching her. His pose was casual, still leaning over with one foot braced on the patio chair, but his eyes were alert. She might have been watching him on his walks through the woods, but he'd been watching her too.

Warmth unfurled inside her and began to circulate through her veins.

'It's getting too chilly.'

He waited for a long moment, almost as if he was debating what he'd say next. When he spoke, the offer surprised her.

'You could use the gym in the main house, if you'd like.'

The main house. She'd made use of the library before he'd returned. There were some valuable resources there that rivalled those she'd found in the NYU library. Yet he was offering her more than that, and she wasn't certain how to interpret it. She doubted he was the type for friendly gestures – although he'd been a renowned philanthropist before the scandal had broken. Or had that all been part of the illusion?

'I found space in the living room of the lake house,' she replied. She had to move the coffee table and she constantly bumped up against the sofa, but he didn't need to know that.

Although, from the look on his face, he probably did. He owned that tiny bungalow.

His gaze narrowed and his lips flattened. Finally, he dropped his foot back to the ground and folded his arms over his chest. 'It's up to you.'

And with that she *was* summarily dismissed.

This time she knew it and she felt it.

She also felt a bit guilty, as if she'd hurt his feelings. Which was just silly and wrong on so many levels. What this man had done had hurt so many people. Yet Elena knew she'd dwell on it all night if she thought she'd been rude. She hadn't been raised that way.

She took a step forward.

His concentration was on the laptop again, but she saw the muscles in his back stiffen. Those long, thick ropes of muscles ... He knew she was still there.

'However ...' she started.

He didn't react, just stood there with his back turned. It unsettled her. Should she continue? Just turn and go?

'The library,' she made herself say. She had Internet

access, but, contrary to what some people believed, not everything could be found with a Google search.

She nearly jumped when he turned. She had his full attention. Only then did she realise she'd had it all along. The signs of fatigue were still on his face and his mussed hair made her fingers itch to smooth it into place, yet it always came back to his eyes. She couldn't look away from them.

'Leonard said you were going for your PhD.'

Her mouth went dry. They'd spoken about her? She nodded.

'What subject?' he asked.

She had to lick her lips to get them to function, and her stomach squeezed when his grey eyes sparked. 'Ec … Economics.'

The expression that crossed his face was at once amused, ironic and resigned. 'Of course it is.'

The knot in Elena's belly turned fiery. 'As it was before you and my father came clean about your Ponzi scheme.'

His jaw hardened, and the lines on his face deepened. The air between them pulsed and, for a moment, she thought she was going to see his anger flare to the surface again. She couldn't have been more wrong. Ice was what she received instead. Cold, hard and unyielding. 'I think everyone knows that I never came clean about that.'

She held his stare, refusing to back down. He had never admitted guilt, and it was something that galled most people. Yet there was something in his tone …

He said nothing more. He just stared at her, daring her to come at him again. She'd seen that look before as he'd done interviews. She recognised it from videotape of the prosecuting attorney questioning him. It made him look cocky, aggravating and sexy as hell.

But she wasn't the one who was going to bring him down.

Better, more powerful people had tried and he'd come away with barely a slap on the wrist. Although ... her gaze was drawn to the ottoman that sat a cockeyed angle.

'Forget it,' she said softly.

She turned towards the lake house, but was surprised when he took a step to follow her. It wasn't a voluntary move, and they both knew it.

'You can use the library,' he said, his tone low and rough.

She looked at him through her lashes, but his gaze was on her body. Or, more precisely, on the way she'd wrapped the sweatshirt around herself. Hot embarrassment ran through her. He wasn't the only one throwing off mixed signals.

'But stay away from me.'

Her chin came up in surprise. Now that wasn't a mixed message at all. It was a direct blow and it stung, but before she could say anything he turned, swept up his laptop and walked away.

\* \* \*

The woman was a distraction.

Alex considered the implications as he did pull-ups in the gym in the basement of the manor. High-tech equipment surrounded him, but he'd learned that old-school still sometimes got the best results. Crossing his feet at the ankles, he kept his body still and made his arms lift his dead weight up and down. The burning became intense, but he kept going until the muscles wouldn't respond any more. He dropped to the ground, flipped onto his back and started doing sit-ups.

She was an unwanted, uninvited distraction who apparently didn't want to be here any more than he did.

He stopped for a moment on the upbeat with his elbows bumping against his knees.

No, that wasn't all true. He wanted her like hell.

His teeth gritted as he started pumping out the reps again. She was beautiful. Heart-stoppingly so. When she'd come upon him down by the lake, he'd gotten his first up-close look at her. It had nearly made him swallow his tongue. She was tiny, but with curves in all the right places. Her hair was so long and silky, it made his fingers itch. But that face. Her skin was flawless and he couldn't look away from her eyes. She had doe eyes. Deep, dark and captivating.

He could drown in those eyes.

Or he could drown her.

He didn't need her here, not now and not like this. He

needed this time alone. He couldn't afford distractions, no matter how gorgeous or tempting.

But he couldn't send her away. He might be a heartless son-of-a-bitch, but he wouldn't feed her to the wolves. Not the kind that stood outside his door, anyway.

'Shit,' he muttered.

Collapsing back, he lay on the gym mat and stared at the fluorescent lighting. This was the first time he'd used the gym in ages. The rain this morning had forced him inside. A little drizzle wouldn't have stopped him, but a constant downpour was another thing. He'd had his share of discomfort. The Precor and Cybex equipment was here for a reason.

He rolled his head and looked around the room. Full-length mirrors on the opposite wall showed his reflection. He'd put in a hard workout. His body felt like mush as he tried to catch his breath. His muscles were warm and his skin was damp with sweat. For a moment, he let his eyes close. Worn out, maybe he could relax.

He lasted for fifteen seconds. Twenty tops.

He heard every little pop and whir in the building. The last year and a half had honed his senses, and he was aware of everything that went on around him. Too aware. That made it all the more difficult to explain how she had snuck up on him yesterday in the garden – and she'd come up behind him. The last guy who'd made that mistake had ended up in the infirmary, yet she'd come upon him like a butterfly on the wind. He'd only known she was there when he'd sensed her watching him.

And felt the responding tightness in his groin.

With a surge of energy, Ax came to his feet. Grabbing his towel, he wiped his face and stalked off to the shower. The woman was like a wraith, so quiet as she floated about the grounds. She was ethereal as she took her morning walks in the mists along the waterfront ... entrancing as she did yoga on the dock ... but so sad, it made him ache.

He needed to get her out of his head. He needed to be sharp. He would be sharp.

But today, instead of feeling like a knife blade, he felt more like a hammer head.

The towel snapped against his back as he flung it over his shoulder. 'Damn rain.'

It had him trapped him inside this house. It might have more rooms than he could count, but so had Otisville. He didn't like being pinned down here by the media any more than his guest did. Wolfe Manor had its own special kind of demons, even for one of its own.

Especially for one of its own.

Something caught at his athletic shoe as he walked into the bathroom, and he looked down quickly. The thick rubber mat that covered the floor had flipped up at the corner. Demons, indeed. They were grabbing for him even now. Walking into the bathroom, he slammed the door shut behind him.

He stripped as the water warmed. When he finally pulled the glass door shut behind him, the steam was already rising. Bracing his hands against the granite wall, he let the dual shower heads spray over him. He was pushing himself, he knew. That snake was still coiled inside his chest. He was doing his best to keep it contained, but she'd seen it lash out yesterday. He regretted that.

He bowed his head and the pulsating water beat against the back of his neck. He needed to get both of them out of here.

Those eyes.

They showed everything she was feeling – distrust, curiosity, anger, *lust* …

Ax felt himself stirring. His tired body was filling with another kind of energy, one that was immediate and gnawing. Hunger started seeping through his veins. His mouth watered and his fingertips ached. His senses heightened, and the images behind his closed eyelids became vivid. Below the belt, he was hard and aching. Damn near throbbing. When the tip of his erection bumped against his belly, he swore and slapped the slick wall.

'Fuck.'

Standing upright, he reached for the soap. He'd had her pegged that first night. She was a temptress, a siren luring him in so she could bring him down.

That was not going to happen.

With their intertwined histories, they could destroy each other.

He soaped himself, shampooed and rinsed off. His body was one big ache, but he ignored it. Screw the rain, he needed to get out of this house.

He turned off the water so abruptly, the pipes shook. The bathroom was cloudy as he stepped out of the shower stall. He'd forgotten to turn on the fan. The mirror was fogged over and condensation covered the fixtures. He dried off the moisture, but it came back just as quickly. He wrapped a fresh towel around his waist and reached for the bathroom door to let in some fresh air.

It didn't give.

His head came up. The tired muscles of his gut seized up as one, and he gave another tug on the door.

It held firm.

'What the hell?'

Stepping closer, he looked to see if a lock had been flipped. There wasn't even a mechanism. Wrapping his fist around the handle, he braced his other hand against the wall. He might be fresh from a workout, but he should still have enough strength to open a stinking door. With a sound close to a growl, he gave another yank.

This time the top corner bowed inward, but the bottom remained lodged. Something had the door jammed.

Ax felt his breaths go short and his chest tighten

unbearably. The air wasn't going past his throat and it felt like it was bulging. He yanked on the door again. Shoved it and pulled. It was like a bank vault.

The walls pressed in on him. He looked over the door, his thoughts pinging about as he tried to force his brain to work. Looking around, he realised he was in an interior room. No windows. No other route for escape.

The snake slithered. He jimmied the door and yanked it harder.

Nothing worked.

He was locked in. Trapped in the tiny space. Those demons he remembered were out and about, taunting him. He slapped the light switches, turning on the string of bulbs over the vanity, and switched the fan on high. The dampness in the air was making it hard to breathe. The moisture coated his vocal cords and clung to his exposed skin.

'Hey!' he yelled, banging his fist against the door. 'Somebody!'

The big old house was silent.

Not wanting to, he turned off the fan so he could hear. The loss of the whirring noise left a gaping hole. He heard nothing. No water dripping, no gym equipment running, no footsteps, no voices in return.

He set up a staccato rhythm that had the door bouncing on its hinges. It set up a racket, but the door was immovable.

'Can anyone hear me?'

He heard a noise now, but it was his heart pounding in his ears and his head. He was confined again. He slammed both fists against the heavy oak door, making contact all the way down his forearms to his elbows.

His control was crumbling.

And then the snake was loose.

'Help! Get me out of here. Anyone. Hey. Let me out!'

# Chapter Four

Elena hurried through the door to the kitchen of the main house and shook herself to get rid of the rain. It was pouring outside. The walk up the hill didn't look that long, but she'd gotten drenched in the time it had taken for her to run the distance. She dropped her backpack onto the floor and tugged off her jacket. She hung it on the metal coat rack beside the door and tried not to shiver when a droplet of water ran down the back of her neck.

'Hello?' she called. A stack of freshly washed kitchen towels was on the granite counter. She grabbed the top one and brushed it over her damp skin. 'Is anyone here?'

She knew that Marta and Leonard were out running errands, because they'd asked her for a list of things she needed. The only other person's location she wasn't sure about was *his*. She hadn't seen any lights on in the main house from her view down by the lake. There'd been no movement or any other signs of life. It was hard to believe he'd be out wandering around in this kind of weather, but she already knew he didn't like being cooped up.

Maybe he was sleeping or off in some distant room. The place had enough of them. She slipped off her shoes and left them on the throw rug by the door so she wouldn't track mud.

'It's Elena,' she called. She didn't want to raise her voice too much. She just needed to buzz down to the first-floor library, but she didn't want to stumble across anyone unexpectedly. That had already happened with a certain person too many times, and she didn't want it to happen here, in his home.

Even if he had given her permission to be here.

Blotting her wet hair, she padded over to peek through the kitchen doorway. 'I'm just here to borrow a book,' she called lightly.

The looming stillness of the house gave her visions of a black hole just waiting to suck her up. She waited another moment, and then yet another for good measure.

Summoning up her nerve, she began tiptoeing down the hallway. She knew which book she needed and where it was. Her plan was to just grab it and go. The problem was that the library was at the other end of the house, a trek away.

She started down the long corridor, trying not to let it unnerve her. The place was just so big and museum-like. She looked into the foyer with its massive stair tower rising overhead. It picked up even the soft patter of her footsteps and made them echo. Squeezing the last bit of moisture from her hair into the towel, she looked in the other direction. It made her pause. The open room was sweeping and expansive, and it offered a wall-to-wall view of the lake – and, off to the right, her house.

Well, not her house. His lake house.

He'd been watching her that first night from the balcony right outside those windows. Had he been watching her since?

The idea sent another kind of shiver down her spine.

Hurrying along, she passed empty rooms filled with oak furniture, priceless antiques and vintage rugs. She felt out of place here, surrounded by so much wealth. Everything felt so heavy, yet so luxurious and tempting. The only context she had was the time she and her mother had vacationed in Rhode Island. Her aunt had taken them on a tour of the famous mansions of Newport – the summer getaways for the likes of the Vanderbilts and the Rockefellers. The only difference there was that the rooms had been roped off. The classic look-but-don't-touch approach.

This was real.

These people lived this way. They kept this mansion that was way too big with way too many rooms. They slept on these beds, walked across those priceless rugs, toyed with those pricey ceramic figurines … Privilege. There were so many aspects to that word. She couldn't imagine how it would feel to not have to worry about money, to have any pleasure or comfort available at the snap of her fingers.

She moved past a study and then a music room with a grand piano and harp. It made her frown. Did someone actually play that thing or was it just for show?

It didn't matter; she was dawdling. Straightening, she focused again on the library at the end of the hall. She was about to walk inside when she realised she was still carrying the kitchen towel. A damp towel and books ... It wasn't a good combination.

There was a half bath just off to her right. She stepped inside to drape the hand-towel over a towel rail. For a moment, she let her toes curl into the rug beneath her feet. Even the bathroom rugs here were thick and sumptuous. Its burgundy colour matched not only the towels that were artfully arranged over the brass rail but also the soapdish and lotion dispenser. She was admiring the heavy ceramic set when a bang suddenly came through the pipes. The sound was so loud, it made her jump.

'Ah!'

Lurching back, she looked at the sink and toilet. Was something wrong with the plumbing?

Another sound radiated through the walls. In the small room, the reverberation seemed to be coming from everywhere. Elena flinched again, warnings flaring in her mind. Shuffling backwards, she braced herself in the doorway.

What *was* that?

She looked for the source of the racket. It sounded as if the pipes were about to explode.

Wait. No, that wasn't the pipes. She could hear them now in a distinct rattle. This was something else ... some kind of impact ... She looked out the window. Had someone made it onto the grounds? Were they trying to break in?

Another series of hard thuds rang in the walls, making her wince. She could literally feel them under her fingertips. No, this was coming from inside.

She looked up.

A strange sound had her quickly reevaluating and looking down. Under her feet. Below her, she'd heard a cry that could only be associated with a wounded animal.

'Oh, God.'

Something was down there.

She didn't think that Leonard had been caring for any pets, but would he have kept a guard dog inside if he'd known she was on the property? She doubted it, but she jumped when there was another explosion of noise beneath her. Banging noises. Desperate sounds.

'Hold on. I'm coming.'

Shaking with adrenalin, she backed into the hallway. Whatever was down there, it needed help. She couldn't ignore the frantic sounds. She looked up and down the hall. How could she get down there? The library was the only place she'd ever visited. She'd never explored; she hadn't wanted to.

*Bang, bang, bang.*

More clanging rang up through the walls and her toes curled with the need to move. Where was the staircase? She didn't try to be quiet as she raced back to the main entrance, though she nearly fell, her socks sliding along the hardwood flooring, when she found an open archway. *There.* Carpeted steps led downwards to the basement.

She flew down the stairs and immediately turned to her right. The sounds were louder down here. The limestone structure had soaked up most of the noise, containing it. On the lower level, they were booming. Her sense of urgency grew, and she ignored the indoor putting green and wet bar as she honed in on the anguish in the air.

'Hello?' she called. 'Where are you?'

Heart pounding, she found the gym. It was nearly as big as the one she'd used in the city, only the equipment was better and it didn't smell like sweaty socks. On the balls of her feet, she scoped out the situation.

There. The door off the end. It was shaking on its hinges.

She heard that raw, guttural sound that had stifled her breaths upstairs. Only this time the keening was clear. It wasn't an animal; it was a person. A man.

'What's wrong?' She raced over to the door, but was

afraid to get too near just in case it exploded outwards. 'Do you need help?'

The person inside didn't hear her. They were setting up a racket, pounding on the door and scratching at it.

She lifted her hands to protect her face when they started kicking.

'Hey!' she yelled.

A roar responded. He'd heard her this time. 'Out! Get me out!'

Her breath caught in her throat. She recognised that voice.

'Now!'

She lurched back into action. 'Stop kicking.'

Again, in his panic, the man didn't listen. He was going at that door like his life depended on it.

'*Alex!*'

The racket fell and the noise level dropped so suddenly, it was jarring. Still, Elena swore she could hear ragged breaths coming through the sturdy wooden door. She approached cautiously and laid her hand over the handle. 'Alex, is that you?'

'Elena?'

His voice was thin, and her name sounded plaintive. Urgency clawed at her.

'Is it the lock? Are you stuck?' She twisted the handle on the door and pushed, but nothing happened. She tried again, feeling him help from the other side, but something was blocking the door's natural movement. Her brain began clicking as she sized up the situation.

'Open it,' he ordered, his voice brusque. 'Damn it. Get it open!'

She yelped when he started kicking again. She could see the door bowing as he made contact, but he was kicking out, while the door swung inwards.

'Wait! Hold on!' She turned the handle and felt the latch open fine. Putting her shoulder into it, she shoved again. The top corner of the door swung in, but the bottom held tight. She knelt down when she found the source of the problem. 'The gym mat is lodged under the bottom corner.'

She reeled back when the door starting shaking again.

'You're making it worse. Alex! Let me help you.'

He stopped abruptly. She pounced while she had the chance, talking out loud to keep him distracted. 'It's wedged in tight. Kicking it will only make it worse, and you aren't Bruce Lee. You can't kick through it.'

Although he'd certainly tried.

How long had he been locked in? Trapped like a wild animal?

No matter what she thought of him, the idea of that kind of suffering made her throat hurt. He wasn't one who was built to be tied down. He could barely stand to be in this gigantic house for a full day. 'Let me just try something.'

She let out a grunt as she fisted her hands around the mat and pulled. The corner of the door only dug deeper into the rubber.

'Elena?' His voice was raw, more a harsh whisper than tone now.

'It's coming,' she promised. Sitting down, she braced her feet against the wall to give herself leverage. 'Don't do anything. I'm right behind the door.'

She tugged again, her teeth gritting at the effort. She could feel him on the other side of that door, hovering and fidgeting.

'Did you try the hinges?' She needed to keep him talking. She needed to calm him down. If she let him slip into a panic, he'd only work against her.

'I broke two combs trying to pry them out.'

He was standing just on the other side of the door, his voice right above her. It was intimidating, but he was focused. That was good. Anything to pull him back from the brink. She began pulling on the mat, working it back and forth. It was malleable, but so heavy-duty she could hardly lift it. It wasn't one of the thick cushy mats everyone did sit-ups on, it was the rubbery kind that gyms laid across their walkways and underneath equipment.

'That was innovative.' She smiled fiercely when the right side of the mat slipped out a good inch.

'Not really,' he said in that raspy voice. 'You should see what inmates can make with those things.'

73

She froze.

'No, I take that back,' he said more softly. 'You should never see that.'

That edge was back in his voice. She had to get him out of there now. She looked around the room for something she could use. For all the shiny equipment and heavy free weights, there wasn't much. Besides, she didn't think cutting the mat was the right way to go.

She kept wiggling it with her feet braced like a rower. Her shoulders began to ache at the effort, but then she fell backwards.

'Ooo, almost.'

She felt his anticipation jump and wondered how she could ever miss him when he was walking through the forest. He was standing on the other side of a slab of wood. She couldn't see him, but she could feel his presence. His heat was blistering.

It made her uneasy. She'd never seen him like this. Every time they'd crossed paths, he'd been cool and contained. Low-key and reined-in.

Except for that time in the garden.

'Can you lift on the handle?' she asked. 'Pull up.'

Before she even finished the question, she felt the resistance give. She yanked on the rubber mat and her momentum swung. She rolled halfway onto her back when the stupid thing popped loose.

'Ha!' She scrambled to her feet and stepped back,

getting out of the way. She brushed off her bottom, but the door stood eerily still.

Why wasn't he –

Oh, God. She'd told him not to do anything, that he could hurt her if he came out suddenly.

She sprang forward and grabbed the door handle. It turned smoothly, and the door swung silently on its hinges as she opened it. It stopped halfway when masculine fingers curled around the edge. Those fingers turned white, and he pulled the door open so wide it banged against the bathroom vanity.

That ache in Elena's throat spread to her chest when she finally saw him. He looked haggard. His colour was ashen, although heat and humidity poured out of the room. The lines of his cheekbones were harsh, and his jaw was set like a master lock. His eyes, though … Those icy grey eyes glinted with something raw and wild. 'Are you OK?' she asked.

He jammed his foot in front of the door and she winced when she saw the bruising and swelling that had already started. He'd been kicking at that door with his bare feet.

Then again, that wasn't all about him that was bare.

She swallowed hard. He must have been taking a shower when he'd gotten trapped, because all he was wearing was a towel. A loose, very insecure towel. It sat low on his waist, with the knot looking like it could slip at any moment.

Awareness prickled along her skin and her face warmed. She'd known he was fit, but this went beyond that. He was ripped. Lean and animal-like.

Beautiful.

He started moving then, determined to get out of the tiny room. Her gaze snapped up and she stepped back to make way.

Only he didn't stop coming at her.

Instinctively, she lifted her hand. To stop him or ground him, she didn't know. He came out of his makeshift prison like a bull coming out of a gate, and her palm spread wide across his warm, muscled chest. The contact was shocking, but she gasped aloud when he touched her. He caught her by the shoulders, his grip hot and urgent. Their gazes locked and her heart kicked like that bucking bull that just escaped.

'You,' he rasped. His hot breaths hit her square in the face.

They stared at each other, chests working. Electricity passed between them, creating a full circuit through touch. His fervency transferred to her; her agitation swam back to him. The tension in the room changed, ratcheting impossibly higher.

Elena watched him with wide eyes as he pulled her close, but then his head dipped and his mouth closed over hers. He kissed her hard, his lips firm. Hungry. Frantic.

The adrenalin that had been rushing through her veins

dove deeper into her belly. Arousal knotted in her gut and her thoughts splintered.

His need; it went bone-deep. She could feel it in the tremble in his grip. He wrapped an arm low around her waist and cinched her up tight. Their bodies connected from mouth to knee. All she felt of him was bare skin as he leaned over her. Smooth, delicious skin. His heat seeped into her and she shuddered.

'Elena.' Something close to a groan rose from his chest.

He was bigger than her and stronger by far, yet he was hanging onto her as if she was the only thing keeping him from going under.

She hesitantly slid her hands up his back. The strength she'd imagined was all there, with nothing to hide. His body was a tapestry of muscles and tendons that jumped at her touch. Her fingertips curled inward. The power she felt was intoxicating.

His tongue pressed demandingly at the seam of her lips. When she gave him access, he swept it across hers. The contact was wet and slow, so erotic she could barely stand it.

'Mmm.' She let out a mew when he hitched her up. He lifted her as if she weighed nothing, and her feet dangled inches from the floor. Her toes curled in reaction. When he slanted his mouth across hers again, she was ready for it. The kiss was deeper, more passionate and intense.

The ache between her legs intensified. Age-old instinct had her wrapping her legs around his waist. She locked her ankles and rubbed helplessly against the hard bulge that pressed between her legs.

'God, yes,' he hissed.

The room spun as he turned. When it righted itself again, Elena found herself on her back on the mat – not the thick rubber kind that had trapped him, but the cushy kind that absorbed impact ... and cushioned the weight of two intertwined bodies ...

He was heavy as he splayed out on top of her. His chest plumped her breasts, and his hips nudged determinedly at hers. She cradled his erection between her legs and wiggled until he pressed against the spot where she needed him most.

He nipped at her lips. 'I have to have you.'

So blunt. So straightforward.

And so sexy.

Arousal clogged her thought processes, and everything honed in on the physical. All she knew was the clench of his hands in her hair, the feel of his bare chest and the press of his hardness between her thighs.

He pushed her top upwards, forcing her to lift her arms above her head, and made quick work of the front tab on her bra. When he cupped her breast, her head rolled against the mat. His hand was big and possessive. Burning. Her nipple poked hard into his palm, but her body bowed when his rooting lips circled her nipple. She struggled to free herself of the stretchy material as he plumped her breast higher and suckled at her with such voraciousness it made her belly contract.

'Alex!'

He dragged his tongue slowly across her sensitive nub, making it tingle. 'That's right, pretty siren. Say my name.'

Elena couldn't believe this was happening, but it was. He was like a man possessed as he worked his hand between their bodies. He yanked down the zipper of her jeans, but she wasn't ready when he shoved them down. Her hips rocked when he cupped her.

'Ahh!' Desire clenched deep in her belly, and she arched against him.

Propping himself up on one elbow, he struggled to catch his breath. They were both breathing hard, and she could felt the hot gusts against her lips.

He was watching her so closely. There was nowhere to hide when he ran a fingertip around her opening. Nerve endings fired, and her pulse jumped. When the tip of one of those curious fingers began to penetrate her, she grabbed at him. Her hands found natural resting places over the curves of his sexy bottom. The towel was gone, and her fingers dug deep.

His jaw clenched underneath the shadow of his dusty beard.

His finger dipped deeper into her wetness, and there

was no way to hide her reaction. Elena became one big shuddering mess. She could feel the strain in his muscles as he kept touching so intimately below. One finger became two. She couldn't find her breath as they rubbed, swirled and plunged.

He leaned his forehead against hers as he touched a spot that made her moan. 'Tell me you want me.'

Want? It was such a tame word for what she felt. She ground her mound against his hand, and her thigh muscles burned. If something didn't soothe the ache deep inside her soon, she was going to go crazy.

'Tell me,' he ordered.

She kissed him instead.

A growl rumbled against her lips. His mouth raked across hers, and his tongue plunged. She let out a cry when his fingers left her empty, but then he was pulling off her clothes. She squirmed as she tried to help, lifting her hips and pointing her toes as he dragged everything down at once. He yanked off her socks along the way and she suddenly found herself naked with him towering over her.

Her breasts heaved as she looked up at him. He'd settled back on his haunches between her spread legs and was looking her up and down.

She looked at him just as fiercely. Her gaze swept over his handsome face. The ashen colour was gone, and the hollow look in his eyes had been replaced by something hot and reckless. She admired the strength in his chest and arms, the definition in his abdomen and –

Oh, my.

His erection stood hard and tall.

He was big, and he was ready.

He toppled over her, taking his weight on his arms so he didn't crush her. Their gazes locked, and she caught at his sides. 'You can't look at a man that way,' he growled. 'Not when he's trying to stay away from you.'

'I didn't come here looking for you,' she panted.

'But you found me.' His gaze homed in on her lips, and some of the tension in his shoulders sagged. 'You rescued me.'

He lowered himself onto her, skin pressing against skin, as he kissed her. He coaxed her to wrap her legs around him, and Elena shivered as his big hands cupped her bare bottom. He tilted her hips up as he positioned himself and then he was pushing into her.

'Oh!' she cried. 'Oh … oh …'

She had to stretch to take him, and the pinch rode right on the thin edge between pain and pleasure. She dug her fingers into his back, and he went still.

'Mmm,' she whimpered. She felt so full. At once, it was too much and not enough. She wiggled beneath him, trying to ease her distress, but his hold locked down, keeping her in place.

'Like this,' he whispered into her ear. Using her wetness

to ease the way, he began pumping in short, slow strokes. With the angle at which he held her, each glide bumped against that tender nub between her legs. It set off a flurry of sensation and her feet arched, her toes pointing hard.

'Alex,' she gasped.

He began pumping deeper and then deeper still until with one surge, he embedded himself all the way.

Elena cried out, her body bowing. Oh, God. He was right. It was good. Better than good. He was perfect.

He held himself still again, and she pressed her face against his neck. 'More,' she begged. 'More.'

The words set him loose and they both began moving desperately. She stroked his back and kissed the line of his collarbone. He thrust into her harder and faster. The tight fit had them both groaning and shifting.

'Damn you,' he grunted.

'I didn't want this either.' She'd tried to stay away, too, but that magnetic pull she'd felt that first evening had been indomitable.

They fell into a hard, driving rhythm, and words turned into cries and groans. The mat hissed and squeaked as it cushioned their lovemaking. Elena's senses were on overload. It was all so fast, so overwhelming.

And so carnal.

She craned her neck when he licked at her ear and she spotted their reflection in the floor-to-ceiling mirrors. She'd never seen anything so erotic. Their bodies were connecting, moving in the most intimate way, and to feel it as she watched …

She closed her eyes as her body began to spiral upwards.

She clung to the stranger who'd just become her lover. He was plunging faster and harder, and her hips rose to accept him. The slap of their bodies sounded naughty and wonderful in the empty room. That energy that always circled around them was now crackling inside them. The voltage was cranking higher and higher.

She cried out when it zapped inside her like a bolt of lightning. 'Ah, Alex!'

He bucked into her and his neck arched as the charge ran through him too.

She felt his wet warmth spurt into her, and an after-shock hit her. They stayed that way, locked together, energy shimmering. It was chemical, magical and out of control. The surge couldn't last. After long moments, the energy ebbed and then dipped.

Elena collapsed back against the blue mat and struggled to catch her breath. Alex relaxed upon her, his body heavy and warm.

'Holy hell,' he murmured. He brushed her hair away from her face. He looked as stunned as she felt. She stared into his grey eyes, happy that the wildness was gone. The panic and anxiety that had choked the room when she'd first entered had disappeared.

Only new feelings were starting to niggle at her.

Feelings of doubt …

Regret …

And, finally, dismay.

She looked up at the virile man she'd just made love to – the man she was still making love to. Their bodies were connected intimately, and she'd played a part in that. A big part, and why not? He was beautiful. Male perfection. She responded to him like she'd never responded to anyone else.

But this was Alex Wolfe.

Oh, dear God. What was wrong with her?

She pushed at his shoulder and tried to worm out from under him. 'I … I have to go.'

His eyes narrowed, but he didn't budge.

'I can't be here,' she said tightly. She couldn't do *this*.

She wiggled her hips, and his hands latched down tight.

'Hold still,' he said sharply. The lines on his forehead deepened as he looked at her, and that muscle in his jaw bulged. 'Let me.'

Heat flared in her cheeks as he disconnected their bodies. Slowly. Almost as if emphasising it. Inside, she felt the flutter of desire and her anger bubbled up all over again. That would be his way, wouldn't it? To lord it over her.

She felt wetness on the mat underneath her, and she bit her lip when his softened erection brushed against her thigh. Horror built up inside her.

She'd always been torn when it came to this man. He epitomised so many things for her … wealth, corruption, excess, greed … sex, physical attraction and lust … She knew both sides of the equation, yet rational thought had gone out the window when he'd touched her.

What was wrong with her? She was a smart, level-headed sort of girl. She knew right from wrong. This may have felt right, but it was so wrong it bordered on stupid.

She scrambled away when he sat up.

'Elena.'

She looked at him as she clutched her jeans and her top to her chest. The expression on his face made her nearly crumple, but she steeled her spine. She rocked back onto her feet and stood. The position made her feel all the more vulnerable. She didn't have the nerve to put on any of her clothes in front of him, and she knew that damned mirror stood at her back, reflecting everything for him to see.

Only he wasn't looking at the mirror. He was still looking at her face.

Her hair swung over her shoulder. 'I've got to go. I'm glad I was here to help you … with *that* …'

She tilted her head towards the bathroom door that now stood open wide.

But she never should have helped him with *that* …

She couldn't stop staring at him sitting on the mat with his elbows draped over his knees and his towel a good three feet away. He stared at her unflinchingly,

85

his expression a combination of satiation, hurt and a determination that made her uneasy.

She backed towards the door. 'I –'

She what? There really was nothing more to say. She'd just made a huge, incalculable mistake.

Turning with her clothes in her arms, she scampered towards the door.

\* \* \*

Alex watched Elena go. He wanted to follow her, but he knew this was for the better.

He rubbed the ball of his hand against his chest and looked around the room. The feeling in the gym had changed. It seemed so quiet, so empty, so dull. He rolled his neck and pushed himself to his feet.

'Ah! Damn it.' Reaching out, he braced himself against the weight bench. He looked at the bottom of his foot and grimaced. It was ugly. 'Hell.'

That was all he needed, something else to keep him contained.

Funny, only moments ago he hadn't felt the pain at all. His gaze swept the mat. She hadn't quite gotten everything on her mad dash. One sock was stuffed under a treadmill, while its partner sat on top of it. Something colourful caught his eye up by the elliptical machine, and his gaze stuck. Her bra. It was a light lavender colour, with delicate lace along the cups. He hadn't even noticed in his ham-handedness in getting it off her.

Bending down, he hooked his finger around a strap and picked it up. It was soft and padded, although she didn't need the help. He clenched the soft fabric in his fist and reached for the towel he'd dropped nearby.

He let out a gust of air when he spotted the evidence of their lovemaking still on the mat. Just looking at the wet spot, he felt himself getting hard all over again.

'Get your head out of your ass,' he chided himself.

She was right about the two of them. They had no business being together – even if she was the sexiest, most fascinating little creature he'd come across in aeons. And the hottest little spitfire. They'd nearly lit up this room with the fireworks they'd thrown together.

But that had been a huge mistake.

The two of them? With their history?

He quickly cleaned up and tossed the towel and socks in the hamper. His thumb swept over the cup of her bra for a moment before it followed suit.

Jaw hardening, he wandered over to the bathroom that had been his second prison in a week. He glared at the rubber mat that sat propped up askew in the corner. He yanked it away from the door and tossed it. The heavy rubber square went flying through the air like a super-duty magic carpet. It hit the floor in the middle of the room with a smack that rang in his eardrums.

How long would he have been stuck in there if she hadn't found him? He braced himself against the door frame, still unable to make himself go inside. He hadn't meant to pounce on her, but he'd been in that tiny eight-by-ten room long enough that he'd been riding the razor's edge. And she'd been so soft and pretty. So warm and welcoming.

He rubbed his chest again, but the ache wasn't easing. At least the snake had settled again.

He propped the door open with a ten-pound weight, washed himself quickly and got dressed. He headed upstairs, more aware of the silence than ever. He'd welcomed the peace and calm when he first arrived, but now it was bringing back memories. Unwanted memories.

He knew without a doubt that she'd gone. The house felt too heavy. He looked up and down the hallway. Why had she been here in the first place?

The books. It was the only way she would have heard him. The library was above the workout room. Thank God.

He headed to the kitchen and looked out of the window down the path to the lake house. It was still pouring outside. Her hair had been wet, he just now realised. Wet and sexy. She had to have gotten drenched on her way back. As she'd run away …

'Move on, Wolfe. You can't get involved with her. You just had to work off some steam.'

Scratch an itch. Slake his thirst.

He sighed and turned towards the coffee maker. That was when he saw the hoodie hanging on the coat rack by the kitchen door. He frowned and went over for a closer look.

The gray material was still damp. It was his, all right, the one he'd lent her down by the lake when she'd been chilled. His fingers swept over the soft fleece. The sweatshirt was too big on her, making her look like a kitten wrapped up in a blanket. He'd told her she could return it, but she'd been wearing it every time he'd seen her since. He'd liked that, knowing that she was warm and comfortable, wrapped up in what was his.

His hand fisted in the material.

Oh, hell no. This wasn't over.

He looked through the paned glass of the kitchen door and saw a light on in the cabin. He knew what they said about sirens, about the temptation and the danger, but he didn't care.

This thing between the two of them? It had only just begun.

# Chapter Five

Elena pushed herself away from the computer and rubbed her temples. She couldn't think straight. Her thoughts had been churning and freezing for the past day – ever since her 'visit' to the main house. Sighing, she looked out the window at the lake. It was agitated. The breeze was stiff, and the surface was choppy. She watched the ripples and the tiny whitecaps as they rolled towards her. The lake looked just like she felt … all roiled up.

*What had she done?*

She rubbed a tight spot in her shoulder that refused to relax. She knew exactly what she'd done. The memory was emblazoned in her head, and her body still felt the delicious after-effects. She'd made love with the last person on earth she should ever be involved with. Alex Wolfe had been her father's accomplice. Their greedy actions had hurt countless people, including her, yet none of that had mattered when she'd found him trapped in the basement.

He might be one of the richest, most powerful men in the country, but in that moment he'd needed her.

There was no way she could have walked away. His agitation and his desperation had called out to the most basic level of human compassion. Her thoughts had been centred on getting him out of that bathroom, no matter how spacious and luxurious it might have been. She'd had to help him, and the relief on his face had been worth the effort. But then he'd touched her …

And kissed her.

Heat bubbled up inside her, meshing with all the uncertainty. Her nipples became sensitive and the tenderness between her legs more apparent. Unsettled, she pulled her feet up onto the chair and hugged her legs to try to crush the sensations.

Things had just spiralled out of control so quickly. One moment she'd been looking for a book and the next she'd been flat on her back with the Sexiest Bachelor of the Year moving between her legs. She pressed her thighs together hard, but it only magnified the memory. Their lovemaking had been so raw, so elemental. So ravening. She'd never come like that. Ever. She hadn't even known it was possible.

But reality had been waiting for her when she'd floated back to earth.

And that, more than anything, embarrassed her. She'd run from the gym like a scared virgin. She wasn't sure how she could have handled the situation differently, but there must have been a better way than running bare-assed through the door. Her fingers dug deeper into the knot in her shoulder that refused to loosen.

She should be horrified by the whole experience, and she was. But, damn it, all she could remember was the way he looked naked ... and the way he felt pressed up against her and inside her ...

A knock at the door had her jerking upright and wincing when the knot in her shoulder popped.

'Ah!' She turned more carefully.

She'd been avoiding calls, and he had called. At least she'd assumed that the number she didn't recognise was his.

Another tap sounded.

Feeling very much like the side of her that had grabbed her clothes and run, she tiptoed to the bedroom door and peered around the corner. She couldn't see who was knocking. Sucking in a breath, she pulled back her shoulders, winced again and made herself enter the living room.

He knew she was here. Her car was parked outside. The only other place she could be was on a walk, but she knew that he wasn't exploring the woods right now. He'd come back half an hour ago. If she was watching him so closely, no doubt he was watching her right back.

She might as well get this over with.

When she reached the door, though, she didn't recognise the woman standing outside.

Hesitantly, she pulled the door open a few inches. If a reporter had made it onto the property, she'd feel no compunction about slamming it in the woman's face. 'Hello?'

'Hi, I'm Tabitha. Mr Wolfe sent me.'

Elena gazed at the woman and then at the area behind her, looking for cameras or microphones. 'Why?'

'I'm a massage therapist. He asked me to give this to you.'

'This' was her backpack, the one she'd left in the manor's kitchen. Elena felt off-balance, and wasn't certain what to do. She opened the door wide enough to take the bag, but closed it again like a barrier. 'Can you give me a moment?'

She felt bad about leaving the woman on her doorstep with the wind whirling around like it was, but she also wasn't ready to let her in the house.

'I'll just get my table,' the pretty blonde said.

Still feeling suspicious, Elena turned away. The backpack wasn't empty like she'd left it. It had weight and bulk to it. Her face flared when she pulled back the zipper. Her clothes were inside, the ones she'd left behind on her desperate escape. She put her socks on the back of the sofa. The grey hoodie made her frown. It was his.

She'd commandeered it for a while after he'd loaned it to her. It was just so soft and comfy. She pressed her face against the grey fleece and inhaled. It was fresh from the dryer and still warm.

She frowned. It didn't smell as much like him any more.

But that didn't matter. She'd returned it. Why was he sending it back?

And where was her bra? That was the one thing she *knew* she'd left behind.

She looked under the sweatshirt, but the only other thing she found was a plain white envelope. Heart puttering a little faster, she unfolded the hoodie and shook it out. Nothing else fell. Her bra wasn't there.

She felt warmth in her cheeks and a sudden heaviness in her breasts. Their clinch had been hot and fast, but he had suckled her so hard her nipples hadn't relaxed for the rest of the day. They perked up again at the memory and she looked worriedly at the door.

The massage therapist was waiting on the threshold, her heavy massage table folded up and leaning against her leg.

Elena opened the door again, this time wide enough to have a conversation. 'I'm not sure I understand.'

'Mr Wolfe said you might be having some soreness.'

Elena's face went from warm to blazing hot.

'From all the hiking you've been doing?' the woman continued.

'Mmm, yes.' Elena cleared her throat. 'And I've been at the computer a lot. Come in.'

She wasn't an idiot. She had proof that the masseuse had been sent by Alex. She wasn't sure if he'd sent her to score points or act as an apology, but she wasn't going to refuse the gift. Her shoulder was about to make her cry, and a massage was a luxury she hadn't been able to indulge in much, especially from a professional. She was sure that whoever he hired would be far superior to the massage-school students who practised their craft on the cheap at the local Y.

Tabitha entered and gave herself a shake. 'It's a brisk one out there today.'

'Yes, it is.'

The woman looked around the tiny cabin. 'Where would you like me to set up?'

Elena bit her lip. There wasn't a lot of room. Finally, she decided to use the space where she did yoga, but that meant moving the coffee table. If the circumstances were strange after what she was used to, Tabitha didn't say anything. She set up her supplies and then washed her hands in the bathroom while Elena stripped down and got under the sheets.

'Any particular spots I should pay attention to?' the woman asked as she came back into the room.

'My neck and shoulders,' Elena said. She couldn't tell her about the other place. That mat in the gym might have been good for sit-ups, but not for the exercise she'd engaged in. Her butt was still tender from bouncing upon it. 'And my bottom.'

The words were out before she could stop them, but why not? Why get a massage and still have a part of her body hurt? She blushed with her face tucked into the table's support ring, but the woman made no comment until she touched her back.

'Oh, hon. You're tight.'

'I've been working a lot,' Elena confessed.

'Too much. It may take a while to work this tension out.'

'Whatever you have time for would be great.'

'Time?' That got a chuckle out of the masseuse. 'I have all the time in the world. Your ...'

She paused as if she didn't know what word to use.

'Mr Wolfe,' she began again, 'hired me for the whole day. I'm supposed to give you whatever treatments you want or need. Hot stones, aromatherapy, reflexology ...'

'The whole day?' Elena would have been thrilled with a fifteen-minute foot rub.

'I believe his exact words were to "leave you limp".'

\* \* \*

Limp was an understatement.

By the time Tabitha left, Elena felt like her muscles

96

were mush. All traces of stress and tension had been systematically removed from her body. In their place was peace, near light-headedness and an indefinable euphoria. She stretched out along the sofa, her lazy limbs falling in comfortable repose. The couch was still tucked up against the breakfast bar, but she didn't have the energy to move it back into place.

'Oh, my God,' she murmured. She felt almost as good as she had after sex.

Almost.

As if she'd summoned him up, her fingers brushed against the hoodie that was still draped over the sofa's back. It had cooled, but the fleece was still soft. Impulsively, she pulled it over herself. It dropped on top of her, but so did a stiff white envelope.

She frowned, but then she remembered taking it out of her backpack. Curiosity got the best of her, and she worked her finger under the flap. When she unfolded the piece of paper inside, her mouth dropped open. She didn't know what she'd been expecting, but it wasn't this. Her gaze skimmed over the results of a check-up from a month ago at the medical clinic at the Federal Correctional Institution at Otisville.

He was clean.

The paper fell from her grip, and she pressed her fingers to her mouth. She'd been so wrapped up in the other after-effects of their encounter that she hadn't even thought about that. To be so reckless … so careless … She'd been so entangled in the emotional and logical sides that she hadn't considered the physical.

Which was ironic, since the physical was what had gotten her into trouble in the first place.

She picked the paper up from where it had fallen across her chest. She'd been avoiding his calls and she'd been avoiding him.

She bit her lip.

She couldn't avoid him any longer. She had to be responsible.

Some of the stress that Tabitha had just dispelled snuck back between her shoulder blades. Taking a deep breath, Elena reached for her phone on the kitchen counter above her and navigated to the list of missed calls. Before her nerves could get the best of her, she hit redial.

The moment the ringing began, her thoughts jumbled. What was she going to say? What would he say? It was all so uncomfortable. They'd gone from avoiding one another to rolling around on the floor together.

His low voice came on the phone much too quickly. 'Hello, Elena.'

The way he said her name made her belly squeeze, and she reflexively drew her knees up towards her chest. 'Thank you for Tabitha.'

It was a safe start. An accepted compromise.

'How do you feel?'

He might as well have reached through the phone line and stroked her side. Her eyelids drifted shut and she swallowed hard. She felt wonderful, relaxed and sensitive, but she chose her words carefully. 'De-stressed.'

'Good. I'm glad you enjoyed it.'

The conversation dipped into one of those uncomfortable pauses that happened whenever they spoke – the quiet moments with so much current moving underneath the surface. Elena ran her hand over the hoodie that covered her like a blanket. 'She returned my backpack,' she ventured.

'You're going to need those socks.'

Her lips curled up at the corners. She never would have expected him to have a sense of humour. 'I'm clean,' she whispered.

There was a quiet pause on the other end of the line, a poignant pause that held so many secrets.

'And I'm on the Pill,' she continued in that same whisper. She'd gone on it when she and her last boyfriend had been together, and she'd stayed on it long after they'd broken up because it regulated her periods.

He'd been honest with her; she had to be up front with him. He had enough problems right now. He didn't need to worry that he'd procreated with her, a Bardot. That just might possibly be the scandal to top The Scandal.

'Have dinner with me.'

The request had her sitting up halfway. It had been firm and authoritative, a powerful CEO re-establishing his control. Yet it had also been wistful, with just enough ache to remind her of the panicked man who'd clung to her as he'd fought off his claustrophobia.

'Up here at the main house. I'll get Marta to make us something, just the two of us.'

Elena scooted back until her bottom pressed against the arm of the sofa. She cuddled deeper into the sweatshirt, pulling it up to her chin. 'I don't know if that's a good idea.'

'We can't keep sneaking around this property, trying to avoid one another,' he said, the powerful side taking over.

No. No, they couldn't. She glanced at the front door to the lake house. Her car was outside. The boxes still lined the far wall.

'Just dinner,' he promised, that crooning tone coming back, almost as if he could read her mind. Funny, but that tone didn't give her platonic thoughts. 'You can get that book you wanted to borrow.'

She blinked in surprise. Ah, there was the conniving side of him, the one she'd always expected.

'We need to talk, Elena.'

Yes, they did. About what had happened and so much more. She had so many questions and so few answers. She glanced at her office. She'd been here for over a month and she'd failed to dig up many of them.

Maybe she needed to go to the source.

'All right,' she agreed before she could over-think her decision.

There was a burst of air, almost as if he'd been holding his breath. 'I look forward to seeing you.'

The last time they'd seen each other, they'd both been naked.

'I'll be there,' she promised.

\* \* \*

Elena was nervous when she knocked on the door to the main house. She tugged her jacket tighter around herself and felt a rock bite through the bottom of her pump. Her ankles were sore from the walk up the hill in heels, but she'd known better than to arrive in jeans or yoga pants. She'd been officially invited to dinner. After her last encounter in Wolfe Manor, she wanted to put on as mature a front as she could. In fact, she'd debated whether she should go to the front door, but that had seemed too formal. So she waited for the kitchen door to open, her stomach swirling and her thoughts racing.

She'd considered cancelling about a hundred times. She'd even picked up the phone twice, but he'd said 'just dinner' and they did need to talk. She couldn't carry on like this, with energy snapping between them every time they came close.

They needed to clear the air.

Still, she had to fight off the desperate urge to turn tail and flee when she heard footsteps approaching.

'There you are, dear. Welcome.' Questions were in Leonard's eyes, but a smile was on his face as he opened the door wide. He stepped back and gave a sweeping gesture, encouraging her to enter. 'Come in before the mist starts up again. We wouldn't want you to catch a chill.'

The kitchen was warm and inviting as she stepped inside. 'It smells wonderful in here. I hope you haven't gone to too much effort.'

'Nonsense. This place was made for entertaining. Wasn't it, Marta?'

The cook looked up from the kitchen island where she was preparing asparagus. Her cheeks were pink and she was beaming with pride. 'It does feel good to fire up the kitchen again. All these professional shiny appliances and nobody to –'

Her words stopped abruptly when she realised where they were leading.

Leonard smoothly stepped in. 'Let me help you with your jacket.'

Elena turned, but prickles of awareness dotted her spine when she heard other footsteps echoing.

'I'll do that.'

The low rumble set those prickles dancing and she glanced over her shoulder. Her gaze connected with grey eyes that reminded her of the clouds outside. Heavy-lidded and stormy. Alex stood in the doorway to the main hall, the one she'd slinked down the other day.

The inquisitive look on Leonard's face intensified, but, ever the professional, he nodded. 'Of course, Master Wolfe. I'll go prepare the table in the breakfast nook as you requested.'

Leonard might have put on a placid front, but the cook stared openly, her gaze darting back and forth between her boss and their guest. Elena bit her lip. She could only imagine what the woman was thinking. *Somebody* had picked up her clothes, washed them and packed them.

'Marta, could you help me?'

The cook snapped upright as if goosed. Backing away, she went to assist Leonard. She didn't allow room for her girth as she headed to the open archway and she bumped into the refrigerator. Her pink cheeks brightened. 'Excuse me.'

Elena's gaze swung back to the remaining person in the room.

Alex looked sharp and important. Intimidating and sexy in a crisp white shirt and black pants. His blue tie brought out the colour of his eyes, and that gaze wasn't moving from her. He held a glass of amber liquid, and the ice in the tumbler clinked as he set it on the breakfast bar. The high-pitched jingles sounded lyrical and threatening as he moved towards her.

Her jacket. Right.

Bending her head forward, she untied the belt. She was pulling the jacket off her shoulders when she felt his hands cover hers. The contact was warm and deliberate. She drew in a fast breath as she felt him come and stand behind her.

'Allow me,' he said, his breath sliding over her ear.

She'd caught her hair up on one side in a barrette, and goosebumps rose on her neck. Whatever she thought of the other day, this was something she hadn't overblown in her mind – the way she felt when he touched her. Her hands dropped helplessly to her sides.

He drew her jacket over her shoulders, his knuckles skimming her bare arms. He wasn't touching her anywhere else, but she was aware of his presence behind her. Big, hard and immovable. He'd been like a ghost ever since he'd arrived home, but now he was manifesting. Real, male and dominant.

The moment she was free, she turned to face him. 'Thank y –'

The words died on her lips when her breasts brushed against his chest. He was so close. She stepped back when his pupils dilated in response, but her heel banged into the coat rack. It rocked noisily, and he reached over her shoulder to catch it before it fell.

'Sorry.' She cringed at her awkwardness, but took the opportunity to duck under his arm and step further into the kitchen. 'I can be a bit clumsy.'

At least around him.

'Really? All I've seen is you trotting through the trees

like a doe or going through yoga poses like a master.'
He hung up her jacket and turned. The raw emotions of
the day before were gone, and he looked different. The
rugged outdoorsman and the sexy athlete were hidden.
She'd been able to relate somewhat to both those sides of
him, but tonight he looked like the powerful executive he
was, rich, confident and used to getting what he wanted.

She smoothed her H&M dress. It was the third outfit
she'd tried on. It had a scooped neck and was of fitted lace
with a sewn-in slip dress underneath. The slender shoulder
straps made the outfit more appropriate for summer, but
the black colour gave it a pricey look. Considering that
she hadn't packed for fancy dinners when she'd come here,
it was the best she could do on short notice – especially
with reporters still blocking the exits.

'You look beautiful,' he said.

She pressed a hand to her stomach as his gaze raked
over her, slow and hot.

He reached for her and she jumped, instinctively
looking over her shoulder in case Marta was still
watching. Colour flooded her face when, instead of his
touch, she heard the tinkle of ice in a glass. A bemused
look came over his face as he swirled the amber liquid.
'Can I get you something?'

Absolutely not. By all rights she should remain clear-
headed, but it would be nice to have something to hold
onto. Something that might ease her nerves ...

'White wine?' she said throatily.

'I'm sure we can find something that will do the trick.' This time he did touch her, his hand settling against the small of her back. With strides measured to match hers, he led her to the open archway. He stopped as they walked through it, though, and looked back. 'How much time do we have before dinner is ready, Marta?'

The cook pirouetted around the corner, biting her lower lip. She'd been caught hovering, and she knew it. 'A while, Master Wolfe. I'm just starting on the risotto.'

'Excellent,' he murmured.

No. Not excellent. Elena pressed her tongue against the roof of her mouth as she walked into the open grand room with the floor-to-ceiling windows. Minute rice would be fine for her. Alex's hand felt huge on the small of her back as he led her to the wet bar, and she could have sworn that his thumb moved over the ends of her hair. The touch was impersonal and intimate at the same time, and she shivered at the coolness she felt when it left her.

'2008 Leflaive Puligny-Montrachet?'

She licked lips that were suddenly dry as paper. 'Whatever you have is fine.'

His grey gaze was steady. 'I think you'll like it.'

Unlike her, he seemed rock solid – unembarrassed by what had happened – although a bit curious. Maybe he rolled around on the floor with neighbours all the time.

He was certainly rich enough and handsome enough to get any woman he wanted. According to the magazines and online blogs, he hadn't passed on many opportunities to 'social network'.

Yet he had been imprisoned for the last eighteen months ...

Elena drank from the glass he passed to her. He might be a man of the world, cultured and suave, but she wasn't as easygoing. She didn't sleep around. She'd had steady boyfriends, but she'd never –

'Mmm,' she murmured with pleasure. The flavour of the expensive wine spread over her tongue like smooth honey. She swallowed, tasting the unexpected spiced notes, and was distracted.

He caught her hand. 'That's better.'

He drew her to the sofa. She kept a respectable distance between them as they sat, but the white leather was unexpectedly comfortable. The cushions were so deep, they sucked her in and defied her to remain rigid. She sat up straighter, near the edge, and crossed her ankles. She couldn't allow her guard to drop, not around him.

Hand tightening around her drink, she took another deep sip. The wind was rising outside. The trees were swaying and those last leaves were fluttering wildly. Inside the mansion, though, she didn't hear the wind's howl.

'Did I ever thank you for what you did?' he finally

asked, his low voice breaking the silence that had taken over the room.

She looked at him through her lashes.

'For rescuing me.' There was no curve at all to his lips. He wasn't teasing or being coy.

'I ... I don't remember,' she replied.

'Thank you.'

The words were honest and heartfelt. They weren't characteristics she'd normally associate with a Wolfe, and they made her chest tighten. 'You're welcome.'

Their gazes connected and, in that moment, something passed between them. Not trust, no, but something maybe closer to empathy. Worried about what that connection might be, Elena focused harder on the windows. The sun was setting, but there weren't any golden flecks on the water. The sky had been overcast all day long, and the lake was just growing darker and more opaque.

'Haunting, isn't it?' she remarked.

His ice clanked. 'More than you know.'

'What do you mean?'

He shrugged, his gaze snagging on the rough water. 'This place is full of memories for me. They keep popping up when I least expect it.'

And not all of them were good. He was hard to read, practically detached, but she could feel how his mood changed. It was subtle, but she was beginning to notice the difference.

'Did you grow up here?'

'No, but my parents would send me here to spend the summers.'

'With your grandfather?'

'This is his house.'

The temperature in the place had just dropped ten degrees. Elena considered her host. She felt an icy rage every time she thought about Bartholomew Wolfe, but why would he? The answer dawned like a light bulb.

His grandfather had gotten away with it.

'Why come here then?' she asked. He'd spent the last eighteen months in prison. Why make this the first place he'd come when he'd regained his freedom?

'The seclusion and the privacy. I'd have preferred to go to my apartment in Manhattan, but I knew this place would be more secure.'

More secure? Or would he have better access to what he and his co-conspirators had left behind?

He drew up his left leg and rested his ankle on his opposite knee. His foot bounced restlessly. 'I'm sorry you got caught up in all the drama. The press tends to follow me wherever I go.'

So he'd known this would happen, while she'd been blind-sided once again. The delicious wine turned a little bitter in her mouth. 'You didn't know I was here,' she murmured.

'No,' he said softly. 'I didn't.'

They watched the water as it slapped against the side

of the dock. It was like observing a silent movie, with action going on all around but no soundtrack.

'Leonard said that the paparazzi harassed you, that it was the reason you came here.'

She ran her finger around the lip of her glass. Reporters and others had run her out of town on a rail, but he didn't need to know that. The less he knew about the power he'd held over her life, the better. 'I'd rather not talk about it.'

His foot stopped bouncing, and his gaze grabbed hers. 'I'm happy to provide you refuge. You can stay as long as you want or need to.'

'I got the impression that you didn't like the intrusion on your property.'

'I didn't,' he confessed. 'I wasn't happy when I discovered you were staying at the lake house, but yesterday I was glad you were here.'

Because of the door? Or because of the sex?

Elena took a gulp of her wine, the flavour returning full and strong. There was a huge pink elephant standing in the middle of the room and they were both ignoring it. They'd had sex. Quick, can't-get-to-it-fast-enough sex. They both knew it. The cook and the butler had to know it. Yet nobody was acknowledging it.

The air in the open room became heavy. Pulsing. It sparked when his hand covered hers where she'd braced it against the sofa.

'I'm beginning to think it would be nice not to be so alone.'

Her eyelids dipped. She'd had to be strong for so long. For a moment, the tiniest of seconds, she let herself sink into the feeling of kinship. The wine, the comfortable surroundings and especially the handsome man at her side tugged at her. The offer of protection was seductive.

His fingers laced with hers, and his palm encompassed the back of her hand. His touch was warm while her fingers were cold. Her fingers curled, digging into the soft leather.

So tempting.

And so very wrong.

She pulled her hand away. He let her go, and she stood on unsteady legs. She tilted her glass for another sip, but discovered it was empty.

He stood in a motion that was so fluid, it made her take a step back. It still surprised her how tall and swift he was.

He took her glass from her chilled fingers. 'Let me get you a refill.'

Not a good idea. She could already feel the effects. She hadn't had much to eat since his unexpected invitation, and she was a lightweight. Literally. She was petite, and alcohol affected her more than others.

'Maybe later.' She smoothed her dress self-consciously. It had cost her a whole thirty-five dollars. The wine glass she'd just clenched like a lifeline was probably worth as much. 'Can I get that book?'

She couldn't sit on that luxurious sofa with him any longer. The cushions just made her want to curl into them ... and him ...

'Of course. Right this way – but you know that.'

His touch settled again on the place on her back, although a little higher this time, under the sweep of her hair. Awareness unfurled in her belly as they began that long walk down the hall. The closer they got to the library, the more she focused on the day before. The sounds she'd heard ... The desperation she'd felt in the air ... That wounded man couldn't have been further from the one she found today. This Alex Wolfe was quiet, composed and focused. Steel-like in his control.

Yet just as rawly sexual.

Which was the real Wolfe? Had she even met him yet?

The library was dark. Alex reached inside to turn on the light before allowing her to enter first. No matter how many times she visited the place, it still made her breath catch. There was no first-floor ceiling in this part of the house. The library went up a full three floors, with books in shelves circling on each level. It was a collection that went back hundreds of years yet still managed to keep up with the latest best-sellers. She didn't know why, but she had an inkling that Leonard had something to do with that.

'Which book was it you needed? Or was there a subject matter that interested you?'

The questions brought her out of her reverie, and she found her host watching her curiously. 'I know what I need. It's right over here.'

She went to the far wall and traced her fingers along the second shelf. She paused when she found an empty space where the book should be. 'It's gone.'

The oddest look settled onto his face. 'That one?'

She nodded.

His mouth tightened in a slight frown. 'I know where it is.'

His eyes narrowed almost imperceptibly, but when he held out his hand she couldn't ignore it. She placed her hand in his and felt his warm fingers wrap around hers. It was the first time since yesterday that she'd touched him back, and that awareness she'd felt began to expand. She couldn't have been more alert to the difference in their sizes, their bodies and, most of all, their places in the world.

They went down the hallway to the small staircase she'd found yesterday but, instead of going to the basement, this time she followed him up to the second floor. The deeper they went into the house, the quieter it was. The more secluded. The hallway was narrower on the second level and the carpet thicker, more dense. Whereas downstairs her high heels had echoed on the hardwood flooring, here her steps were swallowed up like secrets.

113

Elena looked around with curiosity and some uneasiness. Leonard and Marta were puttering around in the kitchen. Up here, she and Alex were alone. She ran her tongue over her dry lips, wishing she hadn't said no to that wine. She wasn't afraid of him physically. She didn't get even the slightest vibe that he'd hurt her. In fact, she got the opposite. It was just … Wild, untamed things seemed to happen whenever the two of them were alone.

They passed an open room. A bedroom. Guest, from the looks of it. She swept her fingers over a polished oak hallway table. The flowers on it were fresh. Another open room stood on the right, and then –

Another bedroom, and definitely not a guest room.

She looked inside for only a split second before she snapped her head straight again. It was his. She knew without asking. The bed was made, the room was spotless, yet it somehow seemed lived in and not by a woman.

It was his. His bedroom. His private place.

'Here,' he murmured.

She wasn't ready when he turned, and she bumped up against him, a tall, muscled brick wall. He steadied her, still holding her hand. 'Sorry. Forgot to use my turn signal.'

She smiled nervously, a little out of breath.

Again, he hit the light switch before entering the next room. When she looked around, she realised that he'd brought her directly into the heart of the wolf's den. Her breath went short and her eyes widened. It was his office.

He walked to the desk and picked up the book that lay open next to his laptop. 'Is this what you were looking for?'

She tilted her head to read the title. 'Yes,' she said in surprise. It was an advanced book on macroeconomics. What was he doing with it? 'But I can wait if you're using it.'

His grey stare bored into her for a moment longer than was comfortable. At last, he closed the pages with a snap. 'I was getting nowhere with it. Maybe you can explain it to me.'

Her jittery insides cooled. Explain market behaviour and trading philosophies to a white-collar criminal who'd secretly managed to rig the entire system?

'I somehow doubt that,' she said flatly.

This was the home office of a billionaire entrepreneur. A software magnate and a perpetrator of a Ponzi scheme whose spider webs were continuing to be found weaving throughout society. There wasn't much that this man didn't understand or couldn't master.

Was this where he and his grandfather had come up with the plan?

She took the book and clutched it to her chest. Her jaw set as she looked about the room. The office furniture was made of glossy cherrywood, and the chairs were that same luxurious leather, only deep red. Wall clocks kept track of various time zones around the world. Two monitors sat on the desk in front of the laptop she'd seen in the garden the other day – along with that red spiral-bound notebook. It was opened next to where the book had been, and a pen had been dropped haphazardly on top of it. Whatever notes had been written were scratched out in a cloud of black ink.

'You already taught me more about the subject than my professor.' She tapped on the photograph on the back of the hardcover book. 'And he wrote the book.'

Alex's face changed subtly, going first to anger. She could see it in the spark in his grey eyes, but it was forcibly dampened. The easygoing charm hardened, but his face went blank. She saw a muscle pulsing in his jaw, an impromptu expression that he couldn't control. She watched that tiny muscle clench, knowing that it connected with deep emotions. She knew because she'd encountered them, up close and personal.

She took a step back towards the door.

'Wait.' His voice was controlled but authoritative. 'There's something else you wanted to see.'

Elena watched suspiciously as he went to the side wall, the one that separated the office from his bedroom. 'You were curious about the situation on the road,' he said as he picked up a remote. 'I have a live video feed from my security team.'

For the first time, she noticed the televisions that were arranged on the wall. Pushing a series of buttons, he brought them to life. The footage was black and white, but it clearly showed the main road. The wolf's head on the front gate was displayed as one camera panned to the left.

Yet that wasn't what made her stomach turn.

She'd been so focused on the danger inside that fence, she'd forgotten what was lurking outside. 'So many?' she gasped. 'But it's been over a week.'

Hugging the book tighter, she moved closer to see. The road was packed with news vans. Some call-signs she recognised; others she didn't. They were parked back-to-back along the side of the remote two-lane road.

'They're curious if I'm going to make an appearance at the Wolfe Financial board meeting later this month.'

Elena couldn't stop staring at the multiple screens. 'Are you?'

She couldn't imagine fighting her way through that horde.

He shrugged. 'I haven't made up my mind yet, but I'd be more tempted to go to the Wolfe Pack company lunch on Friday.'

She mulled that over, along with the fact that he was sharing such information with her. Wolfe Financial was the blue-blood investment corporation the Wolfe family had run for generations. The Wolfe Pack was the financial software company he'd created on his own in his early twenties, the breakout SaaS startup that had become a worldwide phenomenon.

Why tell her such a thing? Was it a test? She had a

phone. All those news vans would gobble up even that little piece of information, and it might lead them away long enough that she could make her escape.

She rejected the idea before it had even fully formed. He'd offered her protection, and it had been an honest olive branch. She knew that in her gut. She couldn't offer him any less in return, not under these circumstances. He was right. They were unwitting allies in this. They'd both chosen the same spot in this grown-up game of hide-and-seek. They needed to make room for one another.

He flicked a switch and the monitors went black. The loss of the two-dimensional world brought her back to the office with the real, three-dimensional man beside her. He folded his arms over his chest. Even in his dress clothes, she could see the strength in the movement, the power of his body. 'That's why I stopped you from hiking up near the gate.'

She bit her lip. If that mob had caught even the slightest glimpse of her ...

'Is there enough security to keep them out?' she asked.

'I've hired the firm that normally does my security detail when I'm in the city. They're the best, and they've been made aware there's a beautiful brunette on the premises.'

Elena felt her cheeks heat. Just when she thought she'd gotten her head on straight about him, he had to remind her why being at such close quarters wasn't a good idea.

'They'll give you your space, but they'll protect you. If you stay close to the lake and the houses, you'll never even see them.'

She pressed her lips together. Funny, but it was sounding more and more like the prison he'd just left, only they were keeping people out rather than locking him in.

He stepped closer to her, and her nerves jumped. She tilted her head back to look at his face.

That muscle was still pulsing in his jaw, but his anger had vaporised. He reached out and brushed back a long curl that had fallen forward over her shoulder. 'We have to find a way to make this work, you and I, living together in this space.'

He'd barely touched her, but she could feel the hot trail his fingertips left on her collarbone. She nodded. They were from different worlds, two ends of a spectrum, but they had to agree on this. For both their sakes.

Off in the distance, a bell rang.

It was soft, but it reminded Elena they weren't alone. She took a step back, but he wrapped his arm around her waist. His hand took its increasingly familiar spot on her lower back, and he dipped his head so his words brushed over her bare ear.

'We might as well start with dinner.'

# *Chapter Six*

Dinner was … unexpected. As on edge as Elena was, the evening turned out to be precisely as advertised. When she relaxed enough to forget herself, the meal was pleasant. With Leonard and Marta hovering nearby, it wasn't the time or the place for pointed questions or fireworks of any kind. She'd forgotten herself with Alex the other day. She was on guard for any signs of manipulation or innuendo, yet all she could detect were signs of a handsome, well-mannered dinner date.

Marta's meal of cider-roasted chicken, asparagus, and mushroom risotto also made her forget her nervous stomach. With Alex supplying more white wine, the experience was a delight for Elena's taste buds. She'd been living on cereal and peanut-butter-and-jelly sandwiches. She could cook, but she'd been more intent on working. It felt wonderful to sit back and enjoy food that had been prepared by someone who obviously loved her craft.

The fact that the meal was in an idyllic setting didn't hurt.

She was still amazed at the little breakfast nook that she'd somehow overlooked. The circular room sat out on the balcony, off the kitchen. The open archway had a door with a rounded top that could be closed for privacy. Other doors opened onto the terrace. They were closed against the weather, and the small room took on the feeling of a gazebo, complete with heat and electricity.

They'd used very little of the latter.

A chandelier lit the table, but it had been dialled down to low and candles provided most of the illumination. They were placed in sconces on the walls, and the ambiance brought her back to times of knights, ladies and castles. Times of chivalry and passion. Out on the balcony, she could hear the howl of the wind and the waves hitting the shore. The darkness would have seemed threatening if they hadn't been nestled in the safety and warmth of the little room.

'When was this house built?' she asked. She'd avoided the manor as much as she could, but now that she was being given access to some of its more unique features she was becoming intrigued.

'In 1892 by Josiah Wolfe.'

'How many greats before that grandfather?'

One of Alex's eyebrows rose and the corner of his mouth followed. 'Too many for me to count, especially with all the wine I've drunk.'

The 2008 **Montrachet** had been flowing. It made everything seem to go down more easily.

Everything, and that made Elena a little nervous.

She smoothed the linen napkin over her lap. She knew who he was and she knew what he'd done, yet he could be charming.

Like a beautiful wolf who wanted to be petted.

Warning signs had been flashing in her head, but now they were dim and fading. He was surprising her. She'd expected the conversation to continue in that stilted, uncomfortable manner they seemed to have perfected, but the truce they'd made upstairs was holding. So far, they'd managed to be on their best behaviour. They'd stayed away from sensitive subjects, which were many and varied, and kept mainly to current affairs, apart from his release, which had taken over the airwaves. He seemed hungry for news of the world, or at least someone to discuss it with. He asked for her impressions, how the public had reacted to certain events and why things had turned out in certain ways.

Elena was amazed to find herself just as eager for conversation. He wasn't the only one who'd been isolated from other people. It had been ages since someone had valued her opinion, and she was interested in more than just the stock market. She was leaning forward to press her point about the Yankees' playoff hopes when a candle over his shoulder flared, seemingly at her.

The admonition cooled her enthusiasm. This was Alex Wolfe. He wasn't her friend.

'Excuse me.' They both looked up when a shadow was cast across the dinner table.

'Yes, Leonard?' Alex asked.

'May I take your plates, sir?'

Her host looked at her dessert plate. 'Are you finished?'

Elena set down her fork. The Bailey's-and-cream cheesecake had been rich and silky. 'It's delicious, but I can't take another bite.'

'Marta will be pleased that you enjoyed it,' Leonard said.

Elena tilted her head. She didn't know the cook well, but she was becoming fond of her. 'Will you thank her for me? That risotto just melted in my mouth.'

Alex drummed his fingers against the arm of his chair. 'I believe you just told her yourself. Didn't she, Marta?'

At his raised voice, the cook shuffled around the corner. Her hands fisted in her apron and she gave a quick curtsy. 'Thank you, dear. I wasn't given much notice you were coming so I had to make do with what I had on hand.'

Elena smiled. 'I'd love to see what you could whip up with the Mac-'n'-cheese and pretzels I have at the lake house.'

Marta grinned. 'I do have a casserole recipe ...'

'Will you need anything else from us tonight?' Leonard asked as he cleared the dishes.

123

'That should be all.' Alex laid his napkin on the table. 'Thank you. Be careful on your drives home.'

'Then goodnight to both of you,' the butler said with a stiff bow.

Marta gave another shallow curtsy, which was actually just a wiggle of her plump knees. 'Sir ... Ma'am.'

Elena didn't know what brought her back to earth harder, being called 'ma'am' or the fact that the staff was leaving.

She watched them go. Suddenly nervous, she hooked her hair behind her ear, only to find it already caught in the barrette. Uncertain what to do, she clasped her hands in her lap. She hadn't anticipated having such a nice time, but that didn't mean she'd forgotten she was having dinner with a sexy, dangerous man. As comfortable as she'd been in his presence, she hadn't lost the goosebumps where he'd touched her back ... or the tickles where his breath had brushed over her neck ...

She glanced across the empty table. In the candlelight, he was even more dark and mysterious. Handsome and tempting.

'More wine?' he asked, lifting the bottle from the wine bucket at his elbow. Between the two of them, they'd nearly finished it off.

She could already feel the languor in her muscles and the cloudiness in her head. More wine was not a good idea. 'I should be going, too.'

'It's early.'

It really wasn't. 'I need to be up first thing in the morning. I have some research I need to do.'

'The book?'

She pushed back her chair. 'The book.'

He was out of his chair and helping her before she recognised the old-fashioned gesture. Once she did, she placed her hand in his and rose to her feet. He hovered over her, tall and muscled. Balancing in her high heels suddenly became tricky, and she tugged at her dress, which had risen too high on her thighs. His gaze slid over the exposed flesh like a warm stroke and she quivered.

'Thank you for dinner,' she said.

'You're welcome.' He didn't step back. 'It's gotten rather nasty out there. Are you sure you want to make that walk?'

She glanced at the windows. The wind was whipping. Trees were dancing and the mist had turned into streaks of rain.

'All the more reason for me to hurry along.' In the small room, she couldn't help but brush against him as she moved towards the archway. She was surprised to find the kitchen empty when she entered. 'Are they gone already? I didn't hear the door.'

'The staff parks in the enclosed garage downstairs.'

The emptiness of the house seemed to echo then. All this richly adorned space for only the two of them? It seemed greedy somehow. Indulgent, yet intimate.

The hollowness loomed, like a well Elena was afraid to fall into.

She had to get away from the edge.

Her heels clipped against the tiled flooring as she walked to the coat rack. Once again, he got there first to assist her.

'I'm not used to men with manners,' she said self-consciously.

'You should be.'

She pushed her arms into the jacket he held for her. When she went to release her hair, his hands were already there. He lifted the dark swath with care, sliding his fingers through it as he smoothed it down her back.

'Your hair is mesmerising,' he said quietly.

Her crowning feature, as her mother called it.

Elena looked at the floor, trying to get herself under control. Her body wanted to lean back into him, but the track lighting in the kitchen was so much brighter than the candlelight she'd adjusted to. It made everything seem so exposed, so glaring. So judgmental. She cinched up her trenchcoat. 'Thank you.'

He traced her barrette. 'Why don't you spend the night? You're going to get drenched if you head back to the lake house, and there are plenty of extra rooms here.'

'I'll run quick.'

'In those heels? They're sassy as hell, but they're not good for a trek in the mud.'

She licked her dry lips. He'd noticed her shoes. 'I'll be fine.'

'All right then.' He took another jacket from the coat rack, and her head snapped towards him.

'The least I can do is walk you there.'

'But ... OK,' she conceded. The book that she was using as an excuse was lying on the counter. Leonard had wrapped it for her. She caught it up against her chest like a shield, such as the knights of old carried for protection.

She waited for Alex to put on his jacket and then opened the door. The wind was waiting. Seeing an opening, it rushed in. The chill smacked into her face and rain splattered against her legs. She wasn't prepared for the force of it and the door swung back, knocking into her.

'Ooh.' She sucked in a surprised breath. Cringing at the thought of going out into that, she nonetheless ducked her head and started forward.

She jerked when the wolf behind her reached past and shoved the door closed, blocking out the howl that threatened.

'Stay.'

His breath was against her ear, and his chest was hot against her back. Elena's knees wavered, and she clutched the book so tightly it dug into her breasts.

This request was different. He wasn't offering her a spare room.

'Why?' she whispered.

'Because I slept the whole night through last night.' His low voice was so close to her ear, she could feel his lips. 'And because this time I intend it to be about you, not me.'

The book slipped from her fingers and became wedged between her hips and the door. She'd never heard anything sexier in her life.

There he was. This was the man who'd made love to her in the gymnasium, uncaring of where they were or who might find them. This was the virile male she'd worried she'd find if she came here tonight.

And, at the same time, feared she wouldn't.

'We ... we shouldn't,' she stammered. That pink elephant was now stamping its feet, demanding attention.

'Why not?'

Because he was amoral and unapologetic. Greedy and self-centred.

Although she hadn't seen that side of him tonight ... or at all since he'd returned to the manor ...

'*I* shouldn't,' she amended.

'Most people would agree with that.' His other hand settled possessively on her hip. 'Then again, they've already got the Wolves and Bardots in bed with each other.'

Warmth spread from his hand around to her stomach and down to her core. She leaned her head against the door. Her resolve was wavering.

He nuzzled against her hair. 'You need to connect with somebody as badly as I do, Elena. We've been drawn to each other from the first moment we saw one another. Yesterday proved why.'

Oh, that wasn't fair.

Talking about their explosive coming together while touching her …

The book hit the floor as she turned around. Her brain felt clogged. She knew she should be thinking a certain way, but she suddenly didn't know which way that was. The wine. The sexual magnetism. Her moral compass was spinning.

He was already leaning towards her. Seeing the look on her face, he moved in those last few inches. 'There's a reason why we were put here together.'

Was there?

Eyes locked on hers, he took off his overcoat. Tossing it aside, he reached for the belt of hers. 'We could be each other's salvation.'

His lips settled over hers and the kiss was slow, full-on and sensual. He kissed with his entire body, his weight pressing her against the door. Arousal seeped through Elena and she clutched at him, her fingers sinking into his trim waist.

At her touch, some of his rawness came through. Hungry. Impatient. Whip-sharp.

It brought her up onto her toes, and he flattened her against the door with his knees and hips.

'You are so unbelievably gorgeous,' he grated against her lips. 'I want you so badly, sometimes I can't think straight.'

A mew left her lips, and the irony wasn't lost on her. Yesterday she'd opened a door and freed him and his sexual needs. Today he was trapping her against one, making her face her own.

She speared her fingers through his hair. It was softer than it looked. Like a pelt, thick and luxurious.

He nuzzled against her neck and smoothed his hands down her body. Her jacket came off in the process and she shivered violently.

'Cold?' he asked, nipping at her ear. Goosebumps ran down her neck and she quivered again. Clipping her hair back had been the ultimate temptation for him. He'd been obsessed with that barrette and her exposed skin all night.

Feeling his lips move along her neck, she was becoming a bit fixated, too. 'I don't know what I am.'

He hauled her up against him, curling one arm around her waist and lifting her. She clung to him, wrapping both arms around his neck. He made her feel tiny and feminine when he did that.

'You just hold onto me, baby.' Sealing his mouth over hers, he carried her through the kitchen on autopilot.

Elena didn't know where he was taking her until he put her on her feet. They were in the grand room in front of all the plate-glass windows. With night fully settled over the landscape, their reflections bounced off the glass like a mirror. As she watched, he reached around and caught the zipper at the back of her dress.

There was a soft hiss and then the material was loose. He peeled it from her body, pushing it down until it pooled at her feet. She instinctively covered herself with her hands. Anyone out in those vast woods would be able to see. Yet seeing him standing over her, fully dressed and businesslike, while she stood in nothing but her underwear and high heels was so erotic she couldn't stop staring.

He traced the strap of her navy blue bra. 'You like sexy lingerie.'

She blushed.

'I'll make a note of it.'

'You didn't give back the bra I was wearing yesterday.'

'I know.' He cupped her breast. She caught at his sides, but arched in pleasure.

He squeezed possessively, watching her face with laser-like focus. She bit her lip, but groaned aloud when his thumb rubbed hard over the centre of the cup.

Determinedly, he pressed her down onto the sofa. The leather was cool, but the sumptuous cushions wrapped around her like a second lover. They pulled her in, warming to her flesh and cradling her in comfort. She settled back and watched him curiously, her eyelids feeling drugged.

That wine had been potent.

Or maybe it was just him.

He was breathing hard as he stood over her. 'Don't move.'

The sensual feeling intensified when the lights were doused. Instead of falling into pitch darkness, the room was lit by a golden glow that flickered and moved as if alive. Her heavy gaze fell on the hearth. Someone had started a fire.

The flames licked upwards, eating oxygen and spitting it back in pops and hisses. The warm glow reached out to her, tickling her flesh. She looked up as Alex stepped in front of her. His tie was already off and his shirt was unbuttoned. With the fire backlighting him, he looked like sin itself as he shrugged off his shirt and threw it carelessly across the room.

She reached for him as he halted in front of her.

'We're going to go slower this time,' he said as he caught her by the wrists.

He dropped onto his knees and pressed her hands firmly onto the sofa. He was looking into her eyes so deeply, she felt like he was staring into her soul. When he let go of her hands, she left them where they were, her fingers biting into the soft leather.

He caught her knees then, drew them apart and inserted himself between them.

Elena's heart began to pound like a big bass drum.

It rumbled in her ears when he caught her hips and drew her forward. He didn't stop until the hardness of his hipbones pressed into her inner thighs and the stiffness of his erection rubbed against the crotch of her panties. Lodged so tightly, only thin layers of material separated them.

He watched her face intently. 'I'm sorry if I scared you yesterday.'

Her breath caught in her throat. It wasn't fear she was feeling now.

Compelled, she reached for him again. His physique was so lean and ripped, so hard and chiselled. He came to her, leaning over her, and her fingertips dug into the muscles of his back. With the fire illuminating him, he looked like a golden Michelangelo.

He hovered over her, one hand still firmly wrapped around her knee, the other stroking her hair. He ran his thumb over her barrette and traced the lobe of her ear. 'Did I hurt you?'

The knot of air in her throat wouldn't move so she answered with a shake of her head.

'I was mindless,' he confessed.

He brushed his lips over hers. 'I'm going to make you need me the same way.'

That knocked the breath out of her in raspy jolts. She sucked it all back in when he ran his hands down her front, palms flat and fingers spread wide. He raked over her breasts, along her stomach and over her hips until he caught the straps of her thong.

The stretchy material was no match for him.

She bit her lip, but lifted her hips when he raised an eyebrow at her. The nylon pulled wide as he coaxed it over her spread legs, the material biting into her skin. He refused to budge from his place, though, and she had to lift her heels high off the floor to rid herself of the nipping garment.

She groaned aloud when the movement rubbed her core over the bulge at the front of his pants.

The sensation was so erotic and naughty. She was bare while he wasn't.

Shyness had her trying to close her knees to hide herself, but the move only caught him tighter. He'd planted himself in the best and worst spot possible.

She groaned.

'Need me yet?' he asked.

'Yes,' she hissed.

'Not enough.'

The front closure of her bra gave way with a pop and he tossed the cups aside, exposing her. Elena gasped when his mouth came down on her. After all the drama with her panties, she'd expected him to tease and coax her.

He did neither.

Instead, he gave her all she could handle.

134

She clutched the back of his neck as his mouth tugged at her nipple. 'Alex!'

'Mmm,' he hummed, giving her a soothing lick. 'That's better. You refused to say my name for too long.'

He caught the tender nub with his teeth. 'I want to hear you scream it.'

She let out a whimper.

Her tummy trembled as his attention drifted lower. His mouth was hot, but his tongue was like one of the flames in the fireplace. It dipped into her belly button and she twisted. Those flames only licked lower and lower still.

She writhed against the smooth white leather as the fire crackled hot and bright. She was rocking from side to side as he kissed his way from one hipbone to the other, but went shock still when he slid his hand between their bodies and cupped her.

'Oh!' Squeezing her eyes tight, she clutched at his forearm.

He ground the ball of his hand in a tight circle. 'So sweet.'

He spread her legs wider and she flushed from head to toe when he removed his hand to look at her. His concentration was so intense, the flames in the fireplace might as well have jumped onto her.

'Easy,' he murmured. His fingertips were gentle as he petted her, spreading her folds. 'You waxed.'

She had. She didn't know why. She hadn't planned for this to happen ever again with him.

135

Or had she?

'I shouldn't ...' she panted. 'It's too ...'

'It's just right,' he said as he leaned in for an intimate kiss.

Her body stiffened when his tongue dragged over her core in a long lick. Nerve endings fired and muscles contracted. He settled in deeper and she let out a cry when he prodded the sensitive bundle of nerves at her apex.

Shyness and self-consciousness left her as pleasure consumed her. More than pleasure – need. With his hands, his mouth, and that raspy beard, he went down on her. Fully and enthusiastically. Her body undulated on the sofa. With the fire and her rising body temperature, the leather had warmed. Beads of sweat rose on her skin as he pushed her body harder and higher.

'Ah!' she cried when she felt penetration.

He pushed a finger deep as he sucked on her, his tugging tight and insistent. Propped up on the cushions as she was, she could see everything he was doing. She cupped his head, threading her fingers through his hair as he buried his face against her. The sight was carnal enough, until she caught their reflection in the windows. The golden glow from the fireplace lit them, caressing them both as it moved and shifted. There was no doubt as to what he was doing to her, and the darkness of the world outside pressed against the windows, looking on. The wind howled and trees clacked as it was held at bay.

'More,' he growled.

SolaceIn Scandal

He was voracious as he demanded her pleasure. He was firmly in control, but this was a different kind of control. His emotions were on the surface. He could no more push them away than she could.

Elena let out a soft cry when he pulled his fingers out of her, but then he was sliding both hands under her bottom and tilting her hips upwards. The position couldn't have been more submissive. She was splayed out for anything he wanted to do, anything he wanted to see.

His head dipped again, and he replaced his fingers with his tongue. The thickness was startling, and she flew into a fast orgasm that rocked her entire body. Ecstasy clashed with need and she pushed her hips at him, wanting more, begging for more.

He continued going at her until she sagged back onto the slippery white leather. With gentle hands he lowered her hips. His grey eyes were stormy as he stroked her body. He cupped her breasts and pushed himself up onto his haunches. She felt weighted down as he crawled up over her, his gaze never wavering from hers.

'Need me now?' he asked, his voice like sandpaper.

Oh, dear God.

'Yes,' she panted, her breaths ragged and uneven.

'Good,' he said in that same rough voice. 'Because I need you.'

He lifted her legs until her calves were braced against his shoulders. It was only then that Elena saw that she was still wearing her black high heels. The picture made her belly contract. He was right. They were much better for this than for walking down that hill. The sight was even sexier when he left her legs where they were and undid his pants.

Their gazes connected as the rasp drew out across the room.

When he leaned over her again, she felt the stretch in the backs of her thighs and the pressure at her entrance. His erection was stiff and thick. Heavy, but he'd made her slick and hot.

He pushed harder and her entrance surrendered. She let out a choked gasp when he moved up inside her. She was small compared to him, and the position made him seem huge.

'Relax,' he crooned. 'Your body is ready.'

She had to stretch to take him. His hands tightened around her shins as he held her legs where they were, pressed against his chest. In instinct or in panic she pushed back, but his shoulders just dug deeper into her calves.

And her hips tilted up, greedy for more.

'Ohhh,' she moaned.

He gave her what she wanted, burrowing into her steadily until she'd taken all of him. Her nipples peaked and tendrils of lighting shot out from her sensitive nub when he ground against her.

'So good,' he breathed.

She caught at him, at the cushions behind her head, anything she could latch onto.

But then he started moving, and she had no sense of time or place. All she knew was him and the perfect way their bodies came together. He pumped into her, slowly at first and then with more insistence. Harder. Faster. His hips swung in a wide arc, pulling back to almost leave her before plunging in deep yet again.

Her toes pointed straight up in the air, her heels close to his ears.

It was overwhelming. Primal. Undeniable.

And then she was coming again, over and over. One big wave came at her after another. She cried out in completion and he thrust hard, driving home. His head snapped back and a masculine groan filled the air. His fingers bit into her hips, and then one last wave took her under.

When her senses righted, Elena opened her eyes. Alex was braced over her, his weight on his arms as he tried to catch his breath. His muscled chest was working and his eyes were bright and clear. Firelight flickered over them, making shadows dance on the wall.

She pulled her legs down, and they both grunted as their connection shifted. His erection had softened, but he was still buried inside her.

A bead of sweat dropped from his forehead and splattered against her chest. He wiped it up with his fingertips, but then cupped her breast possessively.

'No running away this time,' he said, his voice quiet but fierce. He moved in for one last kiss. 'Stay with me.'

# Chapter Seven

Alex was disconcerted when he awoke. For once, his body wasn't tense and his senses weren't on alert. All was still around him. The bed was warm and comfortable. The mattress accommodated his height and the covers didn't scratch. Most confusing, though, it wasn't the dead of night. Early tendrils of light, really just the hint of them, were brightening the east-facing window.

It hit him then. He was out. He was free, and he'd slept the whole night through.

Again.

Rolling onto his back, he stretched. His head was foggy and his body was logy. He wasn't used to getting so much sleep, even though he craved it. He'd developed such a light trigger that the drip of a faucet or the creak of a floorboard could set him off.

Learned behaviour could become as sharp as instinct. And instinct told him he was alone.

He reached for the other side of the bed, but he knew

140

without opening his eyes that Elena wasn't there. Her heat wasn't warming the sheets. Her slight weight wasn't rolling towards him, and he didn't hear her soft breaths.

The fact that she was gone didn't surprise him.

He rubbed his hand over his chest.

With a sigh, he dropped his arm over his head against the pillow. He just couldn't seem to help himself around her. The little waif had gotten under his skin, which wasn't a good thing. He knew the danger of allowing her close. He still didn't know her intentions, although everything Leonard had told him about her had proven true. She was an economics student at NYU, and apparently a good one. She'd ranked near the top of her undergraduate class and had achieved her master's degree with honours. She was working on her doctorate, but he couldn't get past one thing.

She was a Bardot.

At once, his brain cleared. His dulled senses tingled in warning, and he sat straight up in bed.

His office. *Shit.*

His hand fisted in the sheet. It was in the adjoining room and full of sensitive information, business as well as private. There were things in there she could not see.

Had she gone through his papers? Would he have heard her? He'd been out cold.

A breeze sent a chill down his back. He'd sworn to himself he wouldn't trust anyone ever again. Not partners, not family, and certainly not a seductive*femme fatale.*

He shoved back the covers and began stamping towards the other room but pain shot through him unexpectedly. Sucking in a breath, he reached for the bedpost. The bruises on the bottom of his feet looked like storm clouds.

He muttered a curse under his breath.

She made him forget himself whenever she was around. His goals, his promises to himself, his self-defence mechanisms … The ache in his groin was all that mattered.

'Damn hormones.'

He hadn't even considered taking her someplace else. He'd wanted her in his bed. He hadn't given a thought to the risk he might be taking.

His fingers wrapped around the doorjamb as he swung into the next room. His gaze scoured the office, moving fast and then going back for a second, slower pass. On the surface, everything appeared as he'd left it. The chair hadn't been moved, the drawers were shut tight and there was no way she could have gotten into his computer. Still, prickles bit the back of his neck.

His gaze landed heavily upon the red notebook that sat open next to his laptop, and his vision turned nearly the same colour. He slapped the doorjamb viciously, then stalked over to his desk, the pain in his feet fitting his mood. He stared down at the narrow-ruled notebook. It was still open to the page where he'd blacked out most of his notes because he'd been going down a rabbit hole. There wasn't anything to see.

But she'd been in here. He knew it as well as he knew his own name.

He began flipping jerkily through pages. That's what he got for letting his dick lead him around. His teeth gritted until his jaw popped.

She'd been through the notebook. He had no evidence, no proof, but he knew it. It would be unintelligible to most, but she wasn't most people. She was as smart as she was beautiful, and she was willing to use that sweet face and hot body to slip by his defences.

'God dammit.'

He'd known he shouldn't trust her. What was her game here? Had she not gotten her fair share? Had daddy told her there was more for the taking? Had someone made her an offer she couldn't refuse? Appealed to her sense of 'patriotism'?

He dropped the notebook with a splat against the desktop. So help him, he was not going to be played again.

He swept up the desk phone, called his top security guy and skipped right over the niceties. 'I want Elena Bardot checked out.'

He didn't let the man even get started about the first background search they'd conducted.

'Deeper,' he demanded. 'I want to know if she has any connections to the Feds or reporters – television, print, internet, radio or otherwise. Find out how close she was to that bastard of a father of hers. Check her financial situation and if she's ever taken any programming classes. I want to know what kind of toothpaste she uses, damn it.'

He'd nearly hung up before he pulled the phone back to his ear.

'And I want the names of every man she's ever slept with. *Ever.*'

He jammed the phone into its charger base and looked over his desk one last time. He'd brought her here. He'd escorted her right into the room.

He spun away and headed back into the bedroom. The chill intensified.

Frowning, he looked at the sliding glass door. He didn't remember leaving that open.

Mood darkening, he walked over to roll it closed. He was going to have to start locking things, a step he abhorred. If he couldn't stay away from her, it would be the only way to keep –

She was on the balcony.

The sight was enough to temporarily shut down his brain. There she was, plain as day. She hadn't left. She'd stayed with him.

The angry thoughts in his head jumbled.

*What the hell?*

She looked so young and innocent standing out there, wrapped in a blanket and wearing his slippers. His gaze stuck on the outrageously large footwear adorning her tiny feet. She was making a habit of commandeering his clothing. As adorable as it looked, she made the ensemble sexy.

He felt himself getting hard, and it annoyed him.

He stared at her, trying to use his head – the one atop his neck – before he lost the capacity. Had paranoia gotten the best of him? Or was she really that good?

The chill of the morning made him inhale sharply when he pulled the door open. The wind last night had ushered in a cold front. The frostiness hit his lungs like needles. He stepped out onto the balcony, and the iciness was a welcome balm against his feet.

Naked, he walked towards her. 'What are you doing out here?'

She glanced at him and her gaze slid down not so discreetly to his groin. Whatever the cold had shrivelled perked right back up. Her cheeks reddened and she turned her attention back to the horizon. 'Waiting for the sunrise.'

His eyes narrowed. On a frigid day like this? She could have watched it from his bed.

His feet started going numb against the limestone. 'Let me in.'

Again that appealing shyness showed itself. She dipped her chin but opened the blanket. He stepped behind her and wrapped his arms around her. He put her in control of the coverlet again and bundled her close. She was short enough to tuck right up against him and their bodies touched from head to toe.

'Mmm,' she hummed in surprise.

She cuddled closer and his resistance to her wavered.

'Everything OK?' he asked. There might be something to that old saying – keep your friends close and your enemies closer.

He rubbed his chin against the crown of her head. He'd meant to wine and dine her last night and, honestly, screw her until he got her out of his system. That had been the plan, but he hadn't made it past the great room before he'd jumped her.

Already, he knew it hadn't been enough. System-wise, her magic had worked itself deep.

She nodded briefly.

He tightened his hold and dropped his head so he could look at her. 'You tell me if it's not.'

No matter what her objectives were, he'd never resort to hurting her physically.

She nodded again, her chin barely lifting. 'I'm not used to being … active,' she whispered.

Something proprietary rose inside him. 'Get used to it.'

It had been a while for him, too, but he hadn't chosen abstinence. The wolf inside him settled a bit, though, to hear that she had.

The sun appeared in that moment, peeking over the hills in the distance. Only a sliver was visible, yet the bright rays swept over the tips of the trees. The upper floors of the house lit up, but the lake was still dark. It would be a while – a long while – before any sunshine hit those dark depths.

'Beautiful,' she murmured.

He couldn't help but agree, only he wasn't looking at Mother Nature. Her skin glowed under the morning sunshine, and her tousled hair shone. He nuzzled against the soft strands, wondering what it would take to get her back in bed.

Even with the head games, he still wanted her.

She looked over the grounds with curiosity from the lake house to the balconies to the turrets up top. Her wiggling was starting to have serious implications. Icy temperatures or not, Alex was feeling the need to –

'How did you manage to keep the place?'

He pulled back slightly, her fresh scent distracting his thought processes. 'What do you mean?'

She looked him dead on, her doe eyes unblinking. 'Why wasn't it seized by the court?'

His jaw went tight.

And there it was.

He'd thought he'd gotten control of the snake inside him, but it was coiling again, ready to strike. 'The house is in the name of the family trust and has been for over a hundred years. It's not owned by any Wolfe, although my grandfather made it his residence.'

'What about your apartment then, the one in the city? Or your cars? Wolfe Pack?'

She was either brave or stupid – and he'd already verified through background checks that she wasn't feeble-minded. He settled his hands on her hips and turned her so he had her full attention. If his hold bit a little, it couldn't be helped.

'They got me on insider trading. Nothing else,' he reminded her tersely. 'And that was a stretch. I made my own money, and I started my own company. Wolfe Pack has no ties to Wolfe Financial. It's a separate entity entirely. The Feds and the courts can't touch it.'

'But your grandfather …'

'Has never been tried.'

'Because they can't find him.' Her lips flattened and a storm brewed in her eyes. 'Where is he?'

The question hit Alex like a slap.

Especially here on Wolfe property, with Wolfe Lake filling the view behind her. He pulled his emotions in, forcing the snake to wrap around and choke them. He'd dealt with these questions for years, and he'd answered all he was going to. He didn't owe anyone, even her, any more. 'You will never know.'

Tension boiled as the cold settled around them. A breeze lifted her hair as if in fury, but neither of them backed down.

Or pulled away from each other's bodies.

After a long moment, she took a deep breath. She caught the edges of the blanket up in one hand and caught his hand on her hip with the other. 'Why don't you give him up? If you're not involved, why take the fall for him? Why not make him pay?'

The questions came a little too close to home. 'You know, your father was no prince in this whole affair.'

Her face went white, even under the morning sun's soft glow. 'I'm aware of that.'

Turning away, she focused on the scenery. Her body grew stiff, but it worried Alex more when she pulled her hand away from his.

OK, so she and her father hadn't been close.

He circled that hand around her, spreading it wide over her flat belly. 'I'm sorry,' he said, kissing her shoulder. 'That was below the belt.'

'It's the truth.'

The sun was a ball of fire now, punching its way into the sky. It glared down on their conversation, exposing harsh truths.

'They came after my mother and me,' she said. 'The authorities, I mean.'

'You? Why?' It took a lot to surprise him any more, but that did the trick.

'They were looking for funds they could seize, but my parents had been divorced for so long all they could get was my mother's alimony, and that wasn't much. They wanted information even more, but we didn't know anything.'

Alex's teeth ground. He knew what it was like to be in the authorities' crosshairs, but he had resources. Lawyers, assistants, spin doctors and even Leonard. Yet that son-of-a-bitch Randolph Bardot hadn't even protected his own. He'd left his loved ones to face the law, the press and the public's outrage without him. No wonder she'd gone into hiding.

And no wonder she'd be susceptible to pleas from the government or angry investors for help.

'Is your mother doing OK?' he asked. That was another option.

'She's tough. She manages a cupcake bakery now. She loves it, but the owner doesn't know how to run a small business. It has its ups and downs.'

'Is she in New York?'

'San Diego.'

All the way across the country. He did a quick mental calculation. 'Wait. You were here alone when everything went down?'

She shrugged.

Alone and a student at that. She hadn't had to face the real world yet. She hadn't built up the barriers she needed to protect herself before it had all come charging at her.

Ah, hell. If she was here for payback, he understood why.

He wrapped himself around her again, protecting her with his body. Too late, maybe, but the act was instinctual.

'How did you learn about his death?' he asked quietly.

'His suicide.'

The words were clipped and harsh. There was no question at all whom she put the blame on there. Her father had taken the easy way out.

A random breeze ruffled her hair and he tucked the strands behind her ear.

'A cop came to my dorm room.' Her gaze had taken on a faraway look. It wasn't on the sunrise any more, but on the forest the light hadn't yet touched. There were thickets out there that remained dark and dense. 'That was when the other students made the connection and the snowball started rolling.'

'You sound like you hate him.'

She swallowed hard. 'I'm very angry with him.'

Her hollow tone indicated it had taken her a long time to come to that conclusion. Ax knew how that could be. He was very angry with members of his own family, only he wouldn't shy away from labelling that emotion as hate.

'And you're angry with me,' he extrapolated.

'Yes,' she confessed.

Angry enough to want to strike back? To use her feminine wiles to get close enough that she could bring him down?

151

Maybe.

'Still?' His fingers curled inward on her stomach. 'Even after ...'

He might be playing with fire, but he was intrigued by her. Mentally and physically. Maybe even emotionally ...

She'd let him out of that room.

Her long hair caught between their bodies, and it stroked sexily against his chest. The ends of the strands tickled someplace even lower, and he couldn't stop his erection from nestling in that soft curve of her lower back. Instinctively, he rubbed against her.

She caught her lower lip between her teeth.

At least this connection between them wasn't a lie.

He slid one hand upwards to her bare breast. Her nipple poked into his palm when he squeezed, and she let out a soft whimper.

'You confuse me,' she confessed.

'Why?'

'I thought I knew everything about you. I'd read articles and listened to news reports. I watched the streaming feed of the trial.'

'But?'

Her body relaxed against his, melting as if she couldn't fight any more. 'But the way you make me feel ...'

Her body was soft. Trusting. The gesture was unexpected, but powerful. The cold morning air scraped at the bottom of Alex's lungs. She had every reason in the world to despise him and want revenge, yet this connection between them was screwing with her head, too.

Determination settled fiercely inside his chest, along with something infinitely more sensual.

If she could have doubts ...

He toyed with her nipple, rolling it between his forefinger and thumb. 'Bend over, pretty siren.'

She moaned. 'I shouldn't want you.'

'But you do.' He pressed her forward. 'Let me make you feel good again.'

Her breath shuddered out in cold puffs, but she reached for the railing. She kept her grip on the blanket, but opening it up allowed the breeze to sweep under its protective layer and over their heated bodies.

Widening her stance, she bent at the hips. The submissive position lifted her bottom and made her breasts dangle. He caught the lush globes in his hands. They were full and pert, and he loved the way they responded to his touch.

She had a beautiful body, curved and sleek, perfectly proportioned for her small size. It wasn't a secret that her petiteness was an aphrodisiac for him. His superior height and strength made him felt masculine around her, but her trust in him ... This physical trust even when there was so much suspicion between them? ... It made him feel like a man.

Leaning over her, he nuzzled the side of her neck

through her hair. It was draped like a dark, silky curtain over her body.

'Why do you call me that?' she murmured, her breaths growing shorter as he played with her body.

'Siren?'

'Mm.'

'Because you looked like one that first night as you did yoga on the dock. You were so sexy and alluring, I knew you were dangerous.'

'Me? Dangerous?'

He let go of her breasts to rake his fingers through her gorgeous hair. 'Baby, you could be my undoing.'

He caught her hips to hold her still as he thrust into her, slow and deep. Her moan wafted off the balcony and over the grounds. If any of the security staff were nearby, there'd be no doubt what that sound was. Hearing it made him stiffen even harder.

He kept pushing, intent on reaching her soul, and the moan increased in pitch. Her hips rolled as she spread her legs even further. She wasn't letting him bind her up today.

He wasn't complaining. She was like a fist as it was.

He stopped, buried deep. 'All right?'

'Oh,' she gasped. 'Don't stop.'

He had no plans to.

Working leisurely, he pulled out and thrust back into her. She had no idea what she did to him when she was like this, open and supplicant. Free in her pleasure.

154

He loved the way she shook and strained when he took her, as if she was fighting for completion. She had none of the airs that some of his previous lovers had; she knew none of the games. The sexual ones, at least. She was just a sensual, breathtaking woman.

He groaned as he pumped into her with excruciating slowness. She was so tight and wet. He knew he was big for her, but her body readied itself in the most natural of ways. And she let it. She didn't fight her arousal, even though her brain had questions and her morals had reservations.

She did the same to him – made his common sense dim and his internal senses light up.

He knew he was playing with fire, but he liked it.

'Arch up, baby.' He squatted a bit lower and felt the burn in his thighs, but when he penetrated her again, the angle brought him right to her core.

The sensation was incredible and it brought a squeal out of her.

One side of the blanket slipped from her grip. It fell to the balcony floor, baring their bodies as they worked and danced together.

'I can't get enough of you,' he panted as he pistoned in and out of her. He wanted to go fast. He wanted to ram deep, but the sensual pace was exquisite. Heart-grabbing. Watching her rock back to take him and seeing his erection disappear into her was making his teeth ache.

His sexy little spy. Had she intended to let it go this far?

She wasn't used to taking a man this way, he could tell. Her movements were inquisitive and tentative, but she liked being taken from behind. Her body was becoming looser with each deep thrust. Her hips were opening, and her breaths were panting.

He cupped her breast and pinched her nipple tight. She let out a sharp, pleasure-ridden cry.

Off in the distance, a screech owl replied.

The other corner of the blanket hit the deck, and they were one with nature.

'Oooh,' she gasped. 'I can't take it much longer.'

'Yes, you can.'

He had no intention of rushing this.

And so they fucked. On and on.

With the sun spilling over them, Alex's body warmed. His muscles strained, and his skin became slick. Elena's hands were white around the cool railing, and the muscles in her legs were defined clearly as she held herself up on tiptoe.

They'd found their position, and they'd created a rhythm.

He moved inside her hot, clinging depths until the sun had fully risen. Blinding rays reflected off the edge of the lake and he came.

It wasn't cataclysmic, and it wasn't ferocious.

It was like water, bubbling up in a stream and tumbling over a waterfall.

As he closed his eyes and felt her body squeeze around

the most intimate part of him, he felt like he was falling. Free-falling endlessly to somewhere filled with light, warmth and security.

'Alex?'

The tremulous question in her voice made him open his eyes. His body felt like it had just come out of a sauna, but hers was shaking. He pulled out of her carefully, but was taken aback when she turned into his arms. Burying her face against his chest, she clung tight.

He swept his hand under the curtain of her hair and cupped the back of her head. 'Elena?'

Her eyes were deep and dewy as she looked up at him, and her expression cut right through his chest. Oh, God. He'd hurt her. She hadn't wanted it as much as he thought she had. She was about to cry. 'Damn, babe, I'm so –'

She shocked the hell out of him when she went up on tiptoe and cupped his face. His stubble rasped as she pulled him down for an insane, hot-blooded kiss.

It wiped out his thoughts, his plans. Hell, it even kicked out his own name.

She timidly pressed her tongue into his mouth, and his knees buckled. Reaching around her, he caught the balcony railing for support. Leaning into her, he let her do whatever the hell she wanted to do to him.

In the end, it was just a kiss – in the way that Mount Vesuvius was just a volcano.

When she pulled back, Alex looked at her blankly.

There was dampness on her cheeks. She was crying, but it wasn't tears of pain or sadness.

It knocked the arrogance right out of him. Nobody was dominating anyone here.

'You're more than dangerous,' he said gruffly, 'you're lethal.'

She smiled tremulously, but then wrapped her arms around his middle and cuddled close.

He kissed the top of her head and stroked her back.

She shivered again. Without the heat of an orgasm blasting through him, he realised how chilly it truly was. The sun might have lit up the sky for a while, but the temperature still wasn't conducive to buck-nakedness.

Stooping, he swept up the blanket and wrapped it around her shoulders before lifting her in his arms. She weighed about as much as his briefcase, or so it seemed.

He stepped into the slippers she'd left behind. Cold feet hadn't been a problem earlier, but right now he could hardly feel his toes.

He carried her back to the bedroom and closed the sliding glass door behind them. He laid her on the mussed sheets, then climbed in after her. The blanket and comforter were bunched up near their feet. He spread the pile over them and waited for their body heat to radiate.

'Alex?'

'Hm?' He'd found a comfortable spot on the pillow and he tugged her practically on top of him. He was growing sleepy again. Sleep and sex with her could become addictive, despite the cost. This time, though, he'd make sure she didn't leave the bed without him knowing.

'Was it bad in prison?'

He went still. Bad? He'd been locked up, his free will taken away. He'd been lumped in with murderers, drug dealers and wife-beaters. He'd walked away from that place, swearing not to look back, yet it had followed him into locked rooms and into his sleep – or it had until she'd entered his bed. 'I don't want to talk about that.'

Her gaze dropped. She laid her hand against his chest and her thumb traced the edge of his pec. 'What had you planned on doing when you got here? Alone in this big, gaping house? I mean, if you hadn't found me?'

He threaded his fingers through her hair. That was treacherous ground, too.

He looked into her face. Where was she going with this? 'Rage,' he admitted. 'And plan.'

Her hand stopped caressing his chest and hovered right over his heart. 'Plan what?'

He schooled his face. 'It doesn't matter. You *were* here.'

Her eyelashes fluttered and she lifted that doe-eyed gaze to pin him. She watched him for a long moment. 'Don't make me regret trusting you,' she finally whispered.

A muscle worked in his jaw, but he said nothing.

Because that was a promise he couldn't make. Not when he couldn't trust her.

# Chapter Eight

He'd made her mindless.

It was the only explanation.

Elena was still as she leaned against the window frame, staring out at the lake, but her finger traced its edge over and over again. Inside, she was all tangled up. Around Alex, she did things she wouldn't normally do and now she felt guilty, confused and apprehensive. So uncomfortable, it was taking everything inside her not to throw some boxes into her car and leave.

She'd done it again.

She'd slept with him. It was like she didn't know herself any more. All it took was a look from him or a kiss. His touch could make her cast aside her doubts and principles. Was he her enemy or her lover? She didn't know.

It was this place. The situation. It was messing with her head, toying with her emotions. Screwing up her judgment.

Her fingers curled around the curtain, wrinkling it.

She'd looked through his notebook.

She'd spied on him while he'd been sleeping. She'd had every reason in the world, but now remorse was making her sick. She'd only had the nerve to flip through a few pages, and she hadn't understood anything she'd seen. It was all in some programming language. The only things she recognised were the equations from Dr Walters's economics book.

That had confused her even more.

What was he up to? He'd already been convicted of a financial scheme. Was he pompous enough to try again? Or was he simply trying to catch up at work? Wolfe Pack did specialise in market analysis software.

She rested her forehead against the window and the chill felt good against her warm face.

It didn't matter. Justified or not, she felt terrible. She was no Mata Hari. She couldn't continue like this.

Why did she have to respond to him the way she did? She wanted him, regardless of his crimes – and she'd been one of his victims. Was there a part of her, deep down, that recognised something good in him? Was it possible he was telling the truth? Why did she find herself wishing that more and more when a court of law had already decided otherwise?

The phone rang before she could find an answer. Moving back to her desk, she picked up her cell. Her face flared when she saw the caller's ID. Letting out a puff of air, she answered. 'Hi, Mom.'

'Hi, baby. Have you seen the news?'

Her attention focused. Her mother's voice had an edge.

'No, I've been working.' Or trying to. 'What's going on?'

'You're not going to believe this. Bartholomew Wolfe was spotted again.'

'Where?' One word, one name, and Elena's priorities were back on track. Reaching out, she moved her mouse to wake up her computer. She might be developing soft feelings for the younger Wolfe, but his grandfather was another story. The old man had never faced up to his crimes.

'Belize.'

'South America?' She frowned and glanced at the world map she'd hung on the wall. Grabbing a pen, she walked over and marked an X. Stepping back, she surveyed the myriad dots that had been marked across the world. 'I doubt that. Belize has an extradition treaty with the United States.'

'But the man who thinks he saw him is a banker.'

And the last one had been a day trader.

Elena moved back to her desk and sat. Finding this man was becoming like a snipe hunt. 'According to my chart, that's the sixth country where a sighting has been reported.'

'I know it's a long shot.'

But her mother still wanted the man to pay. Everyone did. Elena jiggled her mouse again. She wanted to read the stories for herself and see if there were any bits in them that rang true. She frowned when the screen lit up, but her spreadsheet program closed. 'What?'

She heard the ding of a timer on the other end of the line and the screech of an oven door. 'Sorry, baby. What was that?'

Elena's breath caught when her browser closed next, quickly followed by her text editor. 'No, no!'

'Lainie?'

She put down the phone and switched to speaker mode. She reached for the keyboard, but she was afraid to touch anything. 'My computer is … Ahhh! It's crashed.'

'Uh oh.' The edge had left her mother's voice to be replaced with concern.

'Maybe it was just a glitch. Or it's booting again to install updates.'

She knew it was neither. Her luck just hadn't been going that way. A knot started forming in the pit of her stomach.

'Your paper is on there, and all your notes.'

'I know.' Being reminded didn't help. Tucking her foot underneath her, Elena tried to get more comfortable. She pushed the power button again and crossed her fingers. She winced when a notice popped up about booting up in safe mode. 'This doesn't look good.'

'Can you fix it? When was the last time you backed everything up?'

A couple of weeks ago, maybe? 'Too long.'

'Oh, baby.' There was a swish and then the background noise on her mother's side quieted. She must have moved to another part of the bakery. 'What's it doing now?'

Elena scanned the screen. Her breath caught when it blipped. 'The screen just went blank.'

The conversation fell into silence.

'What are you going to do?' Yvonne asked. 'You're stuck there. You can't go out and get another. Those news vans are still outside your gate.'

'I don't know.' Elena bit her lip. She wasn't a computer tech. She was competent in using them, but the inner workings were beyond her.

'Can you call in a repairman? See if he can rescue it? But ... damn. Who could you call that would keep their mouth shut?'

She didn't know, but ...

There was someone else on the compound who had an above-average knowledge of computers.

'I'm going to have to call A –' Elena broke off, nearly biting her tongue. 'An expert.'

Another long moment ticked by. 'When you say an expert, you mean Alex Wolfe.'

Her mother wasn't stupid, even if the leap was a short one. Somewhere near the phone, fingernails drummed. 'So you're talking with him now?'

Elena searched for the right answer. 'It's kind of hard not to.'

They were doing a lot more than talking, but she wasn't about to get into that.

'What was all that about it being a huge property and you'd never have to interact with him?'

She fidgeted, feeling herself being trapped in a corner. Her mother had a very long and precise memory. 'Do you have any other ideas? Because I'm open to them.'

'I don't want you getting messed up with that man.'

Too late for that.

Elena pushed herself out of the chair. Raking back her hair, she tried to think. She just couldn't come up with any other options, and that made her stomach turn the wrong way.

She might trust the man with her body, but her computer was another thing.

Yet she could lose everything if she didn't do something.

Panic started pushing at the edges of her thoughts. Sitting down again, she tried to clear whatever bug was gumming up the works. It didn't matter what she tried, though, the system wouldn't behave.

She groaned. 'I'm going to have to ask him to look at this.'

'He's a Wolfe, Elena. He's *the* Wolfe.'

'I understand that, but he ...' Elena nearly spoke up to defend him, but stopped herself just in time. One word like that and her mother would be on an airplane to come get her.

'I don't want to, but I need his help.' The more she looked at the things happening on her computer, the more she wanted to cry.

'Well, I suppose he owes you that much,' her mother conceded. She let out a heart-wrenching sigh. 'You be careful, baby. Don't let those dreamy eyes and wide shoulders trick you. There's a Wolfe under that sheep's clothing.'

'I know.'

'A sexy one, but a dangerous one.'

'I *know*!' Her discomfort with the discussion wasn't easing.

The drumming noise on the other end of the line became more punctuated. Her mother was not happy. 'You call me back later to give me an update.'

'I will. Bye.' It was Elena's turn to sigh when she hung up the phone.

She stared at the computer for another ten minutes. Nothing she did worked. By the time she turned to her phone again, the panic was pushing in on her. It took only two rings before she got a connection, but that was almost too long. 'Alex,' she said tentatively, 'can you come down to the lake house?'

'Elena? Is everything all right?'

Her anxiety had moved into her throat. She heard her words shaking, but as she looked around the room, all she could think of was the long nights she'd put into her studies. Now all of that was in danger of being lost. 'It's your turn to rescue me.'

She hung up and gathered her computer and its power cord and moved everything out into the living room. Closing the office door, she looked around for anything else she should put away.

The irony didn't slip past her. She was hiding from him what he should have hidden from her.

The refrigerator hummed and the grandfather clock in the corner of the room ticked as she waited. She stared over the back of the sofa at her laptop. It currently displayed an hourglass of death. It might as well have been counting down her future, flipping it over and dumping it out.

She let out a hiss of air and went to wait by the door. With nervous hands she tucked her hair behind her ear. She wasn't ready to face him yet. Last night and this morning had been too intense.

Yet she needed him. That brilliant, calculating mind …

Every tick of the clock pulled her nerves tighter as she watched the manor. The kitchen door finally opened and Alex appeared. He trotted down the hill, his long legs eating up the distance fast. She opened the door before he even knocked and waved him inside.

'Are you OK? What is it?'

She swallowed hard. 'My computer. Something is wrong.'

The stiffness left his face, but the relief lasted only a brief second. It was quickly replaced with serenity, but the expression looked forced. His eyes were too bright. Bright and alert.

Grabbing his hand, she dragged him over to the coffee table. 'It's had that hourglass for the last fifteen minutes.'

He stared at it for a moment longer than was comfortable. 'You want me to look at your computer.'

She shifted uneasily. 'Yes. Everything is on there – my notes, my bibliography, the first draft of my dissertation. Everything!'

'Me,' he emphasised.

Her hold turned vice-like on his warm hand. Well, no, but yes. He was the last person she wanted around her files, but he had the expertise she needed. 'You seemed like a good choice. You are the CEO of a software company.'

She dropped her gaze. 'And I am sleeping with you.'

He caught her chin and made her look at him. His gaze bored into hers, but the hard suspicion gave way to surprise and that seemed to unsettle him. He cleared his throat, and his Adam's apple bobbed. He nodded grimly. 'OK. I'll see what I can do.'

'Thank you.' She wrung her hands as he took a place on the sofa.

'What happened?' he asked.

'It's been acting funny for a few days. Today, it just

started closing down programs. Now it won't boot up again. I just get that stupid hourglass.'

He nodded, his brow furrowing. 'OK, let's see if I can get to a command line.'

He rolled up his sleeves. She didn't know if that was a good sign or a bad one, but his fingers were confident as they moved over her keyboard.

She sat on the couch next to him, her legs folded underneath her. She didn't know what she was going to do if he couldn't fix whatever was wrong.

He looked at her again, his grey gaze considering. After a moment, he reached out and squeezed her knee. 'Breathe.'

Heat flowed from the contact, startling her but focusing her.

Breathe. Yes, she'd done enough yoga to know that her breaths were too shallow and her body was strung like a wire. There was nothing she could do but let go. She had to trust him in this.

Keeping her gaze locked with his, she inhaled deeply. Her lungs filled and she let the air out through her mouth. It wasn't good, but it was a start.

'Better.' His expression turned contemplative, and he focused on her ailing machine.

Elena fought to keep her breaths even. His presence seemed bigger here in the tiny cottage. Almost overwhelming. The last she'd seen of him, they'd been cuddled up together on his bed. Naked.

'I may be a bit rusty,' he confessed.

'Rusty? Why ... oh.'

It was ironic, but there were times when she forgot how he'd spent his last years.

'Sorry,' she murmured.

Eighteen months wasn't that long except in the software field – and most likely – prison. For him to admit that his skills were out of date, though ... He was less cocky than he'd been before the trial and harder. Scarier, to be truthful.

And sexier. Her mother wasn't blind.

She watched his muscled forearms and big hands as he worked, remembering how they'd felt on her body. Her belly squeezed, and heat settled between her legs. She tugged the nearby pillow onto her lap.

He wasn't rusty with anything.

She hugged the pillow so hard the filling plumped out the corners. Sometimes she felt so naive around him. Forget the scandal. He was a world-renowned business innovator, while she was just a student. Then there was his wealth and the way other people treated him. When he was in a room, there was no doubt who was in charge. Nobody in her sphere came close to him, and sometimes she didn't know how to act around him.

Other than when he kissed her.

They didn't seem to have any problems relating then. Sensing her attention, he turned his head. His gaze settled on her lips, and they tingled. Got puffy.

Her body pulsed and her nipples stiffened. How did he do that? A word or a look and she was his.

The clock in the corner gave a low chime, announcing the hour. She flinched, and Alex's gaze turned to it. Something in his attention shifted, and he relaxed back against the cushions. 'I haven't heard that in years.'

'The chimes?' Trying to cover her discomfort, she looked to the polished wood and brass fixture. She loved that clock, but she'd gotten so used to the melodic tolls she barely noticed them any more. 'Did it used to be up in the manor?'

'It's been here as long as I can remember.'

His gaze was hazy, as if he was somewhere far away.

'One of those memories popping up?' she asked.

His eyes went darker, and he sat up again to return to her computer. 'This was my secret spot,' he confessed. 'It was a good hiding place, but eventually I'd have to go back.'

She frowned. 'To the main house?'

'Yeah.' His fingers stilled on the keyboard. 'Like now,' he said, breaking out of it. He closed the laptop with a snap. 'This needs help I can't give it here.'

Her heart sank. She'd thought he'd be able to fix it with a push of a few buttons.

'I have more diagnostic tools up at the manor.' He held out his hand for her. 'Come on. We'll have some dinner while we're at it.'

171

She tilted her head back to look at him. She'd heard that line before.

His face took on that flat expression again. 'I have no seduction plans. You ran back here pretty damn fast this morning, and I hadn't heard from you. I didn't know where things stood between us.'

She didn't know either.

Yet she put her hand in his.

His fingers tightened around hers. 'That doesn't mean it won't happen again.'

No, she was beginning to understand how it was for both of them. A spark. A glance. Something so little could ignite into so much more.

She followed him to the door, but he stopped and pulled the grey hoodie off the hook. He held it out to her, and she obediently put it on. She tugged up the sleeves and pulled her hair out so it swung down her back. When she lifted her chin, she found him looking at her in that intense way and the air in the room became charged. 'Why did you give this back to me?' she asked.

'Because I like seeing it on you.' He ran his finger around the shell of her ear, sending shivers down her neck. He pulled back. 'I like what it says.'

'What does it say?'

He hesitated a moment, but then cleared his throat. 'That you like me wrapped around you.'

Her stomach flipped. She didn't think that was what

he intended to say, but it made a powerful image. Danger signs flared in her head. Her mother had warned her not to follow her hormones.

Yet she took his hand as he led her up the hill. 'How bad is my computer?'

She could only tackle one dilemma at a time.

'I'm hoping I can rescue the data.'

'But the machine?'

'Probably shouldn't even be siphoned for parts. I'll put everything on a new one.'

Her steps slowed. 'How much will that cost?'

He got a funny look on his face. 'You do know who I am, right?'

'If you have a loaner one I can use …'

'I have a brand spanking new one you can have.'

'I'll pay you for it,' she promised.

He began walking again. 'Don't be ridiculous.'

A damp chill was in the air, and Elena had a feeling the dog days of summer were gone. Fall had settled in, and it looked like it was going to be a dreary one. The colour of the season was fading fast, and everything was blending into a bleak grey.

It wasn't an atmosphere conducive to hope.

She hurried through the door to the manor when Alex opened it for her. Tonight, the kitchen was quiet. She frowned when she didn't see Marta hovering over the stove. The cook seemed to delight in feeding them.

And watching them with curiosity.

'Leonard?' Alex called.

The butler appeared in the doorway, his polished shoes somehow not making any sound on the hardwood floor. 'Yes, sir?'

'How long until James returns?'

'Not long. He called and is almost to Bedford.'

Alex nodded and lifted the laptop. 'We'll be in the tech room.'

Leonard's forehead furrowed. 'Nothing serious, I hope.'

Elena hung up the hoodie and sent a woeful look the butler's way. 'Cross your fingers for me.'

A compassionate look came over his face. 'You've got the right man working on the problem, dear.'

The right man.

She stuffed her fingertips into the pockets of her jeans. Was he?

'This way,' Alex said. 'Marta had a doctor's appointment, so we're having takeout tonight. Is that OK?'

'It's fine.' She hooked her hair behind her ear. 'Your staff doesn't need to wait on me.'

'They like you.'

He led her down the hallway to the left, a direction she'd never gone before. Her eyebrows lifted when he pushed a button on the wall. It was an elevator.

He stepped inside when the carriage door opened,

174

and she frowned. 'Your claustrophobia doesn't bother you in there?'

He punched a button. 'The controls are on the inside.'

'Ah.' She joined him and watched the buttons as they lit up one-by-one. It wasn't necessarily the small space, but the loss of control. For a man who controlled everything, that made sense.

Prison must have been hell on earth for him.

Her heart ached for him, but the sympathy came with a healthy dose of shame. Most people would say that the punishment fit the crime.

She might have, too, until a few days ago. Now, she wasn't so sure.

The ride to the third floor was short. When the doors opened, Elena found herself in a long hallway very similar to the one on the second floor. Like there, the doors were open. She followed Alex into a room. The moment she stepped inside, her jaw dropped.

The tech room, he'd so nonchalantly called it.

Talk about an understatement. This was techie heaven.

There were workbenches filled with wires, circuit boards and gauges. Tables held desktop computers, laptops, tablets, phones and power cords. Surge protectors and monitors were on shelves. MP3 players and televisions filled in the gaps.

'I had a few things brought here in preparation for my arrival,' he confessed.

'A few things?' She walked around eyeing the assortment. It was awe-inspiring, and it reminded her more clearly who he was. Not the criminal, but one of the world's leading thinkers. She was in the home of a tech industry giant. By all rights, she shouldn't even know him.

Much less be having sex with him.

He went directly to a workbench in front of yet another window that looked out on Wolfe Lake. He set her laptop down and turned to a metal rack filled with components and newer, fancier models.

He selected a razor-thin silver laptop. 'Will this do?'

Who was she to argue with him? 'Whatever you think is best.'

Her guilt over accepting a castoff from him was lessening. He had so much. She sat down on a stool and folded her hands in her lap. Once again, she was afraid to touch anything. 'I thought your specialty was software.'

'It is, but I dabble.'

He dabbled. Like he read advanced books on macroeconomics and trained like an Olympic athlete.

He held a tiny screwdriver over her laptop. 'Is it going to bother you to watch me do this?'

Absolutely.

'No,' she said.

He lifted an eyebrow. 'Liar.'

She lowered her gaze.

He'd just unscrewed the first screw when his phone

rang. He looked at the caller ID and then back to her. 'I need to take this.'

She looked around the room when he stepped away. It was organised and tidy, but not pristine like the rest of the house. This was a room that was used, not a showpiece. Everything looked to be top-of-the-line, but where there were communication tools and high-end electronics, there were also gadgets. And toys.

She'd wondered once if she'd ever see the true Wolfe. This might be as close as she'd get.

'You're sure? Nothing?' he asked the caller. She sat a little straighter on the stool when he realised she was staring right at her. 'All right, email me your findings.'

He hung up, and that cool grey gaze settled on her again. Elena tried not to fidget as he walked back over to her. He put down his tools and settled a protective hand over her laptop.

'Why don't I work on this later?'

'Are you sure? It won't hurt anything to wait?'

'Only your nerves.' He cupped her face and ran his thumb over her cheek. He stared at her for so long, it became uncomfortable.

'What?' she whispered.

He shook his head briefly. 'You confuse me, too.' Pushing away from the tall workbench, he caught her hand. 'Let's go see about that dinner.'

They rode the elevator back down to the main floor,

but Elena wasn't hungry. Worry had taken her appetite. The driver was just coming in the kitchen door when they got there. She blinked when she saw the square white boxes in his massive brown hands.

'Grimaldi's?' She recognised the logo on sight, and her mouth began to water. She hadn't eaten there in months. 'From the city? Are you serious?'

Alex shrugged. 'It sounded good. We might have to reheat it a bit. I hope that's OK.'

She looked at him, dumbfounded. He must have been craving New York style pizza.

'What would you like to drink, Miss Elena?'

Leonard took over at that point, ushering them into the breakfast nook.

Elena was still stunned. She looked at the pizza on her plate, unable to fathom that they'd brought it in from the city. New York was an hour away, yet Alex had thought nothing of the extravagance. 'It's a bit overwhelming to be you, isn't it?'

He stopped shaking red pepper on his slice. 'What do you mean?'

'All of this.' She toyed with the napkin in her lap. Somehow, linen didn't seem right. 'It's all so much. The houses and the land, the private gym, a NSA-worthy electronics suite ...'

His brow furrowed. 'That's twice now that you've said something like that. Your father was Randolph Bardot.'

She was well aware of the fact.

'Even before his crimes, he was a very wealthy man.'

She shrugged. 'Because he knew where to scrimp and save.'

Alex's brow furrowed. In the dimmed lighting of the nook, it made him look dark and intimidating. It reminded her of that first time she'd seen him watching her from the balcony, and she fought not to shrink back into her seat.

'Are you saying that he didn't support you at all?'

She breathed very slowly. 'He paid the mandated alimony and child support. The judge also made sure he paid for my undergraduate degree.'

'But nothing more.'

'His lawyer was better than Mom's.'

The air in the tiny room turned downright chilly.

'It was all right,' she said quickly. 'She and I did fine together. We had fun. I ... I just missed him.'

A muscle flexed in Alex's jaw.

She turned her attention back to the pizza. Her appetite had fled, but she folded the slice in half and took another bite. Flavour filled her senses, but it might as well have been cardboard. 'This is delicious. Thank you for including me.'

'You're welcome.'

'I would have been happy with a slice from the convenience store in Bedford.'

'Enough.' That was when he moved in that lightning-fast way of his. Leaning over the table, he speared his hand into her hair and cupped the back of her head. His grey gaze was searching and Elena caught something she hadn't seen in him before. Caution.

The air in the nook changed. The outrage was still in his eyes, but it was accompanied by surprise. 'You're for real, aren't you?'

The words were quiet and almost reverent, but she flinched and pulled back. 'I don't joke about money.'

This might all be a game to him, toying with numbers here and watching results there, but money had value to her. Apparently those who didn't have it valued it more.

'Wait. Stop. That's not what I meant.'

She hesitated, fingers curling into her napkin. His hand still cupped the back of her neck, but it wasn't controlling. It was almost … protective. She looked at him warily.

'Why did you come here, Elena? To Wolfe Manor?'

'You know why. To finish my dissertation.'

'You could have done that anywhere. Why here?'

'Leonard offered and the price was right.'

A muscle in his jaw flexed. With his stubbly beard, it made him look ruthless.

She sighed and shied away from that piercing gaze. 'The same as you, OK? The truth is that I needed to be here. I needed to plan. And *rage*.'

She waited for the flash of anger, but her stomach

squeezed when she saw what was in his eyes. He still guarded his thoughts and emotions like a wolf defending its den, but desire shone dark and clear. Only this time it wasn't purely sexual. The wanting went deeper. To yearning.

'Stay,' he finally said, his voice raspy.

She'd known that, with them, dinner couldn't just be dinner.

He shook his head and his thumb rubbed over her ear. 'Just ... stay.'

# Chapter Nine

When Elena awoke the next day, she was alone in Alex's bed. The room was quiet. The door to the office was closed and her clothes had been picked up off the floor. They were folded on the chair in the corner of the room and an extra blanket had been spread over her. Good thing. The air had a nip to it and all she was wearing was a T-shirt he'd loaned her. The bed wasn't as warm without him.

She curled into the pillow as she surveyed the weather outside. The sun was hidden again amongst the clouds, but she could tell she'd slept later than usual. Her toes pointed as she stretched. She didn't think she'd moved all night long. She barely remembered putting her head on the pillow and curling up in Alex's arms.

Her hand settled against her stomach as she watched a hawk soar against the slate-coloured clouds. They hadn't made love. They'd simply slept together. There'd been a strain in the air, but not with each other. He still seemed angry about something. He was adept at hiding his feelings and protecting his thoughts, but that much was clear. He'd held her to his side protectively. Almost possessively.

She couldn't believe she hadn't heard him get up.

She glanced to his side of the bed and spotted a note. Rolling over, she skimmed the brisk masculine handwriting. It made her come awake fast. He was working on her computer.

She flipped back the covers, got up and headed to the shower. She couldn't laze around when he was doing that. Already she was worried about whether he'd be able to save her files.

And whether he'd look through them.

After a quick rinse, she got dressed in the clothes she'd worn the day before and made the bed. Looking around, she realised she had nothing to do. She didn't want to go up to the tech room. Seeing her computer in bits was more than she could take. She rubbed her hands against her thighs. She couldn't dwell on this. She needed to do something.

She went down to the kitchen and was happy to find Marta.

'Good morning, ma'am.' It came as no surprise that the cook was a morning person.

'Good morning, Marta.'

'You look all pink-cheeked and refreshed.' The welcoming smile on the woman's face turned a bit lopsided.

Elena's cheeks turned pinker. There was no way to hide the fact that she'd spent the night. 'I slept well.'

'Would you like some breakfast?' the cook asked as she flipped a piece of bread on the hissing skillet in front of her. 'I'm making French toast.'

The scent of cinnamon made Elena's stomach growl. She hadn't eaten much of the pizza last night. 'That sounds wonderful.'

Marta grinned at the rumble and pointed to the counter with her spatula. 'There's some fresh fruit to tide you over until it's ready.'

Elena was reaching for the strawberries when she noticed the newspaper. It appealed to the sense of hominess she was feeling. She hadn't read news in print since she could remember, but with her computer on the fritz it was the perfect alternative. She climbed onto the barstool and skimmed the front page. The economy was the top headline as it seemed to be every day.

She opened the paper to the next page. Marta slid a plateful of hot French toast in front of her. Not wanting to let it cool, Elena spread butter on the slices and liberally poured on maple syrup. She rolled her eyes in bliss when she took her first bite.

'Oh, Marta. This is divine.'

The bubbly chef practically beamed. 'Orange juice or coffee?'

'Yes, please.'

She'd made it through half the stack before she glanced again at the newspaper. When she did, she stopped with the fork halfway to her mouth. Bartholomew Wolfe stared up at her, haughty and narrow-eyed. It was an article about the possible sighting in Belize.

Her relaxed mood disappeared.

She read the article carefully, but the story was just as vague as all the ones that had come before it. A man matching Wolfe's description had gone into a bank to exchange a large amount of American money for Belizean dollars. It was a short piece that the reporter had lengthened by tying it to the story of Alex's release. How nice for him to bring the attention back to Wolfe Manor.

She took another bite of French toast and chewed mechanically. She didn't see anything unique in the piece. Nothing stood out as either a hoax or the truth.

She glanced across the breakfast bar. Marta was wiping down the counter adjacent to the stove.

'Did you work here when Alex's grandfather was around?' she asked as innocently as she could.

The woman turned, her gaze going to the newspaper. 'I did.'

Elena waited.

Marta glanced to see if anyone was about. 'Horrible old man,' she whispered conspiratorially. 'Sullen and self-centred. He'd keep dinner waiting for hours and then be unhappy when it wasn't perfect.'

Elena frowned. 'Do you think he's really in Belize?'

'He could be anywhere.' The cook shrugged. 'As long as he doesn't come back here, I'm happy. Master Alex is much better to work for.'

Come back. That possibility hadn't even occurred to Elena. He wouldn't dare, would he?

She was hiding here and nobody had found her.

She swirled a piece of toast in the puddle of syrup on her plate. 'It would be too big of a risk for him to come back, even if he is still in the country.'

'True. Although if he does, his room is ready and waiting.' Marta nibbled her lower lip. 'Come to think of it, I should make sure it's dusted.'

Elena's chin snapped up. 'His room?'

'It's right upstairs.' The cook pointed overhead. 'Above the kitchen, in fact.'

'His things haven't been packed up?'

'Oh, no,' Marta said, shaking her head. 'Master Alex told us to leave everything just the way it was. For the investigators.'

It had been a year and a half since Alex had gone to prison. It had to be more than two years since Bartholomew had last been seen. For real. He'd gone on the run right about the time her dad had died.

Elena's fork clanked against the fine china. She wasn't going to go there.

She scurried off the high stool. Her head was spinning

186

so fast, she nearly forgot Marta was in the room. 'Thank you,' she called over her shoulder.

'Are you done, dear?'

She was already in the hallway, heading for the staircase.

'Oh, dear,' Marta mumbled behind her. 'Maybe I shouldn't have told you about that.'

\* \* \*

The room wasn't hard to find. It was at the opposite end of the hallway from Alex's room – and the only one on the floor with the door closed. Elena approached it determinedly with her fists clenched and her jaw set. She reached out and grabbed the handle. She was surprised when it offered no resistance. The room wasn't locked.

She pushed the door open but hesitated on the threshold.

The place was musty. It was the first thing that hit her. The stale air made her nose wrinkle, although the room was clean as a whistle. There wasn't a thing out of place, but it was a scene stuck in time. A suit jacket was draped across the back of a chair. A book lay on the nightstand, along with a set of gold cufflinks. It looked as if an old man had just stepped out.

The floor creaked when she entered.

Her heart was pounding. She didn't like the feel of

the room, but she supposed it only reflected her feelings about the man. She moved to his desk. It was the messiest place in the room.

She thought of the investigators who must have gone through every piece of paper in the house. Had they found anything here? Had they taken it away as evidence? She didn't know what she was looking for, but there had to be *something*.

Something to explain why. Something to show how.

Her hands were rock-steady as she began flipping through the paperwork. She was spying again, only this time she did it without compunction. He had all the advantages in the world, yet this old man had intentionally stolen from people. He'd taken away their money and their futures.

She scanned every scrap she could find on the desk and in the drawers. She looked at the calendar, flinching when she saw the date she'd lost her father.

Nothing.

There was nothing that gave her the satisfaction she craved. Feeling almost desperate, she flung open the closet door. The musty smell nearly knocked her over. The closet was filled with clothes. Bartholomew couldn't have taken much with him when he'd run.

Of course, with that kind of money he could buy anything he needed.

She let out a sound that was nearly a growl as she

stared into the wardrobe. She wanted to scream at the egotism … the sense of entitlement …

Grabbing hold of the door, she gave in to the impulse to slam it … except that, a moment after she released it, she stopped it with the tips of her fingers. Something had caught her attention.

Confused, she opened the door wide again. There were scuff marks on it. She tilted her head to make sure it wasn't just shadow play. No, the closet door was pockmarked and scuffed on the bottom half. Paint had peeled off in places.

That was odd. Everything in this house was kept in perfect condition. Even the inside of a closet should have merited the attention of the maintenance staff. She knew Alex had left everything for the investigators to search, but the damage looked old. Why hadn't –

Her breath caught in her throat until it felt like a knife jabbing.

Oh, no. Alex!

Her knees wobbled and she sank into an unsteady crouch. Her hand shook as she reached out. The marks were all low on the door … about the height of a child. She remembered the way Alex had kicked and clawed when he'd been trapped in the bathroom downstairs. Her hand pulled away as if burned.

Horrified, she looked into the interior of the tiny space. It wasn't a walk-in closet. The house was over a hundred years old. The storage space was small and dark. There wasn't even a bare light bulb hanging from its ceiling.

The elevator dinged just across the hall and she jerked. For the first time since she'd entered, Elena felt like she was invading. She lurched to her feet and turned towards the door.

She heard movement, but it was too late to hide.

Her gaze locked with Leonard's when he turned into the room and, for a brief moment, she felt relief.

It quickly fizzled.

'Oh, Miss Elena.' The butler wrung his hands in discomfort. 'You can't be in here. You mustn't –'

'What is that?' she demanded. Her finger shook as she pointed at the still open closet.

She knew what had happened. The evidence was clear, but she wanted it not to be true.

Leonard's gaze started to go in that direction, but he couldn't look. Her heart died a little when his woeful face turned back towards her.

'How long?' she asked, her voice barely above a breath. 'How long did it go on?'

The butler blanched until he nearly disappeared against his crisp white shirt. 'Miss Elena, I shouldn't betray –'

Her spine snapped straight and she took two steps forward. 'How dare you defend that monster!'

'Master Alex,' he said, reaching out to catch her arms. He looked sad and ashamed. 'He wouldn't want me talking about this.'

So it was true. Alex had been locked in tiny rooms before. Her stomach squeezed threateningly. She remembered his desperation and agitation when he'd been trapped inside the gym bathroom. His claustrophobia went way back before his time in prison.

No wonder it was so bad.

Her eyes started to well. 'Why?' she simply asked.

'Master Bartholomew was a difficult man.' Leonard let go of her arms and clasped his fingers together. They turned so white, it was obvious he didn't want to talk about the matter. 'He didn't have much patience for children.'

The lake house. It hadn't been a place for hide-and-seek. Alex had hidden there to get away.

'Tell me you stopped it.'

'I did – when I caught it. There were times I'd take the boy to my own home.'

But he obviously hadn't caught it all the time.

Elena's stomach curdled. It had happened more than once. She dashed back the tears that threatened to fall.

'Master Alex stopped it himself,' Leonard admitted. 'When he got big enough.'

'Why did his parents keep sending him?'

'They didn't know. He wouldn't tell them.'

That damn stoic mask he put on.

For protection. She got that now.

Leonard glanced worriedly at the open doorway. 'You really mustn't be in here, Elena.'

No, she mustn't. Suddenly, she couldn't bear to be in the room one second longer. She pushed the closet door back to the way she found it, but couldn't bring herself to make it finally click shut. Leaving Leonard there, she ran into the hallway.

She was standing statue-still when he firmly closed the room behind them. She looked at her old caretaker. He'd left her as a toddler to go care for another, older child. A child who'd needed him much more than she had.

Their gazes locked and the butler let out a very undistinguished sound. It had come from the pit of his throat.

Impulsively, Elena clutched him in a hug.

'He's a good man, Miss Elena. It's a good match, the two of you. You can get past the barriers he puts up. I've seen it.' Again, Leonard let out the anguished sound. 'When I think of what he did ... what he sacrificed ...'

She clutched him tighter, but he shivered and pulled back. Shaking his head, he blinked fast and straightened his tie. His chin wobbled as he tugged the sleeves of his jacket. She touched his arm. 'Leonard?'

Sniffing, he straightened his shoulders and wiped the remaining emotion from his face. 'I need to get back downstairs. The gardeners have just arrived. If you need assistance, could you please find Marta?'

That was all she was going to learn from him.

It was already too much.

Without another word, she and the butler parted ways.

She watched him walk stiffly to the elevator. Wrapping her arms around her waist, Elena turned. She knew they'd never have this discussion again.

She wondered if Alex would ever tell her himself.

Then again, why should he? She'd given him little reason to trust her.

She wandered down the hallway with her chin tucked into her chest. He hadn't been in cahoots with his grandfather. There was no way. She'd felt the hatred he had for that man, and now she understood why.

But money was a powerful incentive.

Could he have partnered with his grandfather and her father solely for the payoff?

She didn't want to think so.

Although all indicators pointed to yes.

She turned into the room they'd shared last night. Like a robot she walked to the closet. She was afraid to open it. When she did, her shoulders sagged in relief.

Not here. Not in this room.

Without really knowing what she was doing, she turned on her heel. Her footsteps gathered speed as she went back the direction she'd come. Halfway along the passage, she turned and headed up the staircase. She was practically jogging by the time she made it to the tech room. As always, the door stood wide open.

Breathless, she stared across the room at Alex.

He was bent over a raised workbench, looking at the

shiny computer he'd shown her last night. At the sound of her panting, he raised his head. Their gazes locked for a long moment.

He frowned. 'What's wrong?'

The ache in her throat turned into a knot. She couldn't tell him what she'd done. 'My computer,' she finally managed to squeak.

His eyes narrowed, but she braved the examination to cross the room. That intense grey gaze swept over her, and her body grew warm. She stopped next to him. Close. She laid her hand on his bare forearm and heat passed between them. Her fingers tightened. 'Was it ...' She struggled for a moment to get her head on straight. 'Was it salvageable?'

'I think I saved your data, but you're going to have to check.'

At the moment, she couldn't have cared less.

Still, she took the wireless mouse from him and began looking through the file manager. Distracted as she was, it was hard to tell if anything was missing, but most of it seemed to be there. She opened a few files. Nothing looked corrupted.

She looked at him and their noses nearly brushed. She stared into his handsome face with his spiky hair and rough stubble. A complicated man with a prickly exterior.

'Thank you,' she whispered.

'You're welcome.' That icy gaze slid to her mouth and then back up to her eyes. He was bracing himself against the table, and the position left him leaning over her. 'It meant a lot to me that you trusted me with that. I know what that computer means to you.' Unable to hold back any longer, Elena leaned into him. Closing her eyes, she wrapped her arms around his middle and kissed him. Slow and deep. Everything she was feeling came out in the kiss, and she felt him rock back in surprise.

It didn't take long before his arms wrapped around her. His hands fisted in her hair and their mouths locked. The heat turned into a slow smoulder. Her fingers dug into his back and he pressed closer. Her head dropped back and she clung to him.

When he finally pulled away, he was breathing hard. His eyes narrowed. 'Are you sure you're OK?'

She wasn't sure of anything, other than the fact that she was going to stop fighting what was between them. Stop ignoring the need. 'I'm just tired and stressed,' she said honestly. 'It's all starting to get to me.'

He drew his thumb over her cheek. 'Well, it's a good thing I made plans for today,' he replied softly.

'Plans?'

'To pamper you.'

She smiled softly. She'd already had the good food and the fine wine. All she wanted right now was to hold him. 'There's no need. The new laptop is more than enough.'

His face turned cloudy and his jaw hardened. It was the same expression he'd taken with him to bed. 'That's where you're wrong. There is a need, pretty siren. There's going to be no more settling for you.'

'What are you talking about?'

'You've done without for too long, and it stops now.' He punctuated the hard sentence with a kiss that seared her down to her toes. 'I've invited some people over to change that.'

Elena didn't understand. He sounded truly angry.

They'd been hiding out, trying to avoid people. They'd gone to great lengths not to be caught together. Tabitha hadn't betrayed their trust, but they couldn't keep taking chances like that. 'I don't think that's a good idea, Alex. I appreciate the gesture, but the press will find out I'm here. Someone is bound to talk.'

'Not at the rate I'm paying them. If they want to continue getting my business, they'll keep their mouths shut. So get ready. You're about to be pampered from the top of your shiny head to the tips of your pink toes.'

'Alex.'

'Deal with it.' He looked at the Rolex on his wrist. 'Now. They should be here.'

They?

He caught her hand and pulled her from the room.

'But Alex,' she protested as they rode the elevator down to the first floor. She tugged nervously at her

T-shirt. When she'd called him down to the lake house yesterday, she'd been working. She wasn't dressed for company – especially his type of company.

'But nothing. You look fantastic.' He lowered his head closer to hers. 'Relax. You're going to enjoy this.'

Feeling nervous, Elena straightened her spine. This seemed important to him. She didn't want to disappoint him, but she'd thought they'd been on the same page about shutting out the real world. Why had he done this?

They turned into a first-floor room she'd walked by many times. The first thing she noticed was that it was different. The furniture had been removed. All that remained was a tufted armchair with a small table at its side. Across the room was a Japanese-style folding partition, screen-printed with cherry blossoms. Between the two was a free-standing cheval glass, something she'd always wanted.

'I don't understand,' she said.

He waved to the racks of clothing that stood at the back of the room, the ones she'd walked right by without seeing. 'You're going on a shopping spree.'

Elena looked from one rack to the next, her eyes rounding. They took up the entire back half of the room. She walked to the nearest rack of dresses and looked at the labels. 'These are designer.'

He signalled at someone in the hallway. 'Jorge?'

A thin man in an exquisite grey suit came into the

room. His dark hair was sleeked back and a pencil-thin moustache rode on his upper lip. Those lips were curled upwards in a smile as he extended his hand. 'Hello.'

'Hello,' Elena said, returning the handshake. She rubbed her ankles together. She felt like such a bag lady in front of these two men who were dressed like power brokers.

'Jorge, this is Elena. Elena, this is Jorge Cruz. He's here to show you a few of his creations. It's up to you to decide what you like.'

'Oh, I –'

Alex's gaze narrowed and he shook his head in warning. They were going to do this.

She rubbed her toe against the calf of her other leg as the designer's gaze swept up and down her body.

'You are gorgeous, my dear. Petite, but sleek and well proportioned.' His eye didn't linger on her curves with sexual interest. 'Alex, you didn't do her justice.'

'How could I?' he asked, going to take his seat. He opened the laptop that was on the table and started browsing business sites.

'I have many pretty things that should suit you perfectly,' the designer said. There were party dresses, gowns and suits. Jorge kept pulling her along, though, until she was staring at a flat table with an assortment of smaller pieces.

Much smaller pieces.

Lingerie. A hot blush settled into her cheeks. She looked over her shoulder. 'Alex,' she hissed.

'It's something I know you like,' he replied, his gaze steady.

'There are more designers waiting to show you their work.' Jorge gestured to the table. 'Lingerie is my specialty.'

Elena tucked her fingers into her pockets, but eyed all the gorgeous pieces in silks, satins, Spandex and every fabric in between. She felt like a kid in a candy store, wanting to touch but knowing she shouldn't. 'They're beautiful.'

'Which do you like?' Jorge asked.

She pointed at a baby-pink set in front of her.

'Ah, soft and sweet. A good choice.' The designer picked up a bra and matching bikini-style panties. 'Why don't you try it on?'

She stared at him.

He gestured at the partition. 'You can have your privacy over there.'

Was he serious?

'Elena,' Alex warned.

It was two against one, but the only one she cared about was sitting across the room. For some reason, Alex wanted to do this for her. After what she'd just learned, she didn't want to hurt his feelings.

He'd been hurt too much already.

Her chest started to tighten, and the anguish built up in her throat. The vision of those claw marks on the door appeared again in her head.

She pushed the vision away, clearing her throat hard. Would it really be so bad to play dress-up? There were clothes here that she'd never be able to afford, much less try on. She wouldn't accept them.

She hesitantly walked over to the corner of the room.

'Let me know if you need a different size,' Jorge called.

'She won't,' Alex murmured.

Her eyes narrowed. He sounded so sure of himself. She stepped behind the partition.

She could say no and stop the whole thing. He wouldn't force her, but he'd gone to such measures. The designer had obviously gone to even greater lengths to bring everything here.

She fingered the pretty bra. She was already in love with it.

She gave up fighting. Setting the lingerie on the table, she peeled off her jeans. The rest of her clothes were next. They might be her comfy favourites, but with all the expensive material in the room she felt like a frump. She put her bra down and picked up the pink one. The difference was there under her fingertips. The quality was better, from the fabric to the stitching. Feeling her pulse begin to pound, she put her arms through the straps and aligned the cups over her breasts. She clipped the tab against her breastbone and felt the change the moment the bra settled over her curves, cupping and supporting them.

There was also a difference in the fit.

Almost naturally, her shoulders pulled back and her chest lifted. There was no comparison to the cheap discount-store brands she was used to wearing.

This felt sublime.

Hurrying, she tried on the panties. They fit her just as well, hugging her curves but not cutting into them.

'Well?' Jorge asked.

'They're perfect,' she sighed.

Alex cleared his throat.

She peeked around the corner of the partition. 'What?'

His gaze was that steady spark of grey ice, the one she'd run into in the forest on more than one occasion. 'Let me see,' he said, making it crystal clear.

Elena looked down at herself. She wasn't naked, but he couldn't possibly be asking her to –

'Come out here.'

She wasn't indecent and he'd seen her in less. Still …

She stepped out into the middle of the room and clasped her hands together in front of her. Alex leaned forward in his chair, the computer forgotten. Jorge nodded, his eye critical. Walking over to her, he examined the fit from front to back. Elena felt like she was under a microscope with both men staring at her so unabashedly.

Jorge's attention was that of a designer, all about the beauty and fit.

Alex's, on the other hand, was so fully sexual, her entire body flushed. His gaze stroked over her hotly, but it turned gentle when he looked into her face. 'Do you like it?'

Her mouth had gone dry. 'I love it,' she whispered.

'We'll take that set,' he said, easing back into his chair. Somehow he didn't look as casual any more. 'What else do you have?'

Elena took a quick step forward. 'This is wonderful, but –'

He pointed a warning finger at her. 'Your day, my money, your fun.' He looked at the way the bra plumped up her curves. 'Our fun,' he amended.

'The red next,' Jorge said with a broad smile on his face. Without awaiting approval from anyone, he chose the new pieces.

The lingerie came at her, one piece after another, and her confidence grew as she modelled it. Alex's preferences ran to the skimpy, while Jorge liked different combinations of satin and lace ... and leather. That combo felt a little outrageous to her, but the moment she saw it on her in the mirror she melted. The set went into the growing pile.

'That's enough,' she finally declared.

'One more,' Alex said, his voice deceptively soft. 'The black lace.'

Jorge's eyebrows rose, along with one corner of his mouth. He fought the smirk as he went for the bra and panty combination Elena had avoided.

She leaned more towards pastels and jewel tones. Black just seemed so dark and mysterious. She wasn't a fan of lace – it scratched and bit – but, if he wanted to see it on her, she could do that.

Although everyone in the room knew they'd moved away from pretend dress-up to the verge of sexual manipulation.

Elena was surprised to find her hands shaking as she tried to connect the hooks and eyelets in the middle of her back. The bra did bite, but then she noticed a strap was twisted. When she had dealt with it, everything settled down into a tight hug. The lace stretched and was softer than any she'd ever felt before. Dollar signs chimed in her ears.

'It's a bit snug,' she confessed.

Jorge chuckled. 'It's supposed to be, dear.'

Oh. Oh, my.

She began to tremble in earnest. She cupped her hands over her breasts. The bottom half of the cups was a shiny silver material, maybe Lycra. It hugged and lifted in all the right places.

She hurried to put on the high-cut panties. She was venturing on dangerous turf here. The faster she finished, the faster they could move on.

Relief settled over her when she had the combination on. It felt sexy, but not as sexually explosive as she'd thought.

Taking a deep breath, she stepped out from behind the partition.

Alex's gaze raked over her from head to toe, and he gave an abrupt shake of his head. 'The granny panties need to go.'

'No?' Jorge said in disappointment. 'High-waists are coming back this season.'

'Not here they aren't.'

The designer let out a huff that Elena almost echoed. The panties felt good. They came up to nearly her ribcage, and the support was nice, although she worked hard to keep her core tight.

She glanced in the mirror and her eyes nearly bugged out. Embarrassed, she clapped her hands over her breasts.

She hadn't known the bra was see-through.

The silver Lycra was opaque, but the line cut right over her nipples. They peeked over the top through the black lace, rocketing the titillation factor of the outfit tenfold.

She scooted back behind the partition and began to take the set off.

'Here,' Jorge said, his hand snaking around the corner to offer her new panties. 'Try these.'

These? Elena's jaw dropped when she held up the tiny thong. It was barely more than a G-string.

'Chop chop,' Alex called. 'The day's a-wasting and you've got dresses, shoes and outerwear to go.'

There was no way she was going to say yes to this set of lingerie, Elena thought determinedly as she pulled off the granny panties. They clung stubbornly as she pulled them down her thighs. The thong was much more amenable. The strip of material slid up and settled into place as if custom made.

She bit her lip as she looked at her reflection. It *was* a G-string.

Taking a deep breath, she stepped out from hiding. Her hands instinctively came up to cover herself when Alex's gaze sparked, dark and intense.

She took a timid step back when he rose from his chair.

That didn't stop him coming straight at her. She jumped when his big hands settled on her waist. He turned her so she faced the mirror and stood behind her as they both evaluated her reflection.

It was the reflection of the two of them together, though, that captured her attention. When he caught her wrists and moved her hands away, she let him.

The picture they made was beyond steamy. Purely sensual. Her femininity and vulnerability were on display as he towered over her, looking male and aggressive. There was something about her near nakedness against his crisp business dress. Something that made the sexuality classier, but at the same time naughtier. Forbidden, yet strict.

Her nipples stiffened, going from peeking to peaking under the snug grip of the stretchy lace.

Alex's grip on her waist tightened, and he turned her. She spread her hands over his chest and looked over her shoulder. The view from behind was even more salacious. Precious few strips of fabric covered her. One rode along the top of her buttocks, while another travelled down between the plump globes. The contrast between her long hair that hid so much of her back and the clothing that covered so little of her bottom was rather shocking.

She watched as his hands came up to cup her. Hide her. Claim her. The hold was bold and firm.

He dropped a soft kiss on the top of her head. 'What else would you like to try on?'

She worried her bottom lip. 'Suits?'

One of his eyebrows lifted.

'I need something to wear at my defence.'

His face softened. 'There's my girl. Sexy and practical.'

His chest lifted and he stepped back. Hardness tented the front of his pants. 'Thank you, Jorge. Would you send in Katrina?'

'Of course.' A sly but happy smile was on the designer's face as he walked backwards to the door. 'Let me know if there's anything else you need.'

\* \* \*

From there, everything turned into a blur of fantasy. Styles changed. Colours burst. The materials felt good against her skin, and the cuts were exquisite. Elena tried on suits, shoes, dresses and jackets. The touch and feel alone told her that everything was top of the line, but the watchful eye of the designers made her feel like a princess.

The watchful eye of Alex made her feel like a princess about to be debauched. He'd stopped working on his computer long ago.

'That one is a definite yes,' he said, eyeing the little black dress she'd put on. Its hemline was high, but not too high, but its neckline was plunging by anyone's standards.

Elena looked at herself critically in the mirror. She seemed like a different woman. The casual, fresh-faced college student was gone, replaced by a sensual-looking seductress. It wasn't a look she was entirely comfortable with, but she liked it all the same. The woman in the mirror showed confidence and poise. Nobody would question her being on Alex Wolfe's arm.

Or they wouldn't if her last name wasn't Bardot.

The designer came over and fluffed her hair, spreading it out in a curtain. 'The trend these days is a curly bob, right above the shoulders. Add some highlights, and that would really make this dress pop.'

'You're not touching her hair.'

The growl came from across the room and was

menacing enough that the woman stepped back. 'Of course.' Her chin dropped an inch in rebuke. 'What would you like to try on next?'

Elena smoothed the soft material over her stomach. Alex's power hung in the air. There was never a doubt as to who was leading this show and some might have taken offence, but she didn't interpret his words as domineering. She felt protected. Turned on. 'That's enough,' she said.

'Are you sure?' Alex asked from his chair.

'I can't lift my arms any more.' She'd shimmied and zipped and tugged all she could.

He gave the designer a nod, and the woman scurried from the room.

Elena walked closer to the chair where he sat. 'Thank you,' she said softly. 'That was like a dream.'

It really had been an idyllic afternoon, sexy and thrilling. She tilted her head back as he rose before her. He wasn't shy about looking over the dress. He hadn't been shy about looking at anything.

She tugged at the hemline, even though it wasn't indecent. She sucked in air when his hands caught her waist. He turned her and walked her back the few feet to the wall. Pressing her up against it, he leaned down over her and nuzzled her neck.

'You are so beautiful,' he murmured.

Her eyelids fluttered. He'd learned right where she

was most susceptible to his touch. Her hands came up to clutch at his waist. 'I'll just pick out a few things,' she promised.

He pulled back a few inches to look at her.

She glanced over the stacks of clothes that had been piled on the 'yes' table. 'Definitely a suit. A dress and maybe the pink lingerie.'

'They're all yours.'

'No, that's all right,' she insisted. She didn't want to be greedy. She knew he'd insist on paying, but it was so much. Too much.

'Yes, it's all right,' he said firmly. 'I didn't just ask these people here so you could play pretend. I asked them here so I could splurge on you.'

She looked at him steadily, the back of her head resting against the wall. 'You don't have to, Alex.'

'No, but I need to.' His hold on her bit, and his eyes turned stormy. He was opening up to her more and more, but it had been a while since she'd seen the deeper emotions that were on display now. The anger and the determination. 'I've spent the last two years fighting to keep what's mine. I made my money honestly with my own company. If I want to spend it now, that's my right. I'll spend it wherever and however I please. Nobody is going to stop me, not even you.'

'OK.' Her hand lighted on his chest. He was breathing too hard, and his heart was racing. 'OK.'

His chest rose at her touch and his head dropped forward. 'Right now, it pleases me to spend it on you.'

She petted him, bringing down the beast. 'I didn't mean to be rude. It's just a bit much to take in.'

'It pisses me off that you think that.' He ground his teeth, but his touch softened as he caught a strand of her hair that dangled close to her waist. 'You should have had pretty things all along. You shouldn't have had to do without.'

He was talking about her dad, and Elena frowned. They'd been partners. They'd taken from people without regret. Did it matter more to him now that he knew her? That he saw the actual difference money made in people's lives? Had he never witnessed the dividing line between the haves and the have-nots?

Maybe not. Yet he was truly bothered by the situation, and that confused her. She'd assumed that only an unfeeling bigot could do the things he did, but he was neither.

How had he gotten caught up in such a mess?

'I had all the important things. My mom, my friends, love.'

A muscle in his jaw worked. 'Let me do this for you.'

There was no defensive barrier in his gaze. No truths or feelings he was hiding.

'OK,' Elena agreed, wanting to make him happy. 'Thank you.'

He sighed and leaned his weight into her, trapping her against the wall. His hands stroked up the sides of her legs, edging the cocktail dress higher. 'Good, because the fun part about buying you new clothes is taking them off you again.'

# Chapter Ten

Elena's body hummed when he finally kissed her. She'd been aroused ever since she'd first stepped out from behind the room divider in that pink lingerie. She couldn't help it. Her body responded whenever he looked at her.

Knowing that she was turning him on revved the titillation even higher.

He kissed his way along her jawline. Wrapping her arms around his neck, she held on. The low cut of the dress called to him, and he was soon at her cleavage.

She moaned as his dusty whiskers woke up her flesh.

'The door,' she whispered. 'What if somebody walks in?'

'I'll fire them.'

He kissed his way determinedly down her breastbone and licked deep. Nuzzling against her, he kissed the sides of her breasts. His hands had already squeezed between her back and the wall to tackle her zipper.

The vee neckline widened as the zipper slid down to her waist.

His breaths were heavy as he looked at the curves he'd exposed. He cupped one breast, holding her possessively. His hand looked sexy against all the black lace. His thumb poked at her nipple, waking it up and making it show itself above the silver demi-cup.

She tugged on his red tie. 'You didn't touch me last night.'

He pushed the dress over her arms and down to the floor. 'You were stressed, and I was thinking.'

'About this?' She gasped when she suddenly found herself in nothing but the tiny scraps of lingerie and a sky-high pair of stiletto pumps.

'About how to make up for all the things you missed.'

A pang hit her chest. She wanted to make up for all the things that had happened to him, too.

She arched when his wandering hands settled on her bare butt. He might as well be branding his handprints onto her curves. She felt the cup of his palm and the outline of each finger. One was dangerously close to the thin strip of the G-string running between her buttocks.

'I didn't miss –'

'Shhh.' He kissed her again, leaning heavily.

She loved the feel of his weight against her, his hard planes and hot skin. She was little, but he didn't treat her like fine china. As his hands stroked over her, she felt like a woman.

And they stroked everywhere. Her waist, her breasts, her stomach and her thighs.

'So ... you can't ... think,' she panted, 'and touch me ... at the same time?'

'God, no.' His voice was strained, too. 'I touch you and my thoughts go haywire.'

She knew the feeling, but she hadn't gotten to touch her fill yet. Hungry, she pushed his shirt off his shoulders and raked her fingers over his chest. It was a like a relief map of muscles and tendons. She flicked his nipple and his abdomen clenched like an accordion.

'Siren.' He nipped at her chin. 'You know it's even worse when you touch me.'

A sexy sense of power consumed her. Power and confidence. She planted her hands wide on him and stroked down all at once. He was as hard as he looked, lean and defined.

And sensitive.

She ran her fingernail along the line of his belt and his hand slapped against the wall beside her head.

The kiss they shared was full-tongued and erotic.

'It's been driving me nuts knowing what you've been wearing underneath all those dresses and proper business suits.'

Her hands trembled as she fought with the zipper of his dress pants. He swore when her fingers glided over his erection, so she went back and did it again. This

214

time she slid her hand inside the opening of his boxers.

His head dropped, and her toes squeezed. He was hot and stiff, way too much for her hand.

She pumped him once, all the way from his base to his blunt tip. 'It's your own fault,' she whispered boldly. 'You're the one who picked it out.'

'You're the one whose nipples got hard wearing it.' He pinched one through the cup to prove his point. 'Did it turn you on? Did it make you wet?'

She groaned as his hand stroked down her belly. She knew what was coming, but she bit her lip all the same when that hot hand pushed right between her legs. The material of the G-string was wider to cover her there, but it was no match for a determined intruder. He kneed her legs apart and his fingers slid along her grooves.

Her body rocked when two of them found her opening and slid right in. 'Alex!'

She was wet and plump, and they burrowed deep. She moaned when they curled and rubbed a trigger point deep inside her.

'Are you ready for me, baby?'

She swirled her thumb over the head of his erection, and his hips thrust.

'Hurry,' she whispered.

He stopped teasing her. His fingers left her body abruptly, but he stopped only to shrug out of his shirt and throw it to the floor. She helped by pushing down his pants. They dropped to his thighs, and he was suddenly more exposed than she was.

His erection pointed at her, thick and at attention.

She inhaled deeply when he caught her by the waist and lifted her. He didn't bother to strip her. Instead, he stretched the G-string aside to get at her. His weight pressed her into the wall, pinning her from shoulder to hips.

And then he was slowly, inexorably boring into her.

Elena moaned as she took him. He could be so overwhelming. So dominating.

And she loved it.

She wound her legs around his hips and locked her ankles. It had only been one night, but it seemed like for ever since he'd been inside her. He began to pump and her body clutched at him, not wanting to lose him again.

'Ooooh,' she cooed.

The lengths to which he pushed her body were indescribable. He drew more out of her than any other man ever had, and her fascination with him wasn't waning. What had been promised in lingering looks out in the woods had come to life.

If anything, it was growing more powerful.

Free. Wild. And ferocious.

He hitched her up higher against the wall and her fingers bit into his shoulders. Leaning forward, he latched onto her breast, lace and all. His tongue swept over her extended nipple, making it perk up ever tighter. Between the lace and his suckling, she could hardly stand it.

Her fingers dove into his hair and clutched at his scalp.

His mouth refused to let her go.

Elena fought the tide running through her. It was too soon. She was rushing too fast.

But there was nothing she could do as pleasure spiked inside her. Her moan filled the room and her head rolled against the wall.

When she opened her eyes, she found the wolf watching her. His grey eyes were lively and sparking. His thrusts became measured and deep. Lodged as he was inside her, he kept a steady caress against the nub of nerve endings at her core.

The nub that was about to shoot pleasure through her all over again.

Lunging off the wall, Elena kissed him fiercely. The impetus forced him to take a step back and support her weight on his own as he thrust up into her.

She wasn't going alone this time. She wanted to take care of him. The need to protect was all-consuming.

Their mouths tangled and she worked her hand between their heaving bodies. When she cupped him, he jerked.

The thrust rammed into her, and she let out a cry.

They banged into the wall again as he reached past her

to brace himself. His breaths were harsh in her ear as she caressed and petted him. In the end, all it took was a soft squeeze from her fingertips to send him over the precipice. His body gave in to hers, shuddering and spurting.

She buried her face in the crook of his neck as a second climax caught her. With a whimper, she let it sweep her along. This thing between them was only growing more potent. Like a drug, its hold was seductive and mind-bending.

It made her forget some things and overlook others. Until all she saw was how good they were together.

She was dazed when she opened her eyes. Looking into his, she saw the same foggy glaze. The fact that the hold was mutual was the only reason she wasn't panicking. It had them both in its grip.

After long moments, he lowered her until her feet were on the floor. Somehow his hands were fisted in her hair.

He combed it out, smoothing the tangles. 'Cut your hair. Is the woman insane?'

Elena straightened her underclothes, which were now sticky and damp. 'No, but I believe we qualify.'

One day. They'd gone one day without making love. How could it have built back up to such a fever pitch? They'd only just met each other, but their bodies couldn't stand to be apart.

She stroked his chest. She couldn't stop touching him.

'Playing dress-up to playing doctor,' she joked, half out of breath. 'What are we going to play next?'

A muscle worked in his temple, but then he was gathering her up and lifting her into his arms. 'House.'

She held on tight as they headed for the door.

\* \* \*

Without discussing it, they fell into a routine. Alex wanted Elena to move up to the main house, but she insisted on working down by the lake. Once evening fell, though, she made her way to the manor. There, they ate together and talked. They found entertainment in books, the in-home theatre, the pool, and the putting green. Eventually, they always wound up in bed.

Alex was still guarded, but he was letting her closer. Knowing even that tiny bit of his troubled background explained a lot. He'd been betrayed so many times. Very few people earned his trust, yet she was seeing cracks in that steely exterior. Flashes of humour. Moments of warmth. He was protective of her as they walked the trails and any sign of her scrimping drove him nuts.

Yet they still communicated best without words. The sex was hot, intimate and addictive. The more he touched her, the less Elena believed the stories about him.

Or his guilt.

She was trying not to let her personal feelings cloud

the facts, but it was hard to understand how he could have fallen in with his grandfather. Her father could be charming, but Alex was smart.

Too smart to be lured into their scheme.

Yet he was driven unlike anyone she'd ever known. Hungry for power and control. Money could buy both.

\* \* \*

It was late one night when she sat in bed with her shoulders propped against the headboard and her new laptop balanced upon her bent knees. Her fingers moved over the keyboard as she browsed the Internet. Night had fallen and the wind outside was howling. She'd stopped working long ago. She wasn't searching for economic models or trends. She had a more personal topic on her mind.

One Alex Wolfe, with an 'e'.

Her teeth worried her lower lip as she looked at old articles from Page Six of the *New York Post*. Ax, as they liked to call him, hadn't lived up to the social awkwardness of most software geeks before his incarceration. In fact, he'd looked a little too comfortable on the social scene.

Her jaw tightened as she looked at a picture of him with a leggy blonde. She read the caption underneath. Barbie was an actress who'd been in two consecutive blockbusters but had planned on going artsy. Too bad that hadn't worked out.

Jabbing the back button, Elena chose a different link.

And found him with a vivacious redhead. Her heart squeezed.

Both of the people in the photograph were stunning. Impeccably groomed and confident. Used to the upper-crust world in which they lived.

Stomach turning, she backed out of that site, too.

She wasn't competing with these women. That wasn't the way things were between her and Alex. She was *not* jealous.

Her gaze fell on a newer article written on the day he'd left prison. Everything inside her went quiet. In the shot, the sun was glinting off his sunglasses as he walked to the awaiting car. The building at his back looked dull and rigid. With his tailored suit and spiky hair, he appeared arrogant and unapologetic, yet she saw the muscle clenched in his jaw – the one that said he was holding everything in tightly.

Darn it.

She pulled back her hand, which had unconsciously reached out to trace that tell-tale sign. She shouldn't know him that well. They weren't having a relationship.

In her mind, that was being disloyal to everyone she knew … everything she was fighting for …

In her body and her soul, though, she knew she couldn't fight the truth much longer. She didn't sleep with just anybody.

221

'Do you need Leonard to get you some more raspberry body lotion?' Alex called.

'I can just use …'

'I'll take that as a yes,' he said as he came out of the bathroom.

He switched off the light and the only illumination left in the room came from the bedside table.

Oh, yes, Elena thought as she watched him through her eyelashes. They might not be a couple, but they had a routine.

She watched as he closed the bedroom door. He only did that when she was with him. Her gaze ran over his back from his wide shoulders to his narrowed waist. He wore black silk pyjama bottoms and nothing else.

Tonight, she wore one of the nighties he'd bought for her. The pale-yellow one.

His gaze was soft as he walked to the bed. 'That laptop still working OK for you?'

She hurried to switch pages on her browser.

'I love it. It's so fast.' The mattress dipped as he took his place in bed beside her. 'Thank you again.'

'You're welcome.' He kissed her temple, and his lips moved down to the shell of her ear as he reached out to confiscate her machine. 'But no computers in bed.'

'You're one to talk.' She arched her neck, but just before her eyes closed she saw something.

'Wait.'

She grabbed the computer and raised the screen so she could see it better.

A random click had landed her on another story related to him, only this one was about business.

Wolfe Pack's stock was down twenty per cent.

'Your company,' she murmured as she scanned the article.

He stretched out beside her, propping himself up on an elbow. 'The stock has taken a beating.'

But not because he'd been released from prison. She frowned as she came to the writer's conclusion. Investors were nervous because he hadn't returned to day-to-day activities. He was the mastermind who powered the company. Without him, people were worried about innovation and sustainability.

'They want you back at work.'

'I am at work. I've been teleconferencing with my people every day. Outsiders just don't know that.'

'Should they?'

He ran his fingertip down her arm, giving her shivers. 'It's my company.'

'You did go public.'

'Because the SEC made me.'

She was seeing some of the stubbornness that had gotten him where he was today. Top of the world and on the wrong side of a federal jury.

'Is there a way you could appease them?' She couldn't

223

help but think of all the people who'd lost money investing with Wolfe Financial due to fraudulent reporting. Wolfe Pack, on the contrary, was a healthy company whose stock price was suffering not from market pressures but because of speculation.

She knew, because she'd run the numbers.

He'd told her he'd made his money honestly. From what she could deduce, he was telling the truth. That company was clean.

She grimaced as a possible solution came to mind. 'Much as it pains me, could you do an interview or something?'

His expression turned turbulent. 'I'm not letting those mongrels inside the gate.'

'No, no. Not the paparazzi. I was thinking of a business reporter. Surely you know a respectable one.' She thought of all the beautiful women in the photos and had to steel her resolve. 'Are you friendly with any of them?'

He cupped her face and ran his thumb over her chin. 'They're all cut from the same cloth, baby. The interview would start out fine, but eventually the questions would drift towards the scandal and my stay at Otisville.'

He practically spit out the last words, and she laid her hand on his chest. He was stretched out casually beside her, but his muscles were clenched.

'I'm sorry I mentioned it.' She hadn't meant to upset him. 'You run your company the way you think best.'

He sighed. 'Actually, my COO wants me to come in, even if it's just for show.'

Come in? As in to the city?

'He thinks that alone would settle some rumours.'

Wind rattled the windows, and a chill washed through her.

Return to the real world? She hadn't considered that as an option. Not this early.

Which really wasn't so early after all. It had been weeks.

Her fingers went numb when he drew the laptop from her grip. He powered it down and set it aside. The chill in her bones got worse and she pulled up the covers. They'd been isolated from everything here on the estate, and protected.

They *had* been playing house.

She'd buried her head in the sand and hadn't had to face the difficult questions or tough decisions. She wasn't ready for that yet. She wasn't prepared for the real world to break in.

'Are you going to go?' The words dragged through her throat like barbed wire. He wasn't hiding out for the same reasons she was. If anything, he was defiant towards the people who wanted to pry into his life. She knew he'd come here to regroup but, based on this article, he could go back and thumb his nose at everyone. His time had been served. He could do whatever he wanted.

So why had he stayed?

He settled his hand wide across her belly. It felt warmer than the computer, and much more personal. The thin satin was like a second layer of skin.

'I haven't finished what I set out to do yet.'

Was that what all the programming was about? Whenever she wandered up to the manor during the day to borrow a book or grab a snack, he was typing all that mysterious computer code and consulting his notebooks. Did he have some big upgrade, some wave-it-in-their-face advances he wanted to spring on all his detractors?

'Your company needs you now,' she said, meeting his steady gaze. She fought the shudder that threatened to rack her body. She knew what she had to say, but it didn't come easily. 'You should go back, Alex.'

His eyes narrowed.

She licked her dry lips. 'For your people and for Wolfe Financial. It needs you, too.'

His fingers curled against her. 'My grandfather's company can go under for all I care.'

The tightness in his body said otherwise.

'The Board meeting is in two days,' she pressed.

'They don't want me there.'

She closed her eyes and resignation settled inside her chest, heavy and immovable. 'If you're innocent like you say, the investors do. They need someone who can straighten out the mess.'

His slate-coloured eyes took on the chill in the air and tension suddenly snapped. 'If I'm innocent.'

She lay beside him, feeling small and vulnerable.

He swore. 'Are you going to make me say it?'

Her hands fisted in the covers. 'I don't think anyone can make you do anything.'

His hand set like a rock on her belly, but he didn't pull it back. 'I shouldn't have to, not to you.'

'I need to hear it.' She held her ground, but the honesty made her throat feel thick. 'I need to look you in the eyes as you say it.'

A howl cut through the room, and the sliding glass door rattled as the wind buffeted it. Inside, the silence was just as deafening.

'I did nothing wrong.' His eyes were fiery and, as belligerent as his voice was, it cracked.

That one weakness, that one true sign of character …

It cracked the shell around Elena's heart, and she melted. She believed him, and not just because she wanted to. She could see the pain in his eyes and hear the anger of injustice in his words.

She rolled towards him, cupped his face and snuggled close. Stretching out her legs, she slid under the covers until her body was pressed tight against his. So strong. So defiant. So hurt.

'Then go help them,' she whispered. Go help himself.

His hand fisted in her hair. Neither said it out loud, but

they both knew it was time to make some big decisions. They'd been living in a fantasy world here, shutting away everyone and everything. It was idyllic, but it couldn't last. He wasn't a man who could be held down long. He needed to go out there into the world and reclaim his rightful place.

His pride would allow no less.

She needed to face the world, too, although she'd prefer to do it in a much quieter manner.

She could do that, though, if he left.

Her grip on him tightened when the realisation hit. When he left, the entourage outside would follow him. She could slip away and they'd be none the wiser.

Her heart broke, splintered really, at the thought of letting him go.

He pulled her down to cradle her against his chest. 'Is it time?'

She pressed her lips together, not wanting to answer, but knowing she had to. 'I think it is.'

His chest rose as he took a deep breath. 'All right – but if I'm going, you're coming with me.'

\* \* \*

Alex stared out of the windows, over the head of a marble wolf, towards the front lawn. Time was quickly running out, and with each second he could feel himself closing in on himself. The weather outside had calmed to the point where it was eerie.

No wind blew. There wasn't even a hint of a breeze. The grass stood green and tall, not wavering.

Inside, everything felt just as still. Like something was impending … a storm, a cataclysm … an ending …

He lifted his chin, ready to face it. He'd prepared himself for this and it was time to confront everything he knew was going to come at him.

And it was going to come at him fast and furious.

In the past few weeks, he'd grown soft. He'd let down his guard. He couldn't be like that in the city.

The memory of the flashing lights and waving microphones at Otisville pushed at the edges of his memory. They were still out there, the hungry buzzards, but he was ready for them now.

Because of her.

In worming her way past his defences, she'd made him face himself and grow stronger. He was ready for the showdown now. In fact, he relished the challenge of it.

The only thing he worried about was her.

He adjusted the band of his Rolex. He wasn't sure she was ready. She was a fighter, but she had a sensitive soul. He didn't know how she'd hold up under the limelight, because it would shine on her like a laser beam.

There wasn't much he could do to protect her from that.

The clippety-clop of a roller bag echoed up the stair-well, reverberating as she came around the corner from the elevator. He sighed. 'Can you not leave anything for the staff to do?'

She propped the plain blue bag up against the wall and began searching through her purse. She seemed ... fluttery. It wasn't a word he normally associated with her. She was graceful as she did yoga, elusive when she hid in the forest, charged when they had sex.

But not fluttery.

'I don't want to leave anything I need behind.' Her laptop bag bounced against her hip. She unzipped it and touched the laptop to make sure it was there, then went on to thumb through pages of notes.

'If you leave anything behind, we can buy new.'

'I don't think so.' Her raised eyebrows told him that the things she was concerned about couldn't be bought. She was concerned about her work, as she rightly should be. It had taken her an entire afternoon to pick and choose what she'd wanted to bring from the lake house. He'd gone down to help her pack her notes, but she'd insisted on working with Leonard. Alex had tried not to take it personally.

But she'd piqued his interest.

She'd taken more care packing that material than she had the new clothes and shoes he'd bought for her. Those she'd left for the staff. Her notes and books she'd packed herself.

'Leonard can ship whatever you need.'

Her lips pursed. It was clear she hadn't thought about that. Her shoulders relaxed.

He walked over to her and relieved her of the heavy computer bag. He knew it was precious to her, so he set it nearby where she could see it. He slid his hands down her arms and gripped her hands. 'Just bring an overnight bag and the computer. James will bring the rest.'

Her brow furrowed in a way that was cute. 'Aren't we going with James?'

'No.' He had other plans for transportation.

Almost on cue, a steady *thump thump thump* could be heard on the horizon. The beat grew consistently louder, invading the tower above them.

Elena's face turned pale. 'What is that?'

'Our ride.' He caught her hand and nodded at Leonard, who'd appeared in the archway to the front room. 'These two bags, please.'

He grabbed his briefcase himself. He understood her paranoia. He had some notes that were irreplaceable himself. 'Shall we?'

He hesitated when she dug in her heels. Her eyes rounded on the window as the helicopter landed in the front yard. 'You could have escaped here any time you wanted,' she said.

'It's not an escape. The news vans outside will catch up in a few hours.'

231

'Then why?' She was looking at the helicopter like it was a big ugly bug.

He smiled. 'I do like playing with them.'

Like a wolf with a rabbit …

Her fair colouring went from pale to off-green. Those doubts nipped at his ass again, and he tapped her under the chin, making her look at him. The fear on her face made his gut twist.

What was holding her back? Heading into New York? Or flying in that metal bird? Either way, he didn't like the idea of making her do something that frightened her.

He stiffened. He'd already made his decision. It was time to go, and he was going big. Yet she still had to have the right to choose.

'You don't have to go with me,' he offered.

Yet his chest hurt as he held his breath. He didn't know if he could leave without her.

Her eyes were huge as she looked up into his face. 'They'll find out about the two of us.'

The words lanced through him and he physically flinched. Out of everything, that wasn't a reservation he'd considered. She was still concerned about her reputation? She didn't want to be seen with him?

The snake inside his chest writhed in pain, but instead of striking out it was looking for a safe place to curl up. Lifting his chin, he gritted his teeth and smoothed his face. 'My security team can get you out of here once I'm gone. You can go anywhere you want ... do anything you want to do ...'

His jaw tightened so hard it popped. 'I'll pay for it.'

Her head snapped back so quickly, her long hair swung. The quiver in her chin disappeared and her hands curled into fists. He'd seen her angry before, almost hateful towards him, yet he'd never seen her livid. Her dark eyes sparked and he felt a charge when she marched forward and planted her hand flat on his chest.

'When are you going to learn that money isn't the answer to everything?'

She pushed him right where his heart was gaping. Ax was so surprised, he took a step backward. She followed, grabbing him by the lapels and going up on tiptoe to get into his face.

He dropped his briefcase. It bounced somewhere near his feet and the thud echoed. He caught her in his arms and kissed her like the earth had just been set on fire.

Maybe money didn't rule the earth ...

But he might have just found what did.

# Chapter Eleven

The view from the Park Avenue penthouse was stunning. Elena looked out of a window that competed with the clouds. The altitude, the opulence and the magnitude of it all made her head reel. The Art Deco limestone building gave a bird's-eye view of Central Park and tree-lined boulevards. It was the most coveted real estate in the city.

Yet the clouds hung low and fat, a familiar sight in a not so familiar world.

She turned away from the view to get her sea legs. They'd only arrived a short time ago. She hadn't yet seen all of the apartment, which took up the entire top floor, but in one sweep she recognised more of Alex here than she'd seen in the entirety of Wolfe Manor. The penthouse was crisp and modern. The style was the reverse of the look-but-don't-touch antiques of the main house. Here, things begged to be touched. Everything from the curtains to the television to the lighting was controlled by the push of a button.

She should have expected nothing less from a technology guru.

Yet even with as much black-and-glass as she found around her, the place had more soul. More comfort. The sofa alone probably cost more than her yearly rent, but it begged her to curl up on it to watch the huge television that disappeared into the wall.

This was Alex's true home. She swept her fingers over a plush recliner. He'd been torn away from this place and all his belongings to be put in a prison. They'd locked him in a barren cell with no diversions for that brilliant mind.

She bit her lip as she felt a pang. She couldn't imagine how that must have felt. He'd had his freedom ripped away, but he was finally home for the first time in eighteen months.

And he'd brought her with him.

She took an uneven breath and perched on the arm of the chair to watch him. He was speaking with his security people. He was in full business-shark regalia: grey suit, blue tie and gleaming Ferragamo shoes. He looked rich and powerful, but the tussled hair and dusty five o'clock shadow pushed the sex appeal into another realm.

She was wearing her Vera Wang blue sheath dress that fit her like a glove. She'd pulled her hair back in the clip that seemed to entrance him so, and new Jimmy Choo shoes smiled prettily from her feet. On the outside, they looked like a power couple. No traces of the nature lovers showed.

Yet he fit into this role so much better than she did.

'Elena?' He held his hand out to her. 'Could you come here for a moment?'

She crossed the room to the foyer. It felt funny to be walking in heels, and it added another element to her gait. As properly as she was dressed, she felt sexy.

Apparently, it showed.

Alex's gaze glinted and the bodyguards averted their gaze to become overly intrigued with the skylight.

'I want to introduce you to the security team. This is Smith, Hanson and Vasquez. If you need anything at any time, you can go to them.'

'Hello.' She looked over the trio and tried not to be intimidated. Smith and Hanson were the size of linebackers, while Vasquez was whipcord lean. They all had that dangerous quality to them that made a woman's radar ping. With their concrete chins and scarred knuckles, she was glad they were on Alex's side.

'Gentlemen,' he said, looping an arm proprietorially around her waist. 'This is Elena.'

So he had seen the male appreciation in their eyes.

'Miss,' Smith said.

'Good day,' Hanson greeted.

Vasquez merely nodded his head.

'Whatever she wants, she gets.'

'Yes, sir.'

Alex turned to her. 'If I'm not around, you go to them, but don't ask them to do anything that would put you in danger.'

'Danger?'

'You never know which way a crowd will turn, ma'am,' Smith explained.

A crowd. The paparazzi, protestors and gawkers would soon be here. She knew they were going to congregate.

Alex nodded in dismissal. 'Thank you. That will be all.'

The three men turned like soldiers who'd been given their marching orders. They left as silently as they'd appeared.

Elena looked up into Alex's face. He appeared calm and in control. He was back in the scene and on his game.

He was also more closed off than she'd seen him in a long time.

He ran a finger along her cheek. 'You're pale.'

It had already been a challenging day. 'I've discovered I'm not a fan of helicopter rides.'

He pulled her over to the bar and took his place behind it. He searched briefly before finding another bottle of the white wine she liked so well.

He popped the cork like an expert. 'You seemed to enjoy the flight.'

That part had been thrilling. She'd loved the views of the lake and the countryside and Bedford. Things had gotten a bit too exciting when they'd made it to the city. 'The flying part is fine. It's the landing I could do without.'

They'd used the East 34th Street heliport, which had the FDR overpass practically on top of it. The approach had been nerve-wracking, but once they were on the ground, the location was convenient. A limo had been waiting only steps away, and the drive to the penthouse had been short.

She took the glass he handed her and sipped. She looked at him over the edge of the flute. 'How does it feel to be back?'

He unbuttoned his jacket and glanced around the place. As she watched, the line of his jaw hardened.

'Like it's about damn time.'

She recognised that cool, determined look, but she could appreciate it better now. 'What are your plans?'

That sharp grey gaze landed on her. 'Our plans.'

Warmth unfurled in her chest. She was glad he considered this a partnership, but she was definitely the weaker link. She wasn't as brave as he was or as focused. People were still angry, and they had questions. His return would poke the hornets' nest.

If anyone recognised her, that would only compound the problem.

'Easy.' Rounding the bar, he took her hand.

She didn't know who needed the other's support more right now.

Together, they walked back to take in the spectacular view.

The sky was heavy. Dark and moody. It was the same sky that hovered over the rural part of the state, but the feel of the city was entirely different. New York had an energy like no other. It was stimulating and scary. Everything was going in top gear. Part of Elena craved that energy and wanted to dive back into it.

Yet a bigger part of her wished she was in the peaceful, secluded confines of the lake house.

She sipped from her glass again, and he squeezed her hand.

'Are you ready for the board meeting tomorrow?' she asked.

'I've read all the materials. It's going to be contentious.'

Couldn't anything be easy any more? She worried about him walking alone into that meeting, but she knew, if she went, it would only cause even more of a distraction. She'd read the materials, too, and the company was in chaos. Alex might not have any connection with Wolfe Financial on paper, but it had been in his family for over a hundred years. Someone needed to do something. The board itself had been floundering.

'How are you going to reclaim your good name?' She hoped he was going to step up. WF needed someone who knew how to take control and wasn't afraid to make the tough decisions. Right now, the financial institution was leaderless.

He looked pensive as he swirled his drink. 'There is no good Wolfe name any more.'

She breathed slowly. That was right. His grandfather was still out there, running from his responsibilities. Then again, the Bardot name had lost its lustre, too.

He tossed back a gulp of whiskey, gritted his teeth and put the empty glass on an end table. 'I'm not going to fight it any more.'

Her hair swished as her head swung around. 'Why not?'

She'd never considered him to be one who would just take the abuse and slander.

'There's no use looking back.' He smiled harshly. 'They say that the best revenge is living well.'

She frowned. 'You don't mean that.'

'The hell I don't.' He waved his hand over the city. 'I'm done hiding, and I'm not about to apologise.'

There it was, that anger that poked through the surface every so often. It had made fewer appearances recently, but she was beginning to understand it wasn't going away. That anger was bone deep inside him.

She put down her drink and moved closer. As warm as his body was, he was stiff and uncompromising. She cosied up to him, trying to take some of that anger away. She knew she had power over it, and it didn't scare her.

His fury was justified. He'd taken the brunt of the blame in the scandal, simply because he'd been available.

Bartholomew hadn't been around and her father had been dead. Alex had a right to be outraged, but she didn't like how it ate him up from the inside.

She spread a hand over his chest above his heart, and he wrapped his arms around her.

'You think I should beg for forgiveness.'

She shook her head. 'No, I don't. But you have to understand the way people think. Your grandfather still hasn't faced the accusations, and you're the closest thing to him.'

'I'm not my grandfather.' Alex snorted in derision. 'And he won't be saying he's sorry, that's for sure.'

Her fingers paused where she was stroking his tie.

Letting go of her, he drew a hand through his hair. 'He never apologised for anything he did in his life. Ever.'

Tears pricked her eyes and she blinked fast. The bastard. How could someone do the things that man had done and not feel the slightest bit of remorse?

Then again, her father had never said he was sorry either.

Not even in his suicide note.

She closed her eyes and cleared her throat.

'I'm nervous about this,' she confessed. 'Maybe returning to New York wasn't such a good idea.'

'There's no going back now.' He cupped her chin. 'Don't worry. I'll protect you.'

'But who's going to protect you?'

241

He laughed, but the sound held no humour. 'I don't need anyone to protect me. They've already done their damnedest. What more could they do?'

She shivered, not wanting to think about that. Going up on tiptoe, she kissed his cheek. 'It's not much, but I've got your back.'

His nose brushed against hers as he looked into her face. 'That's not "not much", pretty siren. It's everything.'

\* \* \*

The press was waiting the next day, milling about on the Park Avenue sidewalk. They knew what time the Wolfe Financial board meeting was, and they knew there was a good chance they'd finally see their target today. Alex Wolfe had avoided them for too long, locked down in the Wolfe compound. He'd travelled back to the city yesterday, though, and all indicators pointed to the meeting as the reason.

They couldn't help but salivate.

It was a juicy story. They'd squeezed as much out of it as they could a year and a half ago, but it was spinning up again. The heartthrob tech whiz convicted of white-collar crimes was returning to the city he'd once ruled. Had prison changed the boy wonder? Was he more humble now? Had the degradation beaten him down? Was he finally ready to admit to his wrongs?

Or had the time he'd spent on the inside made him even more dangerous? The sharp-dressed billionaire had always had an edge.

Would The Ax be out for revenge?

People wanted to know, and it was their job to dig up the facts.

A black limousine pulled up to the kerb, and the mob went on the alert. Reporters checked their mics, and cameramen stooped to try to see through the darkened windows. Was this it? A murmur went through the crowd when the driver stepped out. He closed the door, tugged at his jacket sleeves and made sure they covered his shirt cuffs. He tucked in his chin and pulled back his shoulders as he rounded the car. The guy was built like a Mack truck.

It was the Mr T Mohawk, though, that gave him away. This was the same driver who'd picked up Wolfe at the prison. The man took his place at the car's passenger-side door and glared at them.

Excitement rose. Simultaneously, heads turned to the posh building's front door. The doorman became twitchy. He stared over their heads, ignoring them, but tugged at the collar of his uniform as if it were too tight.

A reporter up front stood on tiptoe and saw movement inside. 'He's coming.'

The message passed swiftly through the crowd. Alex Wolfe was about to make an appearance. The group compacted, bodies bumping and arms tangling as they thrust their microphones forward. Their time would be short. The distance from the door to the car was only about ten feet. They had to make this count.

'Mr Wolfe,' more than one person called as the door finally opened.

Instead of the good-looking tycoon, a mean-looking bodyguard stepped out. He was pumped and amped. His sunglass-covered gaze swung around from left to right, and more than one skinny cameraman took a step back. If anyone got out of line, this guy was ready to squash them like a bug.

The hungry group of reporters waited.

Their caution was thrown to the wind when two more bodyguards bulldozed through the door. The Ax was at the security team's centre.

Questions started shooting through the air like darts.

'Mr Wolfe! How does it feel to be back?'

'What was it like on the inside?'

'What do you plan to say to your investors?'

That one finally stuck. Their interview subject's chin swung towards them, and it was set in stone. 'They're not my investors. I wasn't a part of Wolfe Financial.'

'Yet you're going to their board meeting, right?'

The security team kept their client moving, and the group shuffled along after them. Hips bumped and elbows dug.

'I'll be speaking during the open public comment

period,' the man said flatly. 'At the board's behest.'

Another reporter jumped forward and the front bodyguard blocked him with a straight arm. The reporter kept coming, though, trying to crawl over the sentinel as he threw out his question. 'Do you plan to apologise? Will you tell them where the money went?'

Wolfe slowed. As big as his men were, the crowd was impeding their progress.

'I had no involvement in that unspeakable crime.'

'How can you say that?' the reporter pressed. 'You just spent the last year in prison.'

That got a response. The Ax turned, his body clenched. 'Get your facts right. I was convicted of insider trading, even though I had written orders instructing my traders to sell Wolfe Financial stock if it fell below one-twenty.'

'Are you saying you were a scapegoat?'

Putting down his shoulder, the front bodyguard moved Jimmy Olsen about five feet back from where he'd started, but it was too late. The rest of the reporters picked up his line of questioning.

'What about your grandfather?' someone in the back yelled. 'Have you heard from him? Is he in Belize?'

'No comment,' Wolfe snapped.

The driver wedged open the limo's door and planted his massive form in front of it. The bodyguards became more aggressive and marched forward. The crowd had no option but to part and get out of their way.

One last reporter tried from his position, squashed up next to the kerb. 'Are you back in New York to stay?'

The question was met with silence as Wolfe entered the vehicle and the door was closed behind him. The all-black limousine offered no more answers and no more shots. The opaque windows blocked their view of the elusive, enigmatic man. Still, the news crews took what video they could as the driver pulled out from the kerb and drove away.

The moment the car blended into traffic, the cameras powered down and the crews rushed to their vans. Considering the dearth of communication they'd had with Alex Wolfe since his release, they'd just scored big.

\* \* \*

More reporters awaited in FiDi, the financial district in the southernmost section of Manhattan. They'd been put on alert by their colleagues up on Park Avenue, and they were on the hunt when the limousine pulled up. Microphones were ready, earpieces were in place and cameras were rolling as the black limousine cruised to a stop in front of the building on Wall Street.

The driver eyed the crowd suspiciously as he rounded the car to open the back door. Moving with the synchronicity of a pit crew, bodyguards spilled out and took their positions. A tall, good-looking man rose in their midst, smoothly buttoning his suit jacket.

The press swarmed, hungrier now that they'd gotten a taste.

They jockeyed for position, trying to get the best shots. The Ax had always gleamed under the spotlight. His handsome features and playboy ways had made him a media darling. With one snap of a camera, the reporters could sense the change. This version of the man was different. Harder, leaner and more dangerous. His sunglasses hid his reactions to their presence, but the line of his lips was flat and his steps were clipped.

Put him in a black suit and tie, and he would have blended in with the security detail perfectly.

'Mr Wolfe, what were you doing at Wolfe Manor over the past month? Why the long retreat?' A balding newspaperman stepped forward, his pen and notebook at the ready. 'Were you contemplating your actions?'

Wolfe didn't even blink.

An entertainment reporter held her microphone suggestively, stroking her thumb up and down its side. With her big hair and fake breasts, it was clear she was trying another tactic. 'Barbara Tyson is in town filming a movie. Have you seen you seen her since your release, Ax?'

The bleached blonde was disappointed when the question bounced right off, but the crowd wasn't ready to be deterred.

Another female reporter stepped right into the path of the lead bodyguard. She was just as beautiful, but with her short pixie cut and black-rimmed glasses she had 'intrepid' written all over her. 'How about Elena Bardot?'

That got a response.

Alex Wolfe made an abrupt halt. Around him, his security detail closed ranks.

The sharp brunette's eyes sparked. 'Caroline Woodward, WABC News.'

She held up a crisp 8X10 black-and-white photograph of the billionaire entrepreneur leaving a helicopter with a dark-haired woman at his side. 'We took this shot of you yesterday when you arrived in the city. Sources have identified your companion as Elena Bardot, daughter of Randolph Bardot, former CFO of Wolfe Financial.'

Wolfe snatched the photograph out of her hand and stared at it through his sunglasses. Other than maybe a slight tightening of his fingers, he gave no visible reaction. Yet the chill in the air dropped a good ten degrees.

'What is your relationship with Ms Bardot?' the reporter pressed. Like a hound on the scent, she bore forward. 'Are you romantically involved or is this a continuation of the Wolfe–Bardot business relationship?'

A muscle in Wolfe's jaw clenched. His head slowly tilted and he looked the reporter over from head to toe. Hungry as she was for a scoop, everyone saw the woman inhale in surprise. Her chest lifted and her hips gave a slight swivel. Something sharp and sexy hung in the air.

It snapped and tumbled when, letting go finger by finger, he dropped the photograph like a piece of trash.

'No comment.'

The picture seesawed through the air as it fell to the ground. A beat reporter bent down to pick it up, braving getting stepped on as the security team kicked back into gear.

Gritting her teeth, the reporter followed, her heels clicking against the sidewalk as she tried to keep up. 'Was she involved in this all along? Did she know what her father was into?'

Her cameraman got too close and one of the security men pushed his hand into the lens. 'Step back.'

'Are you saying that's not her?' another reporter called.

The WABC reporter wasn't about to be denied her scoop. Her painted lips thinned and red splotches coloured her cheekbones. Rushing ahead, she walked backwards and sent out rapid-fire questions. 'Have you made restitution to Ms Bardot and her mother? Yvonne Bardot was reportedly an investor who lost her life savings in your Ponzi scheme.'

Wolfe kept on walking, but his neck stiffened.

'Mr Wolfe. Would you like to make a statement?'

They were at the private building's door, the final barrier that the press couldn't cross. The Ax stopped on the threshold. Pulling down his sunglasses, he pinned the not-so-sweet Caroline with a slate-grey stare. 'No. Comment.'

# Chapter Twelve

Elena was worried. The board meeting had run long and, when Alex had returned, he hadn't wanted to talk. It was as if they'd gone back in time to their first days together at the manor, where he'd pass her silently in the woods. The tension between them was there, but it was harder and sharper. It was more than the sexual friction that was ever-present. He'd retreated inside himself. All the anger, pain and pride were bottled up tight.

She feared what might happen if the cork blew off.

He was working out in the gym. Standing outside the door, she heard weights clanging and pulleys whirring. She'd found the room in her explorations as she'd waited for the board meeting to start. It was smaller than the workout facility at the manor, but it had the same topflight equipment. Alex grunted in exertion and the sound grew into a soul-wrenching shout.

Her fingers bit into the tab of her zipper when a loud clang rang throughout the hallway.

It was time. She couldn't let this go on any longer.

Turning into the room, she saw a barbell loaded with heavy weights still bouncing in the bar catches where he'd let it fall. She blew out a breath, relieved that he hadn't dropped it on himself. 'Don't you think you're pushing yourself a little hard?'

He stared up at the ceiling from the weight bench where he lay. His chest rose and fell as he tried to catch his breath. 'I'm just working off steam.'

She leaned against the wall and toyed with the string of the hoodie. 'Want to take a break?'

He shook his head. 'I have two more sets to go.'

'Are you sure?'

He finally rolled his head towards her. When he caught a look at what she was wearing, his arms dropped in slow motion to his sides. 'Damn.'

She ran the toes of her right foot up the line of her left shin. She'd hoped she could get his attention. Looping the tie of the hoodie around her finger, she watched him, smoky-eyed.

He sagged on the bench, some of that enormous cloud of anger over him dissipating. 'Elena.'

She walked towards him, feeling his gaze stroke down her legs. She'd never felt like she had long legs before, but his stare dragged on for ever. It made her feel slinky and sexy.

Even if all she was wearing was a plain grey hoodie.

He sat up as she came near, but she caught his shoulders and stopped him standing up. Swinging her leg over the bench, she straddled him. Watching his expression, she lowered herself onto his lap.

His hands settled naturally upon her waist. Curious, she pressed her palms against his chest. His skin was warm and sweaty, but underneath his muscles were fiery hot. No wonder they looked as if they'd been chiselled from steel. He pushed himself to the extreme.

'Was the meeting that bad?' she asked.

'I've been to better.'

'I watched the streaming video of the shareholder portion online. Bankruptcy?'

'It's the only way. Better to bury this thing and move on.'

The muscles under her fingertips quivered almost imperceptibly. The tiny fibres had been broken down so they could repair and grow back stronger. 'I'm sorry,' she said.

He scowled. 'Why?'

'That company was your family's legacy. It's been around for generations.'

'Until my grandfather killed it.'

And her father. Guilt settled in her chest. 'Are you sure it can't be saved?'

'Only at the expense of the shareholders, and I won't do that. They've already been through enough.' He wiped

252

the sweat from his brow. As confident as he sounded in his recommendation, it still had him worked up. 'Besides, I've already started another company. If there's going to be any family legacy ... Well, that remains to be seen.'

Her caress slowed, and the rest of that thought remained unsaid. For a legacy to be passed on, he'd need to have a family first. Something shifted inside her chest.

But that was a subject for another day. In the distant future.

Right now, they had other issues to address, primarily his bad mood.

She was sitting on his lap, wearing nothing but his favourite fleece jacket. He was bare-chested in nylon shorts and cross-trainers.

And leather gloves.

A few ideas came to mind.

She trembled as his hands stroked her thighs. The weight-lifting gloves covered his palms and the base of his fingers. They protected his hands from blisters, and the wraps around his wrists lowered the chance of injury. The combination of leather and bare flesh felt foreign. Erotic.

He squeezed lightly. 'Speaking of shareholders, why didn't you tell me about your mother?'

Her gaze jumped up to his. 'What about her?'

'She's an investor,' he growled. 'One who got burned.'

Elena looked away. 'It's old news.'

'It's new to me. I should have known.' He cupped her

chin and made her face him. 'Why would she invest her money with your father? Why put it in her ex's care?'

Elena shrugged. 'That was the one thing he always seemed good at, managing money. He spent all his time at work.'

At least, as far as she remembered. She supposed that some of that time he'd actually been with the girlfriend who'd ended up as his second wife.

'And now Yvonne manages a bakery?'

'She likes her job.'

'But she has no savings in the bank, nothing built up for retirement.'

Elena pulled her chin out of his grip. That was a sore point, one that still hadn't scabbed over. After the scandal had come to light, her mother's finances had been analysed backwards, forwards, inside and out. 'Don't worry about my mother. She can take care of herself.'

His thumb ran along her jawline before dropping. 'You both can.'

He took a breath deep enough to jostle her. She clenched her thighs around him to keep from falling off. His eyes sparked, but he wrapped his arms around her protectively. Sighing, he dropped his head. 'They know about us, Elena. There was a photographer with a long-range lens at the heliport.'

'I know. I saw the news report that played before you got home.'

He went still. 'And you're OK with that?'

She threaded her fingers into his hair and massaged the tight muscles of his scalp. 'I don't know about OK. I don't like the idea of my personal life being under a microscope.'

'Personal life?'

Trust him to pick up on that part. Since coming here to New York and seeing him face the pressure of the afternoon all on his own, she'd finally accepted one thing. Their lives had become intertwined. Where one had been, there were now two. They were a couple. 'Very personal,' she whispered into his ear.

His head came up and his slate-coloured gaze bore into hers. 'You didn't want anyone to know about us.'

And trust him to remember that. Brooding and quiet meant observant. She fought not to squirm. 'That wasn't fair to you.'

She pointed her toes towards the floor, trying to find her balance, but they didn't reach. She was dependent on him. 'I've been selfish,' she confessed. 'I wanted you, but I wasn't brave enough to face all the questions and accusations.'

'I wanted to protect you from all that.'

'You have. But watching you take all the heat … It's hurting you, and that hurts me.'

That tell-tale muscle in his jaw clenched. 'I thought you'd be gone when I got home.'

'I'm right here.' She wiggled closer and their chests brushed. 'And if you haven't noticed, I'm wearing your favourite item of clothing.'

'I noticed.' His hands fisted in the excess material. The hoodie was big on her, but it still crept up high on her thighs when he did that. 'I didn't know that you brought it with you.'

'It was in my overnight bag, the one and only thing you allowed me to carry onto the helicopter.'

'Good choice.' He slid his hands up her legs and under the soft fleece. They bit into her bottom when he discovered she wasn't wearing anything underneath.

Elena shifted, settling more comfortably into his hold. 'I've become pretty proprietary about this thing. It brings back good memories.'

'Memories of what?'

She ran her thumb over his nipple and he jerked. Her smile was soft as she let her fingers play some more. 'Do you know what I did that first time you loaned it to me down by the lake?'

He cleared his throat. 'What?'

'I went home and crawled into bed.' She kissed his collarbone. 'And did this.'

She tugged the zipper down. Sliding her hand inside, she cupped her breast. The air began to vibrate when her other hand disappeared between her legs.

'Mmm,' she hummed, her eyelids drifting closed.

'God. Damn. Elena.' His voice sounded like sandpaper.

She'd never done this in front of anyone before, but she heard the desire in his voice and felt the strain in his hands. Watching her gave him pleasure, so she let herself go. This was for him. She needed to get him out of his head, and she knew the best way to do that. Moving her fingers over herself, she felt the heat and softness of her most private place. His hands bit into her bottom, and dampness coated her fingertips.

'Ahhh,' she gasped.

'Let me see,' he growled. He caught the bottom of the hoodie and pulled it up so she was exposed.

Elena felt wanton touching herself with her legs spread so wide. The room had such a hard-edged industrial feel to it, and she was splayed out across his lap. All femininity and softness. Mirrors reflected everything she was doing. There was no place to hide, no soft pillows or blankets with which she could cover herself.

She was on display. The act was brash and explicit, and she revelled in it.

An ache filled her breasts. She ground her palm over her nipple as her fingers down below became more demanding. Rolling her hips, she offered herself up for penetration. Her middle finger slid right in.

'You are so hot,' Alex rasped.

His hands moved restlessly on her hips, petting her and urging her on.

257

She peeked through her lashes and found him watching her unabashedly. The intimacy sent a shudder through her, and her passageway clamped down tight.

'Oooo!' Her head fell back as she began to pump her finger in and out. Slowly at first and then with greater need. Alex's hand fisted in her hair, and her breasts thrust upwards.

He seized her zipper and pulled it down further so he could see it all. A growl filled the air when he saw another intimate piece of clothing. It was the lavender bra she'd left behind in his other gym ... the one where they hadn't made it to a bench ...

'I found it in a drawer in your bedroom,' she panted.

'Your drawer.' He drew the zipper all the way down and spread the material wide to watch her work herself into a frenzy.

Elena squirmed on his lap. Her drawer. Here, in his real home. 'You planned to bring me here?'

'I have lots of plans.' His mouth sealed over hers and his tongue plunged deep.

She kissed him back. Instinct had her reaching for him, but he caught her hands and kept them where they were. A whimper left her when leather bumped against her mound. He made sure she used two fingers this time, and her eyelids fluttered closed.

He popped open the front tab of her bra. Obediently, she cupped her breast and fondled herself.

Her eyes popped right back open when his gloved hand took possession of her other breast. The leather covering his palms felt warm and wicked, while his fingertips were bare and dexterous. He pinched her nipple as he pulled her further onto his lap.

Their chests rubbed as he kissed her again. Elena felt so hot, so out of control. She fingered herself almost roughly as her arousal grew. Wriggling forward on his lap, she rocked right against his ridge.

Swearing a blue streak, he pushed her back far enough to untie his shorts, thrust them down and free his erection. Elena was nearly gone. Watching her turned him on. She'd do nearly anything to please him.

'Hurry,' she whispered. She was close to coming as he caught her by the waist. It was clear his strength had returned. His arm felt like a steel band around her as he lifted and positioned her.

Her fingers bumped against a rock-hard erection. That was what she needed. That was what her body craved. She caught him, and his breath hissed in her ear as she guided him to her core. Her toes reached for the floor and, this time, found it. Taking control, she lowered herself onto him.

Their groans blended as she took him inside her.

'Sexy siren,' Alex murmured. His gloved hands swept up her back as she began a slow, tortuous rhythm.

Elena's senses went into overdrive. The hoodie was caught

between them and the zipper abraded their skin as she humped up and down. The feeling was raw and electric. The cold tab of the zipper caught in the crease of her leg, and she let out a cry. She could barely stand the stimulation.

'You told me you liked seeing this hoodie wrapped around me,' she struggled to say.

'Hm' was all he managed to get out. His hands were cupping her bouncing breasts and his face was buried in her hair.

'What ... what were you really going to say when I asked you? Why do you like seeing this oversized old thing on me?'

His teeth raked over her throat. 'Because it says you're mine.'

From that point on, there was no more talking. Only touching. And kissing. And deep, fast penetration. Alex held Elena tightly as she established the rhythm and the pressure. The weight bench grew slippery as their hips rubbed back and forth. She was taking all of him, as far as he could go. She heard the sounds they were making, the sighs, the groans and the squeaks against the vinyl.

Her thighs burned. She was his. All his.

He pulled the hood up over her head as he kissed her. It focused her solely on him. For her, there was no other. It was the two of them, alone and always.

The supple leather stroked over her. The zipper bit and caressed. But most of all she felt him. Her Alex.

Her lone wolf.

Her body suddenly arched. She pressed down hard, her body milking his as she thrust her breasts into the air. He cupped her possessively, the leather capturing her nipple and pressing against it tightly. His thighs bunched, and then he was jerking up into her.

They came so hard, the barbell clattered in its holder. The weights rang loudly as the tremors continued.

At long last, the tempest died. She leaned her head on Alex's shoulder and fought for air. His arms locked around her, holding her on his lap. He cupped the back of her head and whispered soft, sexy words.

Elena's body went slack, but her brain came back to life. Synapses fired and thoughts sprang up. Hopes for the future. Concerns about today. Solutions for all their obstacles. The ideas were brilliant but, in her state of bliss, fleeting.

'How are we going to handle this?' she asked. 'We have to make this work.'

He leaned back against the bar. 'We've already been outed. I could deny it, but –'

'Don't.'

He peeled back the hood to look at her face. Her hair was loose and wild. 'You need to think about this.'

'I have. I want them to know. I want everyone to know.'

'Elena,' he cautioned.

'I'm sure.'

He shook his head, unconvinced. 'You're getting involved with an ex-con. People are going to think the absolute worst of you.'

'They thought that when I was a student whose father had just died.' Lifting her head, she looked him in the eye. 'Let them see us together. Let them talk. I don't care what they say.'

'I do. I can't protect you.' His expression turned fierce and proprietary – and maybe just a bit panicked. 'You're going to be hurt.'

'I've been hurt before, and I'm not going to let you take on all of it.'

'Baby ...'

'What matters is the two of us.' She gave him a fast kiss. 'Come on, Wolfe. Take me out. Show me your New York.'

\* \* \*

He took her out to dinner at Jean-Georges in the Trump Hotel. Elena felt the stares and heard the whispers as they entered the dining room. The attention bothered her, but, seeing Alex's stern face, she could tell it bothered him more. There were massive picture windows on two sides, and it felt like they were in a fishbowl. When the waiter tried to seat them at a table out in the middle of the room, Alex demurred. They chose a cubbyhole table off to the side instead.

262

Elena was happy she'd accepted the clothes he'd bought for her. If she hadn't been wearing the classy burgundy cocktail dress, she would have felt out of place. The restaurant and all its diners practically dripped money, but even amongst his peers Alex commanded attention.

The waiter and sommelier were respectful, and Chef Jean-Georges himself even came out to greet them. Yet all around them diners were taking furtive looks. Some were even texting.

She took his hand. It felt stiff and cold. She squeezed tightly. 'What's good here?'

He blinked at the menu as if he hadn't realised it was in front of him. 'Everything.'

His attention focused on her, and his shoulders relaxed. 'Order whatever you'd like.'

She chose the scallops with caramelised cauliflower, while he went with the black sea bass crusted with nuts. They sat quietly as a waiter poured their wine. The table they'd chosen wasn't exactly hidden in a corner. They sat together on a bench seat, tucked in the cubbyhole but facing out into the room. They had a wonderful view of the trees and small flower garden outside, yet it also put them in the situation of facing the crowd. Only the waiter serving them hid them from curious onlookers.

'Did you play football?' Elena asked as she took a sip of the Chardonnay. It sat nicely on her tongue. He'd chosen well.

Alex frowned. 'Where did that come from?'

She crossed her legs. 'I'm trying to figure out what you were like growing up.'

She was also trying to distract him and make him relax. People were still stealing looks, but most had gone back to their meals. She was nervous about showing her face, but they couldn't constantly be on guard.

'I can see you being a quarterback,' she decided.

He finally settled back in his seat. 'I played lacrosse.'

'But you were the captain, right?'

The corner of his mouth twitched. 'Somebody had to be.'

She rolled her foot in circles underneath the table. A woman at a table way over in the corner had just pointed at them.

'I just can't picture you as a computer nerd,' she confessed.

That got almost the hint of a smile out of him. His gaze flicked to the far table, and the nosy woman snapped forward in her chair. Elena relaxed a little when he laid his arm protectively along the back of the bench seat. 'I was an only child, and I bored easily. To keep myself entertained, I took things apart and put them together again. Computer games and programming were a natural extension.'

His brow smoothed and his look turned pensive. 'My curiosity got me into hot water more than a few times with my parents.'

It was the first time she'd ever heard him talk about them. 'When did they pass away?'

'When I was in high school.'

A difficult time for any teen. And he'd been left with that monster of a grandfather? She laid her hand on his leg.

'I'm sorry.' The touch was hidden by the crisp white tablecloth, but she didn't care who might see.

That pensive look deepened. The table setting was military precise, but he realigned his salad fork.

Her fingers tightened around the delicate wine glass, and she set it down before she broke it. The woman over in the corner had stopped trying to steal glances, but her friend was talking into her phone. She had a straight-on view, and she wasn't even trying to be discreet.

Elena smiled politely when the waiter approached with their food, but she forgot everything else when she saw what the chef had prepared. She didn't want to appear unsophisticated, but it was hard not to stare at the creations. Both dishes looked like works of art.

The seafood tasted like culinary art, too.

Jean-Georges was out of range for poor college students, and it was her first experience at a three-Michelin-stars restaurant. She wasn't going to waste the experience worrying about gawkers.

She took a bite that melted in her mouth. 'From what I've read, you started Wolfe Pack while you were still in college.'

'I didn't think I was being entrepreneurial. It was another project built out of boredom, but it kept growing. More and more pieces were fitting together in my head.'

'Enough so that you left school?'

'It wasn't a decision that was easily accepted at the time. Believe me.' He buttered a piece of black bread that had come with his meal. 'But I knew I was onto something. I was determined to see where it would take me.'

She'd seen that unflinching determination. It had brought him far but, truth be told, it hadn't been that big of a risk. He'd had old Wolfe money to fall back upon.

Or maybe that was exactly what he'd been trying to get away from.

'I think you've done OK for yourself.'

Their gazes locked, grey to brown. For a moment, she thought she'd put her foot in her mouth. There was the scandal. He'd spent time in prison. Yet the molecules in the air between them started vibrating. She felt a pull, almost like gravity, in his direction.

His voice dropped low. 'Yeah, I really have.'

His leg brushed against hers. His eyes twinkled with secret knowledge, but the light in them went steady when he focused on someone beyond her.

Elena straightened, concerned. She looked to her left, but it wasn't what she expected. The press hadn't gained entrance and there were no protestors with signs. Her stomach tightened all the same. A tall, buxom blonde was headed towards their table. She recognised the woman instantly. It was Barbie, the movie star from the website pictures.

'Hello, Alex.' The woman's voice was sultry and cultured.

'Barbara.' He stood and took the hand she offered. She kept coming and he greeted her with a kiss to the cheek.

'I'm sorry to interrupt.' Her mouth curled upwards when she glanced in Elena's direction, but the smile held the warmth of a reptile. 'Hello.'

Elena returned the smile through gritted teeth. 'Hello.'

The blonde had bombshell written all over her. She dressed to highlight her assets, and she knew just how to pose to best show them off. Her dress even sounded sexy as the silk brushed against Alex's suit.

'I'd heard you were in town,' he said. 'A new movie?'

'Yes.' The expression on the woman's face brightened. 'I was hoping we'd run into each other. Why haven't you called?'

Elena began to tap her foot underneath the table. She was sitting right here!

'We always had so much fun together,' Barbara pouted.

It didn't take a brain surgeon to understand what kind of fun that was.

An ill-tempered light came into Alex's eyes and he gestured to the table. 'Barbara, this is Elena.'

'Bardot. I know.' The condescension in the woman's

voice couldn't have been clearer. She lifted her chin and her hair moved stiffly. 'I'm a friend of Candace.'

Candace. Her stepmother. Elena's jaw clenched. The plastic blonde was about the same age, she thought cattily. Although it was hard to believe that this woman was still friendly with her stepmother after her fall from grace. No money, no brunches. No cash, no wardrobe. Last she'd heard, the Bardot apartment had been taken away and the family had moved in with relatives. Candace had taken her misfortune much harder than Yvonne had. The loss of her husband hadn't affected her as much as the loss of wealth. She'd whined and cried but had taken no steps to support herself.

The elegant movie star bit her lip and looked back and forth between the two of them. 'Sorry if I'm interrupting a business meeting.'

Elena cocked her head. *What?*

That muscle ticked in Alex's jaw. He was not happy. 'We're here on a date.'

'Really?' The woman patted her hair and swivelled her hips. She pressed her hand to her cleavage, but she quickly realised that her former lover's attention was no longer on her. She followed his gaze to Elena, and her astute eyes narrowed. 'You are very pretty.'

Elena was taken aback. 'Thank you.'

She bit the side of her cheek and lied. 'I'm a big fan.'

Barbara's lips pursed, and her gaze swung back and

forth between the two of them. 'I apologise for the confusion, but I heard that the two of you worked together on that Fonzie thing.'

Elena had taken a sip of wine, but she nearly choked on it. Half of her wanted to laugh and the other was outraged. 'Excuse me?'

'We just met recently,' Alex said, his voice like glass.

Barbara's expression went innocent. 'Honestly? Because Candace swears that Randolph and his daughter talked all the time about the markets and that type of thing. Maybe I just assumed ...'

They hadn't talked all the time. One call every three months or so was not often. So what if they did talk about economics? It was the one thing they still had in common.

Elena's fists curled. Everything inside her propelled her forward. She didn't know what she intended to do, but she started to get up.

Alex's hand settled heavily on her shoulder.

'Barbara, I think your date is trying to get your attention.'

The woman looked over her shoulder. Almost as if a switch was thrown, she arched her back and waved flirtily. 'Sorry, that's my director.'

She was smiling when she turned to say goodbye. 'Have a nice dinner. I'm glad you're out, Ax.'

She moved in for another peck, but he pulled back. The look on the woman's face faltered, and fear flashed momentarily in her eyes. She stepped back quickly, but gathered herself enough to walk back slinkily to her table. Alex stood stiffly, watching her go. His face was hard and the air around him bubbled. With that dark five o'clock shadow, he looked dangerous.

Elena took a sip of wine that went more smoothly down her throat. She looked around discreetly, hoping few had heard the exchange. She was mortified to find people staring again.

He held out his hand. 'Let's get out of here.'

She caught it fast. 'Yes, please.'

\* \* \*

'I'm sorry,' he said in the car.

'It's not your fault,' she murmured as she watched the lights outside the Bentley go by.

'She was a shiny bauble to have on my arm as I went to society events.' He spread his legs wider in the back seat and raked a hand through his hair. It had grown somewhat, but still seemed tussled. 'And she was an easy lay.'

Elena flinched.

He caught her hand. 'I didn't say a good one.'

She inhaled deeply. 'If she's a friend of my stepmother's, I know exactly what type of woman she is. Candace is the queen of the gold-diggers.'

And a bitch.

But that went without saying.

She rubbed her temple and felt Alex's grip on her hand tighten.

'I'm sorry I didn't stop her sooner,' he said.

She'd come perilously close to stopping the woman herself. The comment about her father had been cheap, and it had blindsided her. Yet the way the woman had touched Alex with such familiarity and thrust her breasts in his face had almost been worse.

Elena let out a breath and her eyes fluttered closed. She'd almost put her fist in the woman's overly white teeth. She couldn't imagine the brouhaha that would have caused. In Jean-Georges? With the press watching their every move and hanging on every word?

'James, pull over here,' Alex instructed suddenly.

Her eyes popped open. They were stopping? All she wanted to do was get back to the penthouse.

Alex caught her chin and lifted her face. The garish lights of New York City spilled into the car, and she couldn't hide her mood. His thumb ran across her lower lip. 'You need a drink.'

She needed a pitcher.

Elena wasn't in the mood, but she got out of the car, accepting Alex's hand. She glanced up and down the street but didn't see a pub. She didn't see any camera flashes, either. Apparently James had lost the paparazzi. The driver was good.

271

The wolf in Alex was still looking for threats. He wrapped an arm around her waist and guided her across the sidewalk to a building. They stood on a landing where three steps led down to a basement level. The blues club was hidden away and there wasn't a name on the door. The nightspot was shadowy and exclusive, and Elena felt more relaxed the moment they stepped inside.

The crowd here was looser and more accepting – or they just didn't care who'd stepped into their midst. Compared to the white starkness of Jean-Georges, the club was a panacea for the eyes. The lighting was dim, and the air was hazy. The tables were small, but visitors were more into each other than into their neighbours. Heads were bent together and glasses clinked.

Alex pulled out a chair for her, and a waitress appeared the moment he took his seat. She wrote down their order and moved along.

Elena turned towards the stage when she heard a bass being tuned. 'Live music?'

'It's what they're known for.'

By the time the waitress returned with their drinks, the band had started their set. The music had a throbbing beat and a seductive melody, but that was the way blues were. It suited Elena's mood perfectly. Heartache and pain. Temptation and soulfulness. She swayed in her seat, drawn in by the ambience.

The second number was slower and sexier. They hadn't

even hit the chorus when Alex stood and held out his hand.

'Dance with me.'

Her heart gave a little flutter. She hadn't expected dancing. Taking his hand, she slipped from the chair. They moved to the tiny wooden floor and she turned into his hold.

They said that some men danced the way they made love. Her thighs turned to jelly when she discovered he was one of those rare few. He drew her so close, her breasts plumped against him. She rested her head against his chest, and their thighs brushed as they moved. 'I thought it was your mission to go incognito tonight.'

He'd chosen tables on the edge of the rooms and had discouraged anyone who paid too close attention. Here, though, they were the only ones on the dancefloor. The mood-lighting wasn't bright, but they were still out in the open and on display.

'I changed my mind.'

'Why?'

His hand stroked the small of her back. 'Barbara.' He frowned down at her. 'She thought we were business partners.'

'Oh, the *Fonzie* thing.' Elena rolled her eyes and followed as he circled them over the polished floorboards.

Alex wasn't laughing. 'People are seriously asking that question. I had a reporter throw it at me this morning.'

273

She rubbed her lips together, considering how to answer. She'd been through this thing once before. She didn't want to go through all the questions and suppositions again, yet she cared for him. 'I can take it.'

He stopped moving. 'I've got a better solution.'

There, in the middle of the pulsating dancefloor, he kissed her long and slow. A hoot went up, followed by cheers and a smattering of applause.

And cellphone flashes.

People were taking pictures of them. The club might be discreet, but people knew who they were and they were putting on a show. They'd be in all the newspapers and supermarket rags by morning.

Spinning her around, he dipped her sexily. 'It's time we dispelled the rumour that I'm into you for your criminal mind.'

# Chapter Thirteen

They went out to dinner the next night, too, and then to a Broadway show. The more appearances they made on the social scene, the more Elena found her poise. Alex was protective wherever they went, and the merest hint of a television camera would have him snarling. In those times, a soft word or touch from her could ease him.

And circumstances did improve.

Once high society determined that The Ax really was back – and as rich and powerful as ever – they welcomed him into their midst. His notorious reputation took on a strange kind of cachet. Everyone who was anyone wanted him at their parties and events.

The press wasn't exactly warming to them, but their focus had shifted. Reporters and pundits alike were intrigued by the Wolfe–Bardot alliance. Their romance was at once considered scandalous and dreamy, a dark turn on Romeo and Juliet.

Through it all, Elena stood at Alex's side. He fit into the scene like an integral cog that made it all work, but she could see the defence mechanisms he had in place. Everything he did and said was strategic. He planted himself at her side whenever he saw a socialite with a nasty or gossipy reputation sidle up to her. He avoided delicate topics such as stocks or Wolfe Financial when talking with old friends.

In essence, he became The Ax.

At home at night, though, he was her lover. The emotions he bottled up came pouring out when they were in bed. The sex was hotter and greedier. Their connection was becoming closer, almost obsessive. He seemed intent on protecting her, insulating her and pleasuring her.

It was at Wolfe Pack where he was calmest.

He pushed himself there, too, but it wasn't punishment. Elena felt comfortable at the company's offices, and she liked seeing Alex secure enough to lower his guards. He loved his work and he trusted his people. He'd grown Wolfe Pack from scratch and it was now an industry leader. Even with a blue-blood CEO who'd come from old money, the company had an X-gen culture. Located in the FiDi neighbourhood, the office was nonetheless outfitted with beanbag chairs and comfy sectionals. The kitchen was filled with free snacks and drinks. The techies dressed like college kids, but they worked like maniacs.

Elena tended to stay in the penthouse to work, but on some days like today she'd work in the Wolfe Pack office.

'Hi, Elena,' a fresh-faced programmer said. 'How's the dissertation coming along?'

'Hi. Josie.' Elena pulled her ear buds out of her ears and sat back in the chair. The young woman was a user interaction designer about her age. 'I'm so close I can taste it.'

Her new friend looked over her dress and high heels. 'What fancy party is the boss taking you to tonight?'

'I don't know.' Alex had only told her the event was dressy, but not too dressy. 'It's a surprise.'

'Ooh, a mystery. That's fun.'

It was fun, because he'd actually seemed excited about whatever he had planned. Excitement wasn't a quality she saw much from him. He was more reserved these days. Distrustful.

She glanced towards the conference room where he and his team leads were working. They'd been in there all day long, writing things on the white board, staring at computer screens and pasting post-it notes on the wall. 'What are they working on in there?'

Josie shrugged. 'Dunno. Something big. All I've heard is that it's called Project Alpha Wolf.'

'Hm.' Through the windows, Elena saw a developer write something on the board. Alex shook his head, erased part of it and wrote something else. Apparently the Alpha Wolf was being a rogue.

She stood and stretched. 'Hungry?'

Josie held up a plastic cup filled with Gummy Bears. 'Already got my snack.'

Elena felt her back pop. She really needed to get back into doing yoga more regularly. 'I need some tea.'

Leaving her things in the cubicle, she walked towards the kitchen. Her path took her right by the conference room. As if sensing her, Alex looked up. His gaze settled on her, bright and alert. Heat settled inside her, way down low, but she smiled and waved, not wanting to bother him. Her steps slowed, though, when she saw the notebooks spread out on the conference room table.

Understanding dawned in her head. Project Alpha Wolf.

It was the project he'd been working on obsessively since she'd first met him. The one she'd tried to spy upon. Her smile dimmed as guilt caught her, but that didn't stop her curiosity. At least now she knew for sure it was a project for the company.

She poured herself some tea and was walking back to her desk when the receptionist turned the corner.

'Oh! Excuse us, Elena.'

Elena held her tea away from her body and narrowly missed spilling it on herself. 'Oops. That's OK. I should have been paying more attention.'

She grabbed a tissue from the desk next to her and wiped the cup.

'Elena?'

She looked up at the sound of the familiar voice and saw a familiar face. 'Dr Walters?'

'Hello, dear.' The rumpled professor tucked his leather notebook under his arm and reached out to shake her hand. 'How are things coming along with the dissertation? I see you're on my calendar for your defence in a few weeks.'

'I am. It's coming along well.' Confusion gripped her. Dr Walters was on her evaluation committee. What was he doing here? Checking up on her? Had Alex called him to help her? 'I'm sorry,' she said. 'Did we have an appointment?'

The older man chuckled. 'No, no. I've been asked here by Mr Wolfe. He's asked me to consult on a project.'

Her head swung around, and she saw Alex watching their little group.

'Oh, there he is,' the cheerful professor said.

'What are you working on?' She knew she shouldn't, but she couldn't stop herself from asking.

'A very intriguing question, I must say.' The professor caught himself and frowned. He tapped his folder. 'Ah, I'm sorry, dear. I've signed a confidentiality agreement.'

'Oh, well.' She stepped aside, being careful with her tea. 'Have a good meeting.'

Curiosity consumed her as she sat back down at her desk. It had been Dr Walters' book that she'd been trying to borrow at the Wolfe Library. Alex had been reading it, too. They must be working on a new financial analysis program or a new feature. Professor Walters would be the obvious consultant for that.

Although seeing him here reminded her that she had work of her own to do.

It could have been minutes or hours later when she noticed the shiny black loafers stop beside her desk. She looked up to find Alex standing over her, putting on his suit jacket. Even after a day of work, he still looked crisp, professional and sexy.

'Ready to go?' he asked.

She smiled. 'You still haven't told me where.'

He grinned, and her stomach tightened. It was the first smile she'd seen out of him in weeks, maybe ever. 'You'll never guess, but hurry up. We're the guests of honour.'

She was sure that he was the guest of honour, but he had her intrigued. He attended events strategically, but since he'd returned to the New York scene he'd stayed away from the limelight. This was a change-up for him, and it intrigued her.

Especially since it was honouring him.

'Just a minute.' She turned off her computer and put the laptop and power cords into the carrying case. She kicked her shoes out from under the desk and reached down to put them on.

Her breath caught when he knelt to do the task for her. A warm hand circled her ankle, protecting her Achilles heel as he slid the slingback over her toes. He hooked the strap around her heel and butterflies swirled in her stomach.

Looking over his shoulder, she found Josie watching wide-eyed. Her friend patted her heart as if she was having palpitations and then dramatically swooned.

Elena smiled self-consciously. He made her swoon, too, only for real.

'There.' He caught her hand and pulled her to her feet. 'James is waiting outside.'

When they started on their trek, Elena became even more confused. The driver was heading north. That ruled out the symphony, ballet and opera. She frowned as they continued north and east. A Yankees game, maybe?

She scooted closer on the limo seat. 'The Bronx?'

Alex toyed with her hair. 'Maybe.'

'We're awfully dressy for a ball game.'

'We're not going to a ball game.'

'A friend's house?' she guessed.

'You're not very patient,' he said, tickling her ear. He leaned closer to give her earlobe a soft nip. 'Then again, I knew that.'

'Alex!' She glanced towards the driver, but the divider

was up. She pushed the button that would lower it. 'Where are we going, James?'

He grinned and shook his head. 'I'm not allowed to tell you, Miss Elena.'

She peered through the front window as they travelled along, trying to find landmarks or clues. They were a few blocks away when she had an idea. She tilted her head. 'The zoo?'

Alex smiled. 'They're dedicating the Grey Wolf exhibit today.'

Her mouth dropped open in surprise. 'You funded it?'

He tugged her hair again. 'I wasn't going to support a cat exhibit.'

She grinned so wide, her cheeks ached. They'd been to plays and shows, dinners and art exhibits. She'd enjoyed them, but this sounded special. Impulsively, she leaned over and kissed him. 'I love it already.'

She loved it even more when they got inside. An employee in a golf cart picked them up at the gate and drove them directly to the new exhibit. Alex sat next to her, his legs spread out casually and his arm looped around her back. The terrain turned from savannah grassland to rougher, wooded hills. The paths might be made of asphalt, but Elena was immediately taken back to Wolfe Manor and the lake.

'It reminds me of the trail where we met,' she whispered.

His grey gaze lingered and his thumb moved over her hair.

A yearning began inside her chest. She really did miss that place and the time they'd shared alone, away from the world.

The tour guide drove them around the exterior of the large enclosure, stopping when they saw the pack. Elena got out of the cart to watch them. She moved cautiously, not wanting to spook the wild animals. 'How many are there?'

'Eight,' Alex replied. 'With three new cubs.'

'Aw.' The wolves looked back at her with just as much curiosity. Their eyes were bright and intelligent. Their coats were growing thicker for the impending cold weather, but they played as if the chill didn't bother them. They nipped each other and played tag.

'There's the alpha,' he said, pointing at a wolf with a coat entirely of silver.

Once she began watching the larger canine, his status was clear. The other wolves deferred to him, playing along but always submitting. When they were caught, they'd roll onto their backs and the alpha wolf would stand over them.

'Is its name Ax?' she joked.

'Actually,' the tour guide said with a chuckle, 'it is.'

Her jaw dropped and she looked at Alex.

'Money can buy you some things.' He grinned and helped her back onto her seat. 'I've never heard you call me that.'

'Because that's not who you are to me,' she said quietly.

He ran his finger across her cheek.

The tour guide started up the golf cart again. 'Dr Hoff wanted me to bring you directly to the medical centre.'

Elena frowned. 'Oh no, is one of them sick?'

'No, it's time for the pups' check-up.'

She shot Alex an excited look.

'I thought you might like to watch.'

She laced her fingers through his and squeezed tight. Out of everything they'd done since they'd returned to the city, this was the most special. They followed the zoo employee through a door disguised to look like a wall of rocks, and put on white lab coats and gloves.

When Elena walked into the examination room, it was all she could do not to squeal. Three wolf pups were in a box on the ground. The cardboard was softened with a towel that had already been gnawed threadbare in places. The pups tumbled together and tried to climb over each other to get out.

'Mr Wolfe,' a blonde woman called. She was decked out in medical scrubs. 'Welcome.'

Alex shook her hand warmly. 'Dr Hoff. This is Elena Bardot.'

'I'm glad you could join us. Thank you for all your support.'

'What are you doing today?' Elena watched as another caretaker lifted a pup out of the box. It squirmed in her arms, but the woman held it close as she carried it over to a scale. It took a while before they could get an accurate measurement. The pup was curious about the shiny stethoscope hanging around her neck and a red ball that had been left nearby on the table.

'We're taking weights and measurements. We want to make sure their growth is on track.' The veterinarian pointed to the two pups on the floor. 'Do you want to help us out?'

'I can touch them?'

'We try to keep human contact to a minimum, but you're geared up properly.'

Elena looked at Alex. He was right. Money could open doors that some people could never break down.

For once, they were out together in the city and he looked relaxed. He squatted down beside the box and scratched the head of a grey and white pup. It appeared to like the feel of it. Twisting its head, it yipped and pressed harder into the palm of his hand.

Elena tried to coax the shyer pup that was cowering in the corner. It was dark, with a coat the colour of sable. 'Come here, sweetie.'

She picked up the pup and held it close to her chest. The poor little thing trembled, but she stroked its back until it snuggled close. Alex had more trouble with his energetic charge. The grey pup was full of vigour and devilry. It scrambled out of the box before he could catch it. Bounding across the room, the little predator attacked another red ball.

'That's OK,' the veterinarian said. 'He's working on his hunting skills.'

Alex tugged the ball away from the alert little pup and tossed it. The grey wolf chased and pounced so dramatically everyone laughed.

'They're so cute.' Elena could hardly bear it. She scratched under the chin of the pup she was holding and tried not to squeeze it too tightly.

'They're six weeks old today and starting to wean.' Dr Hoff signalled to Elena. 'Could you bring the female over, please?'

She was careful as she sat the little pup on the scale. The assistant marked down her weight and picked up the tape measure. She measured the wolf's length and the circumference of her chest. Throughout it all, Elena stroked the dark little fur ball. It seemed to trust her and kept wanting to cuddle close.

Alex walked over with her rambunctious brother. It was licking his chin and trying to bite his ear.

The titan of industry couldn't have looked happier.

The medical team went on to do a thorough check of both babies' health. They looked at their teeth and their vitals. Soon it was time to put them back in the box with their triplet. In the den, the alpha female was getting anxious to see her litter.

'Just one last thing,' the doctor said, snapping off her

gloves. She tossed them into the trash and turned with a clipboard in her grip.

'What's that?' Elena asked.

The veterinarian looked at Alex, but he nodded his head, smiling. 'Go ahead.'

'We had a public contest for the two males, but the female needs a name.'

Elena's breath caught. 'Alex,' she said softly. 'Really?'

'Really.'

She melted on the inside. He'd wined and dined her, bought her an entire wardrobe, but this was a gift. It almost felt too important to accept. She knelt beside the box and stroked her little friend. The wolf rolled onto her side and offered up her stomach.

'What do you think?' he asked. He offered up the red ball. Finally feeling playful, the little girl batted at it with all four paws.

'You name her,' Elena insisted.

His grey gaze swung up to meet hers. 'It's why I brought you here.'

'But she's yours.' He'd funded the exhibit. He was the one who'd given the wolves a home.

His grey gaze turned soft and intimate. 'Her coat is the same colour as your hair.'

'Not Elena,' she whispered.

'No,' he agreed. He stroked his big hand over the small pup and twirled his finger around its tail. 'How about Siren?'

Elena tilted her head. 'I like it.'

Dr Hoff chuckled. 'That's perfect.'

They both looked at her, confused.

The woman rolled her eyes. 'You should hear her howl.'

\* \* \*

From there, the evening turned more sophisticated. A reception was held in the den viewing area. It was a cool underground space where the public could look in on the den through glass windows without bothering the mother and her litter. All the pups, including Siren, had been returned to the pack and seemed none the worse for their experience.

All around, champagne was served along with appetisers. Elena enjoyed herself immensely. She'd known Alex had a philanthropic bent, but she hadn't known he'd contributed to something like this. From what she was able to learn, he'd funded the project years ago and it was finally coming to fruition.

It was nice to see the good that money could do, even if the zoo had had to deal with investigators.

She set her empty wine glass down on a passing waiter's tray and waited for a break in the discussion Alex was having with a researcher before touching his arm. 'I'll be right back.'

Wandering down the path, she searched for the ladies'

room. The designers and construction team had really outdone themselves. She felt like she was in a cave out in the woods. She finally saw the familiar sign.

She used the facilities and freshened up. A smile was on her face as she smoothed her hair. There was a flush to her cheeks and a lightness in her mood.

'Siren,' she whispered.

Her heart squeezed. That man might have just taken it.

Eager to rejoin him, she left the restroom. She nearly bumped into a woman standing outside the door. 'Oh, excuse me.'

'Elena? Elena Bardot?'

Elena looked at the woman, trying to place her. She looked familiar. 'Yes?'

A bright light suddenly turned on, blinding her. The woman lifted a microphone and grinned like a crocodile. 'Caroline Woodward. WABC News.'

Elena took a step back and lifted her hand to shield her eyes. 'Excuse me?'

'As the daughter of former CFO Randolph Bardot, how do you feel about Wolfe Financial declaring bankruptcy?'

Elena didn't know what was going on, but any mention of her father put her back up. She looked around for help. The restrooms were around the corner from the party. Nobody else was nearby but this reporter and her cameraman.

'Shouldn't the Wolfe family be trying to pay back the

investors they swindled?' the reporter demanded. Her eyes gleamed behind her black-rimmed eyeglasses. She'd caught the scent of fresh meat. 'On that note, shouldn't the Bardots?'

Elena tried to sidestep the duo, but the reporter blocked her way. She was trapped, and her heart began beating inside her chest like a snare drum. Flashing back, she remembered the reporter who'd trapped her in the stairwell of her building. 'No comment,' she said hoarsely.

The reporter smiled smugly, pulling the microphone back in for what would surely be another loaded question. Elena heard the clinking of glasses and the chatter of cocktail conversation. Dare she call out? Would that make things even worse?

'You seem to be doing very well for yourself,' Caroline said, rocking her head back and forth on her neck like a swivel. 'How long have you and Alex Wolfe been seeing one another?'

'No com –'

'Was this your way of pulling yourself up by your bootstraps?' The reporter bulldozed right over her, not waiting for an answer. 'What are your mother's feelings on the pairing?'

Elena's mouth dropped open in shock. 'I don't think this is an appropriate discussion to be having.'

'Not appropriate. I'd say that's what most people are thinking about your relationship. The two of you have been seen all about town. Does Mr Wolfe feel no remorse? Have you no shame, eating at Jean-Georges while the common man is out there trying to rebuild his retirement portfolio?'

The common man. Elena didn't know what to say. Technically, the majority of people affected by the Ponzi scheme had been high-end earners. She knew. She'd analysed the numbers. Bartholomew and her father hadn't gone after chump change, but there was no way she could make that statement without seeming haughty and condescending. After all, her own mother had been a victim.

'No comment?' Caroline said saucily. 'OK, what can you tell us about Bartholomew Wolfe? Has The Ax spoken about him at all? Are you aware of the man's whereabouts?'

'No, I don't know anything about that.'

'You haven't asked?' The cameraman panned to his partner and she gave an overly dramatic look of miscomprehension. 'Do you think that the elder Wolfe is even alive?'

'I –' Elena's brain froze. It was a low blow, and it took the wind right out of her.

Holding up her notebook, the reporter read off the facts. 'Authorities have never found a flight manifest with Bartholomew Wolfe's name in the days surrounding his disappearance. There hasn't been any activity on his accounts. Do you give any credence to the long-held suspicion that he did not leave the country? And perhaps met the same fate as your father?'

Elena reached back to the wall for support. Revulsion was making her stomach churn.

The over-aggressive news reporter stepped into her space. Elena held up her hand to protect herself from the camera, but she couldn't keep them both at bay.

'Alex Wolfe has a reputed black temper,' Caroline said salaciously. 'Is there –'

'Yes, he does,' Alex said, stepping into the middle of the confrontation. 'Caroline.'

The way he said the woman's name made Elena shiver. She reached for his hand, but he pushed her behind him, blocking both the camera and the reporter's view. Rage radiated from him. The air resonated with the violence of his mood, practically humming.

The reporter's eyes widened and the reaction was magnified by her lenses. She licked her lips. 'Mr Wolfe, what would you like to say about your grandfather?'

'Absolutely nothing,' he growled.

Seeing she'd tweaked a nerve, the reporter smirked. 'Back to your relationship with Ms Bardot, then. Did you seduce her, knowing the public would consider her a sympathetic figure? Were you trying to rehabilitate your reputation?'

He took a threatening step forward and Elena reached out. Settling her hand upon his, she wove their fingers together and clamped down tight. His fist bunched, but he gathered himself. She could feel him reining his temper in.

He let out a sharp whistle. 'Security.'

The reporter's energy turned frenzied. She knew her exclusive interview was coming to an end. 'Or perhaps your relationship with Ms Bardot goes back further than that. We've learned from classmates that she's followed in her father's footsteps and is somewhat of an economics savant. Was she complicit in the Ponzi scheme?'

Vasquez and Hanson converged on the scene. One went for the reporter and the other went for the camera. Vasquez planted himself like a wall in front of the video guy, and the man lost coverage. He tried to come from another angle, but everywhere he turned, he was hindered. Vasquez wasn't that much bigger, but he was stronger and he was faster.

'Back away from my client,' Hanson ordered. Using a move that was deceptively simple and amazingly effective, he used his mass to bully the reporter away.

'Don't you touch me!' she snapped.

He held up his hands. He hadn't put a finger on her, but it was clear he would if she didn't stand down.

The bulldog reporter went up on her toes. 'Elena! Do you know where those hundreds of millions of dollars went?'

Elena hung her head. She was about to make a break for the bathroom again, because she felt sick. Such a wonderful event had been ruined. People were starting to come around the corner to stare. She'd learned to be oblivious to the whispers and finger-pointing they received at the restaurants they visited, but this was entirely different. Their supposed crimes were being shouted out so everyone could hear, but none of it was true.

'Do you really want to talk scandals, Caroline? Underhanded schemes?'

Alex stepped forward, dropping Elena's hand. She reached for him, but the tables had turned. Hanson was now keeping his client away from the reporter. He'd planted his heels into the ground and was pressing his shoulders back into Alex's chest to keep him off the nasty little journalist.

'Is it true that you slept with the sixty-year-old station manager in Buffalo to get an anchor spot?'

The look of glee on the reporter's face froze.

Vasquez had his cellphone out and was making his own documentation of the confrontation.

'Alex,' Elena breathed. She didn't want to go down this road. They had to take the higher ground. She'd been dragged through the muck for too long. They both had. She hated what this was going to do to him. She knew how reporters twisted things around.

His voice dropped to a cutting tone. Ax, indeed. 'I have it on good authority that you're doing the same here. Is that how you plan to get to the top, Caroline?'

'Cut,' the woman hissed at her cameraman. She made a slashing motion across her throat. 'Stop filming.'

The man merely stood there, gaping at her. Anger flooded his face and his brow crumpled. From his response, there might be some truth to Alex's angry words.

Elena caught Vasquez by the back of his jacket. They didn't need to stick around to see any more. 'Go,' she ordered. 'Get us out of here. Now!'

# *Chapter Fourteen*

Back at the penthouse, Elena thanked the bodyguards. They'd showed why Alex had hired them. They'd whisked them out of the zoo so fast, she barely remembered riding in the golf cart again. James had been waiting with the car running at the gate. They'd all executed their jobs with the utmost of skill, and she was grateful they'd been there.

But it was time for them to go.

She politely shooed them out of the penthouse and into the elevator lobby. Vasquez hesitated. He didn't say anything, but he did lift an eyebrow.

'I'll be fine,' she assured him.

Alex was inside the apartment and at the bar. He'd already knocked back one shot of whiskey. He was still steaming from the reporter's ambush – not of him, but of her – and he wasn't in good shape.

'Will he?' the bodyguard asked.

She nodded. 'I've got him.'

She'd take care of him. All he'd been doing since they'd returned to the city was try to take care of her.

Vasquez nodded. 'I'd like to post one man here and another downstairs.'

He lifted his hand when she started to protest. 'In case any reporter tries to use the stairwell.'

She rolled her eyes. She hadn't even considered the idea. It would be a long haul, but after tonight, there wasn't much she'd put past the media.

'OK. Thank you for everything.' The security detail hadn't only protected them physically. Vasquez had forwarded his recording of the incident to both Alex's lawyers and his PR team during the ride home.

'You're welcome, Miss.'

She waited until the elevators closed before she went into the penthouse. She shut and locked the door behind her. Leaning back against it, she considered her options. Alex wasn't at the bar any more. He was pacing across the living room like a wolf locked up in an enclosure that was too small.

He dragged a hand through his hair and shot her a look. 'I knew I should have stayed away from you.'

She flinched.

His eyes held a wild cast, but he knew exactly what was going on. He knew the security personnel had left. He was on top of everything, but he'd lost the key with which he usually locked down his emotions.

'Why?' she asked, bracing herself.

'Because I'm no good for you. I've dragged you back into this mess, when you'd nearly crawled your way out.'

She let out a breath, but her tension didn't ease.

'I had some part in the decision.' As rapidly as he was pacing, she was holding just as still.

He pulled off his jacket and tossed it on the sofa as he strode past. 'They're never going to give up. They're going to keep coming after me until –'

Elena pushed away from the door, her heart nearly stopping. Until what? Until he couldn't take it any more?

He stopped abruptly, swore and pivoted in the other direction. 'The only thing that might satisfy them is for me to repay the investors. I've tried to find a way to do that, but I can't. I won't sacrifice my own company. I won't bastardise it, and I won't jeopardise my people.

'Damn him.' He swept up the empty shot glass on the bar and slammed it down. 'Damn them both.'

Elena cried out when the thick glass broke. 'Alex.'

She rushed over so fast, she didn't feel her feet touching the ground.

'Careful,' he warned, holding up his hand to keep her away.

'You be careful.' She caught his wrist and made him open his hand. 'Are you cut? Did it get you?'

Amazingly, she saw no traces of red. Instead of shattering, the thick glass had cracked, and the web had widened near the lip. She dragged him around the bar, turned on the faucet and made him wash away any splinters that might remain. She threw the broken glass in the trash and patted his hand dry with a bar towel.

She let out a long breath when she finally assured herself he wasn't injured. 'Don't scare me like that. None of this is worth it.'

'But you are.' He looked straight down at her. That muscle in his jaw was going strong.

She trembled, adrenalin and emotion pushing her to the brink, too. 'You can't let these things bottle up. The only way for it to come out is in an explosion.'

'I can keep it contained if it's just me, but they came after *you*.' He cupped her face with shaking hands. 'I'm sorry I didn't get there sooner. I didn't know that news crews could even get on the premises. It's a public place, but the party was private.'

'It's OK.' She laid both hands on his chest. It was one of the only ways she knew to soothe him, and he was further gone than she'd seen him in a long time.

Because of her.

She'd known she was the weak link, and tonight had proved it. That vindictive reporter had separated her from the group and gone after her with teeth bared. As calm as she was trying to make him, Elena felt her own hands balling into fists. 'I'm OK,' she insisted. 'I'm not that thin-skinned. I'm angrier about the things the woman said about you.'

The wildness in him practically clawed at the surface. 'You're *not* OK.'

Gripping her by the waist, he lifted her and planted her on the bar. Bracing his hands flat by her hips, he leaned in so they were eye-to-eye. 'After that stunt, that witch won't work in this town again. My lawyers are already on it.'

'The things she said about you and your grandfather!' Elena smacked her hand on the countertop. 'I wanted to claw her eyes out.'

The sound sliced through the air, and Alex paled. 'The glass.'

Catching her wrist, he turned her hand to see. It wasn't cut, but it might be bruised. She hadn't realised how hard she'd hit the granite. Cursing the reporter's name, he kissed her hand gently. He wiped the countertop down and braced himself again.

His weight was held on his arms, and all his emotions were right there on his face. His walls had crumbled and his defences were laid flat. The ferocity was still in his eyes as he looked at her, and the expression was raw. 'They can say whatever they want about me, but I can't deal with them going after you.'

His head dropped and Elena cupped the back of his neck. His muscles were strung like piano wire. She caressed them gently and he shuddered.

'They can lock me up again, I don't care, but I will not tolerate them hurting you.'

'Alex.' She couldn't bear to hear that. Not that.

He took a deep breath that rocked his whole body. She kissed his temple and wrapped her arms around him. 'She's nothing. Don't do this to yourself. She's not worth it.'

Elena's heart ached. They were caught in an impossible situation. They never should have come back to New York, but they couldn't stay at the manor for ever.

Where was their place in the world?

There had to be one. She remembered the omega wolf she'd seen at the zoo tonight. It was at the bottom of the pack structure. It took nippings and beat-downs from the rest of the pack, but it was still loved. It was still included and valued. The world outside their door was trying to take her alpha male and reduce him to less than even that.

She couldn't bear the thought of him beaten and broken.

Especially because of her.

She ran kisses over his cheek. Cupping his face, she brought his mouth up to hers. The kiss was soft and poignant. Gentle and heartfelt.

Words were barely reaching him. She tried to show him how she felt through touch.

He kissed her back. Their mouths moulded and their breaths meshed. His hands came up to cup her head. His fingers tangled in her hair as he kept the kisses slow and drugging.

There was no flashpoint, no rampaging drive to tear off each other's clothes.

What they needed was to connect.

He stroked her hair away from her face. 'I need to hold you.'

She scooted forward on the counter.

He didn't even allow her feet to touch the ground. Sliding his arm underneath her knees, he picked her up and cradled her against his chest. Elena held him tightly, snuggling into his neck. Those jagged emotions were smoothing out, but his heart was still pounding. She could see his pulse. She brushed her lips over the fluttering vein.

He was twice her size and muscularly honed, yet she still felt the overwhelming need to protect him.

He carried her down the hall, his footsteps muffled by the plush carpeting. The only sounds in the whole apartment were the refrigerator humming and their breaths. That silence was punctuated when he carried her inside the bedroom and firmly shut the door behind them.

He used his foot, but he didn't kick. That gave it all the more meaning.

He was shutting the world outside and locking them in together. Willingly. Intentionally.

She shivered.

'Are you cold?'

'No.' She was moved.

302

He set her on her feet, and they shared another lingering kiss. Neither hurried as they undressed. As difficult as the evening had been, there should be scars and open wounds, yet all the hurting was on the inside.

He pulled back the covers and she slid in. She held out her arms and he came to her naturally. His athletic movement was so graceful. He turned out the lights and they lay facing each other.

His hand swept up her side and came to a rest on her breast. She ran her hand down his ribcage. So strong, yet so vulnerable. He only let her see that. As much as he'd fought against letting her in, he'd become crystal clear to her. Her palm found a resting place on his hipbone, and her fingers lay softly against his thigh.

He kissed her forehead and the tip of her nose before finally meeting her lips.

'I'm sorry I'm not as strong as you,' she whispered. 'If I'd just ignored her or walked on by ...'

His hold on her breast tightened.

'I'm not strong,' he replied. 'I've been hardened. I don't want that to ever happen to you.'

She sighed and kissed his collarbone. She felt such a connection with him like this. It was the calm in the eye of the storm. Rubbing her cheek against his chest, she thought back to when they'd first met. They'd somehow found a way to each other, even with all the obstacles in their path. They'd found the heart of each other. Why wouldn't others do the same?

At the very least, why couldn't they just let them be?

She stroked his shadowy beard and kissed him with more heat. They were damned if they did and damned if they didn't. They might as well take solace in one another.

'Do you need me, Siren?'

'You know I do.'

He caressed her breast and stroked her down to her flank. Catching her knee, he pulled her top leg over his hip. The position was easy and free. Elena stretched and rolled her hips towards him. That same wicked hand glided over her bottom, and her toes pointed in pleasure when he explored the heart of her.

He rubbed her intimately, preparing her.

She bit her lip to hold back a moan, but it came out when he tweaked her sensitive nub.

'Don't hold back with me.' His mouth covered hers and his tongue pressed deep. 'Ever.'

She worked her hand between their bodies. She explored him fearlessly with palm and fingers. When her nails scraped ever so gently along the underside of his erection, he jerked.

It was enough for him.

They shifted on the covers until they were positioned just right. Elena hitched herself up and then he was there, at her entrance. Their mouths locked together and their fingers laced at her hip. With one long, continuous thrust, he took her.

Her moan was soft and airy.

He inhaled the scent of her hair.

And then they began to rock.

Slowly. Passionately. Their coming together wasn't frenzied and feral, but that didn't make it any less momentous. The need was just as strong, but it was accompanied by emotion and meaning.

Maybe it always had been.

Their bodies undulated together, finding a rhythm. They weren't racing towards an end. It was all about the connection.

Alex groaned. 'You are so tight, so hot. It's like you don't want to give me up.'

Elena tucked her face into the pillow. 'I don't.'

He felt so good moving inside her. Hard and thick.

Words fell into touches. Their bodies warmed and their skin clung. The air in the room became steamy as they rode one another. Sighs blended with grunts. Caresses stoked the fire.

When they came, it was as one. Their bodies arched. Their muscles tensed. Elena let out a soft cry and Alex whispered her name.

When they finally floated down from the high, neither was ready for it to end. They stayed connected, physically and emotionally, as the night darkened the room. They fell asleep in each other's arms with the world held at bay. The night was theirs.

But they both knew that daylight would come much too soon.

\* \* \*

Things changed after that. They worked from the penthouse the next day, and Elena made dinner for them the next night. The following day was the same. And the next.

Nothing had been discussed, but their adventures in New York stopped.

They didn't attend any more events. They didn't even consider the invitations.

Alex had food delivered on nights when neither of them felt like cooking. They watched movies on the big screen and worked out in the gym. They even saw people. He invited programmers over from Wolfe Pack for a code jam one day and, when she needed to consult with someone on her dissertation, he sent James to pick up Dr Walters.

It was insular and protective, but it was driving Elena out of her mind.

At least at the manor they could go outside. She'd gone on long walks and had felt the air on her face. She'd smelled the flowers and had swept her fingers through the lake's cold water. Even switching between the lake house and the manor had offered a change of scenery.

Here, she felt like Rapunzel in her ivory tower. Her knight in shining armour might be with her, but it wasn't the fairytale that it seemed.

She tried begging, and she tried rationalising. Alex just wouldn't hear of it.

'The bankruptcy decision for Wolfe Financial is still too volatile,' he told her. 'The press is still looking into you.'

And they were. They just weren't finding anything – much like when they'd tried to find anything a year and a half before.

Only Caroline Woodward wasn't giving up. She'd taken some heat for her romantic relationships, but that had just made her more dogged in her determination. Alex had promised she wouldn't be a problem any more, but not even his lawyers could fight the freedom of the press. The reporter was coming after them like a hyena after fresh meat.

Last night, she'd interviewed Candace. The talk had been full of supposition, lies and venom. It hadn't been pretty, and Alex had been pacing around the room by the end. His lawyers probably didn't get much sleep.

Elena's patience was waning. The two of them couldn't bury their heads in the sand. It wasn't helping. It was only making the media wonder why they wouldn't face them. Were they plotting something new? What were they trying to hide?

After nine days of it, she couldn't take it any more.

She sat cross-legged in an easy chair in the office Alex had set up for her. A three-drawer desk with a reading lamp sat unused across the way. Her laptop was open on the table at her side, but she hadn't touched it for nearly half an hour. Its screensaver was spinning random shapes.

She watched the blue oval turn into a yellow square. 'I don't what to do any more,' she confessed into her phone. 'I'm going stir-crazy, Mom.'

'Can't you just run down to the corner shop? Maybe grab a cappuccino?'

'Caroline Woodward would be there within minutes asking her nasty questions.'

'Don't you have security people?'

'We have lots of people. If I wanted a cappuccino, any of them would go get one for me. It defeats the purpose.'

'Oh, honey.' Her mother sighed. 'I hate to say it, but –'

'Please don't say I told you so.'

'I wasn't going to.' In the background, a beater whirred. 'Hard as it may be to believe, I was about to say, "Maybe he's right."'

Elena cocked her head, certain she'd heard incorrectly. 'What?'

'I know. Listen, I wasn't happy about you getting involved with him, but you had to go back to the city eventually to finish your degree. I can't say I'm unhappy that he's there, protecting you. *Especially* after what happened at the zoo. Honey, that was scary for everyone.'

'But I feel smothered.' Trapped. She was beginning to understand what he felt like when his claustrophobia kicked in. They had an entire floor to stroll around in, yet she craved her freedom. She wanted to buy a hotdog from a vendor on a street corner. She wanted to feel the chilly air whip down the streets as if they were wind tunnels.

Even the crummy drizzle outside today would be refreshing.

'He cares about you, Elena. I can see it in the photographs in *People* and the stories on *Entertainment Tonight.*'

'I know he does, but he's afraid of what might be lurking around every corner. I just can't say that to him.' The big bad wolf wasn't supposed to be afraid of anything. 'I'm worried about him,' she confessed. 'He's not meant to be held back like this.' She watched the shapes spin and morph as they bounced off the corners of the laptop's screen. They weren't able to escape either; they just kept spinning round and round. 'Neither am I.'

'I understand,' Yvonne said. 'His intentions are good, but the results are not.'

'He's not doing well, either.' Elena was quick to defend him. 'I can see how it's wearing on him, but he feels a responsibility to his company now that he's returned. He's as stuck as I am.'

'Have you told him how you feel?'

She sighed. She'd tried, and he did understand. He just wasn't willing to compromise. 'He's stubborn.'

'Have you tried getting him out?'

Elena toyed with the cuff of her slipper. 'He won't even go into the office. I know he's comfortable there, and the whole company is wrapped up in some big project. He says he can do everything he needs to by teleconference.'

'How about something fun?' her mother suggested. 'Is there any way you can lure him out for something like that?'

Elena grimaced. 'I made the mistake of suggesting we go visit Siren and the pups the other day. It was a bad call.'

One she hadn't thought the whole way through.

'Oh, baby.'

'I thought we could replace a bad memory with a good one.' At the very least, they could apologise to Dr Hoff. The reception had been so delightful until they'd created such a commotion.

Well, they hadn't created it. The reporter had. Clips from that ambush were still trending on YouTube.

'He's richer than God, Mom. He can get anything that he wants delivered.' Anything. They'd even had dinner from restaurants that supposedly didn't cater.

There was a long pause at the other end of the line. 'OK, I'm with you now,' Yvonne said. Her voice was calm but clipped. 'But you're not going to like what I have to say.'

Elena bit her lip. They both knew that was why she'd called.

She just needed to hear it aloud.

'The behaviour you're describing isn't healthy. It's controlling and it's disturbing.'

'He's not –'

'You have to look out for yourself, Elena. I know you care about him, and you've convinced me he wasn't that involved with the Ponzi scheme, but you have to take care of number one.'

'I'm trying to think about myself.' It was why she'd called. 'But I don't want to hurt him.'

She'd tried adjusting, and she'd tried working with him. If they'd never met … If she hadn't gone to the lake house, she'd probably be in exactly the same situation, only she'd be a hermit in a tiny studio apartment. Yet he *was* involved, and she'd become stronger than that.

She couldn't stand to see him do this to himself.

He'd already been imprisoned once. The penthouse might be cushier and better equipped, but it had become a prison of his own making.

'Sometimes you have to make tough decisions,' Yvonne said quietly. 'Even if they sting.'

Elena bit her lip. The screen saver had timed out and her laptop had gone black.

'I was with a man with money once.' Her mother's voice became raspy. 'I know how it can creep into the corners of your life and burst out the seams.'

'Oh, Mom.' They'd rarely talked about the divorce. She'd been so little, and then it had merely been a fact of life.

'I loved your father, Lainie, but I had to do what was right for you and me.'

Elena swallowed hard. She had to do what was right for Alex and her, too. 'I understand. Thanks, Mom.'

It was painful, but it was what she'd needed to hear. Sometimes a kick in the butt was necessary.

It was time. He'd protected her. It was time for her to do the right thing for him.

Terrible as it might be.

They said their goodbyes, and Elena picked up her laptop. She traced her fingers along the outer edge. It had been a gift from him, one of the many ways he'd rescued her. She tapped a key to bring it back to life and stuck a flash drive in the USB port.

She had it clenched in her hand as she walked into his office down the hallway.

She'd told her mother he could do anything here he needed, and his office was proof of that. It looked like a war room with two monitors on his desk, a work flow diagram spread out over two tables, and a big screen TV on the wall. Any technology he needed was at his beck and call.

Any but one.

'Hi,' she said softly.

He glanced up from his desk. He was scanning through another economics textbook. 'Hey.'

That observant grey gaze ran over her, first to check if anything was wrong and then with more leisure.

She held up the flash drive. 'I need to go to the printer.'

His pen clipped down on the desk, and he straightened. 'Are you finished?'

'With the paper.' She inhaled deeply, but the sense of relief and accomplishment was muted inside her. She couldn't summon up the excitement that was warranted.

He came around his desk and hugged her. 'That's fantastic, baby. I'm so happy for you.'

She was happy, too. It was an accomplishment, but this was just one milestone. She could take a day or two to refresh, but she needed to start preparing her presentation next. A committee of tenured professors was going to pepper her with questions, and she had to be ready to defend her findings.

She turned the flash drive over in her fingers. 'I need to print out copies and have them bound.'

'Send it over to Wolfe Pack. They can handle that for you.'

She scowled. Not that she didn't trust his people, but she was going to do this herself. After all the blood, sweat and tears she'd put into it, she was going to make sure

313

it was done right. There weren't going to be any missing pages, smudges or crooked printouts.

'I'd like to get everything over to the committee by the end of the day.'

'Not a problem.' He picked up the phone. 'We'll get a courier.'

She shook her head and covered the keypad before he could dial. 'No. Alex, this is something I want to do myself.'

'I know it's important to you, baby.' He rested his hips against the desk. 'How about this? We'll have James run them by here so you can check everything before he delivers them. Does that work for you?'

She sent him a sad look. No, it didn't.

He saw the less than excited expression on her face. Catching her chin, he brushed his thumb along her jawline. 'Let's order Grimaldi's tonight to celebrate.'

Her eyes started to sting, and she clenched the flash drive in her fist. She didn't feel much like celebrating. 'I'm not very hungry.'

She was frustrated and discouraged, but determination gelled inside her chest.

She turned and left the room. She grabbed her laptop, then headed past the living room and bar to their bedroom. Carefully, she tucked the computer into its bag. Her hand was shaking as she zipped the flash drive into a pocket of her purse.

Moving almost mechanically, she took the time to change out of her yoga clothes. A pair of jeans and a knit top made her feel more like her old self. Her throat was thick as she tugged on her boots.

She stared at the dresser for ever. The dresser with her drawer … which had become two. When she felt herself wavering, she turned towards the closet instead.

It was time to get to work.

She was halfway through the hangers when Alex poked his head into the bedroom. Elena lifted her chin. She hadn't tried to be quiet, and the rustling couldn't be helped.

His gaze immediately latched on to her suitcase. It was open on the bed and full of clothes. His eyes turned flinty, and his lips flattened. 'What's this?'

His stoic phase had come and gone long ago. He couldn't hide his feelings from her any more.

She folded her black suit carefully and tucked it in the bag. 'I'm going away for a while.'

He was leaning in the doorway, braced against the doorjamb. His posture didn't change, but everything else about him did. His body stiffened and the air snapped. 'Why?'

'Because I can't breathe here.'

She forced herself to face the dresser. Rummaging through her drawer, she found the black lace lingerie. She hesitated for a moment, her breath shaky, and chose something simpler.

315

His voice took on a measured patience. 'Elena, I've told you. It has to be this way, at least for a while.'

'And I don't agree.' She packed her toiletry bag. She was about to zip up the suitcase when she thought of something. It made her chest ache, but she couldn't leave it behind.

'We could have a picnic lunch on the roof.' His words were coming more quickly. 'It's supposed to clear up later on.'

She looked at him sadly as she returned to the closet.

'A walk around the block.' He dragged a hand through his hair. 'Smith and Hanson will have to accompany us.'

Her resolve strengthened. 'I've lived in hiding, Alex, and I'm done. It can't be us against the world any more. We need to find a way to coexist.'

'Elena.'

She took a hanger off the rod. He paled when he saw the hoodie. It impelled him out of the doorway and he stood over her, hands on his hips. For once, the all-powerful Ax looked helpless, as if he didn't know what to say to keep her.

She folded the hoodie with the utmost care. More than anything, she wanted to put it on, but in comforting herself she would hurt him. She was already doing enough of that.

The air was raw with emotion.

'I know you think you're protecting me, Alex, but

the world needs us out there in it. Things are difficult right now, but you need to get back to work. Go back to Wolfe Pack. Do good things.'

'I'm trying,' he ground out.

She zipped up the bag and pulled it to the floor. He reached to help her, but then stopped himself.

Elena hooked the computer bag over her shoulder. Gathering the rest of her things, she walked past him. The walk down the hallway to the penthouse's front door was the longest she'd ever taken. Her eyes were damp, and her breaths were pummelling her lungs. She didn't want to do this, but she had to. The roller case clattered along after her, the wheels sounding loud in the quiet apartment. It couldn't compete with the roaring in her head.

'Elena, please.' He caught her shoulder. 'Don't.'

She looked him in the eye, even when a tear slipped out and trailed down her cheek. 'I love you, Alex, but I can't live like this.'

She opened the front door before she could change her mind. Vasquez was waiting in the foyer. His astute eyes measured the situation.

'Vasquez,' Alex warned.

The bodyguard's jaw turned rock hard. 'I'm sorry, sir. Your orders.'

The wiry man took the roller bag and planted himself firmly at her side. 'What the lady wants, the lady gets.'

It wasn't what Elena wanted, but this was the way it had to be. Something had to break them out of this self-defeating cycle. It was up to her.

Still, it took everything she had to leave behind the man she loved.

# Chapter Fifteen

Alex wasn't doing well.

He knew it, but there wasn't a damn thing he could do about it. He missed Elena like hell. He couldn't sleep. All the doors in his place stood wide open. Project Alpha Wolfe had become Project Dead Dog. He'd been taking out his frustrations in the gym, but he was working out so hard, his body was starting to break down. He'd run on the treadmill so long the other day, he'd barely been able to walk when he'd gotten off it.

He stared out of the window of the penthouse with his hand fisted against the glass. Everything she'd said had been the truth. Right, dead-eye centre of the target. He had to grow back that thick skin that she'd peeled away. He needed to toughen up and turn a deaf ear to all the critics. He knew that, but they'd come at him through his soft underbelly.

They'd gone after her.

They'd noticed just as quickly that she was gone.

He'd stayed in the apartment for another two days after she'd left, but his claustrophobia had expanded until even the entire top floor of the building had seemed too small. When she'd been in the penthouse, he'd had everything he needed. Once she'd walked out that door, the walls had pressed in. He'd gone back to work, and he'd even cut the ribbon at the public opening of the wolf exhibit at the Bronx Zoo.

All the news stories, though, had focused on why a pretty young brunette was no longer at his side. Fortunately, she'd turned into the sympathetic figure Caroline Woodward had predicted. Nobody blamed her for leaving The Ax behind.

He was the only one who felt split in two.

She'd told him that she loved him. She just couldn't live with him.

Not many people could. He was finding it difficult these days to be around himself. She'd been gone two weeks. An eternity. He should just let it be.

He couldn't.

Turning away from the view of the New York City skyline, he swept up his jacket. He put it on and smoothed it. He tugged at the cuffs and lifted his chin. 'Let's go.'

Vasquez was waiting just inside the door. When Alex moved out into the elevator lobby, the bodyguard nodded at the briefcase on the bar. 'Will you be needing that?'

'Not today.'

The ride in the elevator was silent, and James was waiting with the car on the street. Vasquez swept the area before letting Alex slide into the back seat. The Bentley pulled away from the kerb, its well-tuned engine nearly silent. Traffic was already busy. James put on his blinker, but was having trouble getting over into the next lane.

'We're not going to the office today,' Alex instructed. 'Head to NYU. The economics building is on West 4th.'

'Sir?' Vasquez said sharply.

Alex looked out the window. 'I'm not going to make a scene. I just want to support her. It's her big day.'

The stern man nodded.

Alex looked at his watch when James reached the edge of campus. They were early, but she would be, too. Knowing her, time would feel as if it were dragging by. She was ready for this. She'd been diligent in her work, and she'd sacrificed so much. He knew she was going to knock it out of the park.

He slid on his sunglasses as he and his bodyguard walked across the campus's white sidewalk. In a world where students cruised around in jeans and sweatshirts, they stood out. He took no interest in the hive-like activity around him, and the realisation made him take a deep breath.

It wasn't really the world he'd been avoiding.

He knew what building she was in and the front office gave directions to the room where she would be defending her research. He headed to the third floor, but his steps slowed when he heard the growing chatter. His jaw clenched. Vasquez sent him a questioning look, but he shook his head. They weren't turning around now.

Vasquez pulled out his cell.

The bodyguard took the lead. His sharp eyes took in the situation. Reporters were gathered everywhere with their cameramen.

The balding newspaperman was the first to see them. 'Mr Wolfe.'

A collective gasp went up. People fumbled with their equipment, and Vasquez made the most of the opportunity. Acting like the tip of the spear, he made his way towards the conference room.

Alex summoned his control and looked straight ahead.

'Are you here to wish Ms Bardot luck?' a reporter called.

'Are you two back together?' another asked.

Questions flew left and right, but the crowd parted to let him through the doorway. They followed him inside and the small passageway soon bottlenecked. They didn't just want a shot of him on campus. The money shot would be of him and Elena together.

At the ruckus, the university representatives turned. Disapproving looks settled on their faces. It was a public oral examination, but they would not put up with a disruption.

Reporters quickly began claiming seats. Alex looked around the space. It was one of those large, stately academic rooms with tall windows that climbed high up the twelve-foot walls. The moulding was ornate, and the smell of books hung in the air. A projector screen had been set up at the front of the room. His gaze settled upon a familiar laptop on the podium. It was already hooked up and ready to go.

He spotted Elena immediately. Like a magnet, he felt her pull. She was heads-down, going through her printout one last time. She was studiously avoiding looking at the audience, but from the stiff set of her shoulders she knew what she was about to face.

It wasn't fair. Most PhD candidates went through this alone or with a few fellow students in the room. Speaking before the evaluation committee was stressful enough, but she had to face a crowd of media. Everything she said, every move she made, would be broadcast by lunchtime. He scowled at the row of distinguished-looking professors from the Economics Department. They'd better not give her a hard time or NYU would see his charitable donations drop next semester.

He noticed Dr Walters, but the professor was headed over to the large audience that had formed. Behind him, Alex heard the man start laying ground rules.

Good.

He took advantage of the opportunity and headed up

to the podium. Behind him, he heard a hush come over the room. 'Elena?'

Her head spun around and her hair swung forward over her shoulder. 'Alex?'

For a moment, excitement lit her face. She looked young, fresh and full of life, but then she caught herself. She paled when she saw the packed room and her hand went to her stomach. 'What are you doing here?'

The reaction made his jaw clench. He caught her by the elbow and pulled her behind the projection screen where they could have some privacy. 'I'm sorry. I didn't mean to bring them here.'

She shook her head. 'They were here before you. Caroline Woodward is in the front row.'

Alex jerked in surprise. His fists clenched and he leaned back to look. Elena caught him before he could make a scene.

'I'll deal with her,' she promised.

He let out a frustrated breath. None of this was going the way he'd planned. 'I'm not here to upset you. I just wanted to wish you luck and give you this.'

He pulled a jewellery box out of his pocket. He'd had it for weeks.

She looked at the velvet-covered box, her eyes widening.

'It's a graduation present.'

Her shoulders relaxed, but she threw a look back at the academics who were still in view. Seeing that they were busy in a heated discussion about the overcrowding, she tilted her head at him. 'Alex, you didn't have to.'

'Of course I did.' He put the box in her hand. 'Open it.'

Her hands shook as she opened the clamshell box and she let out a tiny gasp. Her gaze snapped up to his and back to the box. She pressed her fingers to her mouth.

He took out the necklace and undid the clasp. 'You can wear it for luck.'

He moved around behind her. Her hair was gathered back in the gold clip. She held the dark curtain of it aside as he threaded the dainty gold loop through the latch at the back of her neck. She touched the necklace where it lay between her breasts. He'd had an artisan specially craft the black diamond pendant in the shape of a wolf's paw.

'It reminds me of Siren,' she said.

'I saw her the other day.'

'Did you? How is she?'

'Growing fast.'

She took a breath that shook her shoulders. He slid his hands down her arms, but stepped back. Maybe it hadn't been a good idea to come. He was piling stress upon stress. 'I'll go.'

'No, don't. Please.' She glanced towards the long table where the committee was lined up like a firing squad. Her hand fisted around the necklace. 'I'm so nervous.'

'Dr Walters will keep control of the room.'

'Not about that.'

He stuffed his hands in his pockets to keep from reaching for her again. She'd gotten past the reporters easier than he had. They weren't her concern; it was the presentation. 'Don't be. You've worked hard. You know your material.'

She looked at him with those big, scared doe eyes. 'What if it's not strong enough?'

'Don't be ridiculous.'

Behind them, someone cleared their throat. Looking over his shoulder, Alex saw Dr Walters. The man was pointing at his watch.

Elena's breath caught and her voice tightened. 'It's time.'

He gave in and squeezed her hand. 'Good luck, baby. Knock 'em dead.'

Alex felt the eyes upon him as he walked to the seating area. Cameras were clicking fast and video recorders were rolling. There was only one seat left. His jaw clenched. They'd left him a seat next to Caroline Woodward from WABC News. She smirked up at him.

The bastards.

He spotted Vasquez along the back wall. The university's Department of Public Safety were lined up next to him, ready to handle any disruptions.

Alex smoothed his face and put a lockdown on the snake slithering inside his chest. Not-so-sweet Caroline was not going to rile him today. He sat down beside her in the hard wooden chair.

'Mr Wolfe,' she said gleefully.

'Ms Woodward.'

The head of the committee raised her voice. 'Silence, please. We're ready to get started. Ms Bardot, if you would.'

Elena nodded politely and gestured to the screen where her presentation was showing. She began to talk and Alex eased back. The chair was rigid and uncomfortable. Trying to find a more relaxed position, he hooked an ankle over the opposite knee. He drummed his fingers against his thigh as she got started and felt Caroline's gaze take in the nervous gesture.

He couldn't help it. Elena was nervous. She was talking too fast and her voice sounded high and tight. Her blank stare was skittering along the audience and off the back wall. He finally caught her eye. Their gazes locked and he took a deep breath. She did the same. He nodded at her and her shoulders relaxed. She slowed down. Gathered herself.

Addressing her audience, she finally got into her flow.

She began going through slides, and his pride in her grew. The subject was dry, but she was doing what she could to spice it up. Some reporters took notes, but others just watched. The sexy suit was probably the reason for that. It was black, with a modern edge, yet so professional the edges looked like they could cut steel. The fit was tailored and the style didn't require a blouse underneath. It emphasized the black diamonds that lay nestled between her curves.

Curves that were supported by some kind of sexy lingerie, he was sure. Was it the black lace? The innocent pink? He shifted on the hard seat. Whatever it was, he'd bought it for her. That thought alone was enough to make him rock hard.

From that point on, the crowd of reporters just disappeared. They didn't matter now.

'I began by looking at Case A, which followed market trends,' she was saying.

So this was what she'd been doing all those hours she'd spent alone in the lake house. He ground his teeth together. Would they still be together if they hadn't left the manor? Or would he have driven her away from there, too?

'I tracked all the known market indicators,' she continued.

She'd said she loved him.

The snake that always sat inside his chest hissed. It was impatient. It wanted him to make things right.

He wanted her back.

She loved him, but she'd left him. If he could just come to grips with the way things were, could he convince her to give him another chance? The world might just see the rotten image they'd created of him, but she'd dug beneath the surface once.

She pulled up another colourful chart. 'I then turned to Case B, the Wolfe Financial scenario.'

Alex's ears perked up and his attention focused like a laser. He read the chart more closely, and his long body unfolded. He planted both feet on the floor and gripped the arms of the chair.

Next to him, Caroline started taking notes furiously.

'I tracked the very same indicators,' Elena said, her enthusiasm mounting. She was addressing the evaluation committee directly now. It wasn't a student trying to impress her teachers. She'd gone beyond that and was so immersed in her subject, she'd become the expert. 'You'll notice the trend is the same, however the variance is more pronounced. This made me question if the deviation was something that could be quantified.'

Alex's heart began to beat a bit faster. She hadn't just been reading textbooks down at her lake house office and thinking in hypotheticals, she'd dug into a real-life scenario.

Her life.

And his.

He looked at the chart on the screen. Unlike most of the reporters in the room, he understood exactly what it meant. She'd analysed the scandal that had put him in a cell and knocked her to the ground.

329

He homed in on the sound of her voice until the room felt hollow around him. Every muscle in his body was clenched until his bones ached. His brain raced as he listened to the theory behind her work. She was more advanced than he was in the area. Hell, the committee was looking at her with stunned expressions.

'The data proved problematic, however,' she confessed. 'The algorithm I developed here didn't accurately predict the fraudulent reporting of Case B.'

She pointed out the difference between the predicted and the actual values, offering up the limitations of the results freely. 'I struggled with this until I realised that I needed to account for parallax.'

She moved to the next slide of her presentation and Alex's mouth dropped open. It was a shot of Wolfe Lake.

'It's like when you look into water and see a shiny rock,' she explained. 'I could calculate the position of the rock, but that calculation assumes that sunlight is moving through air. If you turn around and consider the rock, it's looking up to the sky through water. The two environments don't jibe, even though the rock hasn't moved.'

She was energetic now, walking right up to the professors' table. She wanted them to understand. She wanted verification of her work.

Alex looked to them, wondering the same thing.

Was she right?

She directed a laser pointer at the screen. 'I needed

to combine both views. I needed to look through air and water. Or, in this case, I needed to determine the variance using both macroeconomic and microeconomic principles.'

With a flourish, she pulled up an advanced mathematical formula. 'Ladies and gentlemen, I give to you my findings on how to determine if a fund is achieving questionable results.'

One professor squinted while another ran numbers on his notes. A woman with her hair in a bun pointed a pen at the screen. 'So this is from the microeconomic side of the pond, so to say.'

'Yes, ma'am. Said simply, using this formula, investors can determine if their investment results in a stock or fund are "too good to be true".'

'Wait a minute,' Caroline Woodward piped up from her seat. She raised her microphone. 'Are you showing people how to play the market?'

The crowd started tittering.

That was stopped fast.

'Security,' the head of the committee snapped. 'Please remove this person from the building.'

'No,' Elena said sharply.

Heads turned towards her.

She didn't flinch. 'In answer to Ms Woodward's question, the answer is no. This is not a "how to" guide. Think of it as a mine detector, not the mine.'

Caroline gestured belligerently at the screen. 'But couldn't someone reverse engineer –'

'Enough,' the committee chairwoman said, rising to her feet. 'Get this woman off of campus property.'

The reporter's eyes narrowed behind her black-rimmed glasses. 'This presentation is open to the public, and freedom of the press –'

'Does not allow you to disrupt the proceedings. You were given the rules of participation, and you broke them.' The chairwoman was radiating power in all her glory. She pointed at the door with the authority only a schoolmarm could pull off. 'Out.'

The university cops took over from there. Standing over the fuming reporter, they waited impatiently for her to collect her things. When she stood, one took her arm. She ripped it out of his hold. She signalled to her cameraman to stay. When the security team realised she wasn't alone, one of the bigger men cocked his head. The intimidation was enough to make the cameraman jump out of his chair to follow, too.

Alex felt the muscles of his face pulling in an unfamiliar direction, but then he caught the look of horror on Elena's face. She was looking at the evaluation committee with trepidation. The urge to smile left him. They'd better not count this against her.

The crowd was still shifting and the committee looked discomposed.

Professor Walters adjusted his glasses. His hair was ruffled from where he'd tugged on it, and his cheeks were rosy. 'So if I may summarise, Ms Bardot, you're talking about determining fraudulency in real time – that is, Ponzi schemes?'

She lifted her chin. Everyone in the room knew who she was. 'Yes, sir. I am.'

The crowd of reporters couldn't help themselves. A gasp went up and pens began scratching fast against paper.

Alex dropped his head, his breath leaving his body. Holy. Shit. She'd been doing all this right under his nose.

\* \* \*

'Are there any more questions?' the committee chair-woman asked.

Elena waited with bated breath.

Seeing there were none, the woman nodded at her. 'Thank you, Ms Bardot.'

The professor stood and turned to the crowd. More than one reporter cowered in his seat.

'Thank you for your attendance. We'll be going into closed session now. Please leave the room in an orderly fashion.'

Elena caught the woeful looks aimed in her direction. The reporters had more questions for her, but they knew better than to ask her now. She felt as if she were stepping off a rollercoaster ride as they started to disperse.

She knew they wouldn't be going far. They'd be waiting when she left.

Bowing her head, she concentrated on collecting her things. She'd just gone through the most intense interview of her life. Her knees were wobbly and her stomach was tight, yet the thrill in her chest was near euphoric. She'd done it. It was over. One way or the other, she'd given it her all.

She had to be happy with that, but she had a feeling things had gone well. She hadn't let even Caroline Woodward rattle her.

She took her first deep breath of the day.

'Elena?' Professor Walters said.

She raised her chin. Did he have more questions? What more could she tell him?

'If you've collected your things ...' Seeing that she had, he gestured to another door at the end of the room. 'You can wait in my office if you'd like.'

She looked around. Everyone had left.

He was offering her an escape route, and she felt nearly light-headed with relief. 'I'd appreciate that.'

She gathered her computer bag and the rest of her things. Passing the committee's long table, she smiled at them nervously. Her heels clonked against the old wooden floor as she headed for her getaway. It opened up to a side hallway, she knew.

Still, she was careful when she opened the door. Peeking out, she surveyed the scene. Students milled about, but apparently none of the reporters were familiar with the building. She slipped into the hallway and hurried down to Professor Walters's office. She whipped the door shut behind her and sagged against it.

Oh, thank God. It was over.

When she opened her eyes, she realised it had only begun.

Alex was in the room. The rollercoaster ride started all over again. His grey gaze locked with hers and she set down her computer bag before she could drop it.

He'd stayed.

She felt a pang in the middle of her chest. She'd missed him so much. He was leaning back against the office's cherrywood panelling, looking like a *GQ*model. He had one foot propped against the wall and his hands were in the pockets of his natty blue suit. He wasn't wearing a tie today, and his hair was mussed.

He looked classy yet casual, and so sexy she wanted to launch herself at him.

She ached for him. The two weeks they'd been apart had seemed like two years.

But she couldn't forget why she'd left. Things had gotten too intense between them. She couldn't go back to living that way. A gilded cage was still a cage, no matter how pretty the trappings.

Movement nearby broke her out of her trance. Flinching, she turned to see who was watching them.

'Congratulations, Miss,' Vasquez said.

She pressed her hand to her stomach. 'Thank you, but it's early. They're still deliberating.'

'There shouldn't be any question,' Alex said.

The bodyguard moved away. 'I'll scope out another exit for us.'

Elena's nerves intensified when the man left and she and Alex were alone. Today was one of the most important days of her life. There was only so much she could handle.

'How do you think it went?' he asked.

'OK. They threw a few curve balls at me, but I handled them as well as I could.'

'You were prepared.'

She nodded, once again feeling the tension. All she'd done over the past two weeks was study and give practice pitches. Now that she'd come out of that protective shell, she was starting to feel again.

He raised one eyebrow. 'Ponzi schemes?'

The question was posed calmly, but all the clattering in her head came to a screeching halt. Oh, God.

For the first time, she took in his body language. She was a chaotic mess, but he was eerily still. Friction burned in the air, and it was all directed at her.

She reached for the door behind her. Her knees suddenly felt more than wobbly.

He was angry.

She hadn't even thought. The Ponzi scheme was a sore point for him. She'd never told him the crux of her research.

'I needed to understand,' she said, her mouth going dry. When the scandal had first come to light, questions had consumed her. She'd wanted to know why but, more so, she'd needed to know how. Her father's actions had mortified her and pushed her.

It had become an obsession for her.

'The lake?' he pressed.

She shouldn't have shown that picture. It was private property. It had been their safe place, the one where they'd kept people out, yet she'd waved that photograph around like it was her right. 'It all came to me one day when I was looking at it.'

'Why didn't you tell me?' he asked.

'I don't …' But she did know. 'It was such a touchy subject, especially at that house.'

'And you didn't trust me.'

No, she hadn't. At first. 'Not in the beginning.'

She swallowed past the rock in her throat. 'I went to Wolfe Manor looking for answers. I found them, but not the ones I expected. I was … I was hoping to find the money.'

'You moved in with me, Elena.'

She folded her arms over her chest. 'I didn't know if what I was doing had any merit, and I didn't want to hurt you.'

He'd gone to prison for the racket.

Her arms dropped limply at her sides. 'I'm sorry, Alex.'

His head snapped back. 'You're sorry?'

He came off the wall as if propelled. 'Elena, it's *brilliant*.'

Her lips parted. The way he'd just come at her reminded her of when she'd freed him from the locked bathroom, oh so long ago. His body was primed and his eyes were bright. Her body melted, and her mind went blank.

He raked a hand through his hair. It had gotten longer. 'It's genius.'

She spread both hands against the door behind her. Her brain had just tilted.

Breathing hard, he leaned into her. The lines of his cheekbones were like slashes across his handsome face.

'I can't do this right now,' she whispered. Adrenalin was pumping through her system. Once it ran its course, she'd be a puddle on the floor. She was exhausted, and she just needed to get through the day. If she thought about him or their relationship, she wouldn't make it.

'You have to. You just made a public disclosure. We need to get started on the paperwork as soon as possible.'

Her brow furrowed. 'What are you talking about?'

He jabbed a finger towards the room where the committee was still debating. 'That. Your research findings. We need to go talk to NYU's patenting department. Did they have you sign anything before you gave that talk? Have they started proceedings on protecting it?'

She stared at him, not comprehending.

His gaze slid over her face, and some of the tension drained from his body. He gave her a soft smile. 'Sorry, that was Ax coming out.'

Elena slumped against the door, letting it take all of her weight. She was so tired.

He stroked a curl of her hair. 'I'm not talking to you as your lover right now.'

Her heart jumped. Were they still lovers? She hoped things hadn't become too strained for them to fix.

'I'm talking to you as CEO of Wolfe Pack, a Fortune 100 company that wants to license your technology.'

'Wh–what?'

He sighed, but pulled his hand back. 'Sexy, compassionate and brainy.'

There were footsteps on the other side of the door, and he backed away from her. Scrambling away from the door, Elena pressed her hands to her cheeks. She knew they were flushed. When Dr Walters stuck his head in, it didn't matter.

Because she felt her blood drain right out her feet. So soon? It couldn't be good news. The committee had found a flaw.

A wide grin split the professor's beard in two. Juggling a folder of papers, he thrust out his hand. 'Congratulations, Elena. I mean, Dr Bardot.'

# Chapter Sixteen

The emotions of the day were starting to wear on Elena when they finally made it back to the penthouse. She couldn't believe it was over, that her studies were through at last. There was still the final official paperwork and ceremony, but she'd reached her goal. She hadn't known if that would ever happen. With all the drama and stress, it had become questionable.

The accusations and suspicions had beaten down her confidence. At the very heart of it, she hadn't been sure she was onto something, even though it had made sense to her. She couldn't even describe the sense of pride that had gone through her when the committee had declared that her research had merit.

Alex certainly thought there was something to it.

She rubbed her head as she sat down on the sofa. It had all been such a whirlwind. She hadn't expected him to show up at her dissertation defence, much less drag her down to the university's intellectual property office. She still didn't understand what was going on.

With this licensing agreement ... Or between them ...

She watched as he set her laptop on the coffee table. Contrary to her, he was bounding with energy. He took off his suit jacket and tossed it over the loveseat. She swallowed hard. If anything, he looked harder and leaner. She'd forgotten the intensity of his physical presence. He was so raw, so male.

She pressed her thighs together.

She hated sleeping alone. She'd hated tearing them apart the way she had, but things had gotten toxic. All-consuming. If she hadn't gotten out when she had, she would have drowned in them.

She tore her gaze away and clenched her hands together in her lap. She couldn't go back to that – not now, when she was just getting her feet underneath her.

'I need to show you something,' he said, moving to the bar.

She bit her lip. At least he was getting out of the apartment now. That was a step in the right direction. And he seemed driven again. Back in control. The NYU licensing associates had certainly been dazed when The Ax had strode in to their little closet of an office to start negotiating.

But had things really changed?

Her stomach dipped when he pulled out a stack of familiar spiral-bound notebooks from his briefcase.

There was a spark in his eye as he stood over her, holding the rainbow of paperwork. When he sat next to her, he was so close his shoulder brushed against hers and their thighs nestled together. She felt his muscles clench, and she couldn't stop her response.

She squirmed as warmth unfurled deep inside her.

'Did you look at these?' he asked, tackling the subject head on.

She wanted to cry. 'Yes. I was curious, but I didn't understand them – and I felt so guilty about spying I was sick.'

His chin dipped. 'I didn't feel right looking through your computer files, either.'

Her wet eyes snapped up to meet his gaze.

'There were too many files,' he said with a sigh. 'I didn't put it together until you did it for me at your dissertation.'

He opened the blue notebook and held it so she could see. 'This is the last year and a half of my life.'

She hesitantly touched the narrow-ruled paper. It still made zero sense to her. The pages were filled with gobble-dygook. His lips curled when she scrunched her nose, so he pulled out another notebook. At least she could read some of what was in it. The green notebook had comments in what she recognised as his tight, cropped handwriting.

Something about architecture and action scripts ... 'Were you coding in prison?' she asked.

'They wouldn't give me access to a computer, so I had to do it all by hand.'

She grimaced. There were pages upon pages of chicken scratching. Reams of them. Some lines had been crossed out while others had been circled for emphasis. Were all the notebooks like this? 'You've been transcribing all this?'

'Using it as more of a guide, really. I've been refactoring as I go and fixing things as the quality testers send them back.'

'Wolfe Pack is working on this.' She remembered the meeting in the conference room with all the department heads. And Professor Walters. 'This is Project Alpha Wolfe.'

He closed the notebook with care. 'I should have named it The Siren Project.'

She frowned. Her brain could only take in so much, and it had already done its work for the day.

For the month, actually.

Taking a deep breath, he spread his arm over the sofa behind her. Something twirled in Elena's chest when he began to play with her hair.

'We're a lot alike, you know,' he said.

Really? She'd never thought that. He was driven and aggressive. She was motivated, but quiet. Studious. But they'd meshed well.

She locked her ankles together. Very well.

The muscle in his jaw twitched. 'That Ponzi scheme that my grandfather and your father developed was an evil concoction. It nearly cut me off at the knees when I found out about it, but there was nothing I could do to protect anyone. The damage had already been done to the investors ... to the Wolfe family ... to you.'

His Adam's apple bobbed, and his fingers tangled in her hair.

'There was no avoiding it. No explaining it. No stopping it or turning it around. That nearly drove me crazy.'

She heard the rasp in his voice, and she laid her hand on his thigh. His muscles bunched, but she didn't pull back. His gaze met hers, and she could see right to his soul.

'When they put me in that cell, I knew I had to find a way to fill my time or I *would* lose it.'

She stroked his leg, hating to think of him being held down that way. The vision of those scratches on the closet door still made her want to howl.

He shook his head. 'I realised that the only way to settle matters in my own mind was to find a way to turn everything around. Power needed to be given back to investors. They needed financial software that could protect them. It's always been an elusive thing in the industry. Companies self-report. The SEC has become much more powerful, but not even it has the tools to detect the kind of activity our family members conducted. So I started building that tool – useless as it was at the time. There was only one problem.'

'No computer?'

'No *you*.'

She smiled gently. 'Alex, I'm glad I inspire you, but –'

He gave a short laugh. 'You inspire me in other ways, Siren.' His gaze touched on the necklace nestled between her breasts. 'What I needed at the time was your beautiful brain.'

She looked at the notebooks and then to her laptop on the table in front of them. Was there a connection? 'My research?'

He laid his hand over hers and threaded their fingers together. 'I had everything mapped out. I knew how the software would function. I even designed the user interface, but I kept banging into the same brick wall. I'm not an economist. I couldn't come up with the way to detect when conditions are questionable. That dizzying equation you had on slide eighteen of your presentation? That, baby, is the golden bullet.'

He tossed the notebooks onto the table, and they landed on top of her computer bag. Two combining.

Her weary brain finally started firing. 'My algorithm. You needed that to make your software work.'

'And I nearly fell off my chair when you handed it to me today on a silver platter.'

She twisted on the sofa, tucking her leg up underneath her. 'So all the time when I was in the lake house working on this ...'

345

'I was up in the manor coding my fingers off.'

The possibilities were making her pulse rush. 'So we ... we can help people.'

'The financial industry has been looking for something like this for a long time. People need to know if and when their money isn't safe so they can move it. With the combination of our innovations, we can put control back into investors' hands.' He shrugged. 'The SEC will probably be interested in it, too, but I think we'll have to charge them more. A *lot* more.'

After what the regulators had done to him, the way they'd gone through his life with a fine-toothed comb, she could understand why. 'People will actually buy this?'

'In droves.'

'But ...' Her thoughts were now flying by at light speed. No wonder he'd been so aggressive back in Dr Walters's office. 'Shouldn't we give it away? Seeing how ...'

His jaw tightened, his stubborn streak showing. 'I didn't get where I am today by giving things away. People will pay, and we will profit.'

She couldn't help it, she cringed. Her stomach actually flipped at the thought. The press would go rabid if they were to produce software that benefited again from their families' crimes. Hundreds of millions of dollars were still missing.

Seeing the look on her face, he caught her chin. 'What I

would like to do is donate a portion of the proceeds back to those who were robbed – starting with your mother.'

Pay people back.

The light bulb dawned inside her head with the brilliance of a beacon. He'd said that before. He'd talked about it as being the only way to get people off their backs. She knew how they hounded him. They went after him like rats in a sewer.

But ... 'Is this to improve your image? *Our* images?'

Sighing, he leaned his forehead against hers. 'It's to make us feel like we've done all we can. You and me. You were right. We can't make up for our families' mistakes. We need to live our own lives, no matter what people think.'

He looked at her almost cautiously. 'I'd like to collaborate with you on this.'

She cupped his bristled chin. It felt prickly and sexy. She'd thought of him once as being calloused and detached, but those were just protective mechanisms he'd built. His feelings went deep.

'I want to work with you, at the very least. I need more, but if that's all you can do, I'll take it.' He closed his eyes. 'I'm sorry I chased you away.'

'You were just trying to protect me.'

'Because I love you.' He opened those brilliant grey eyes, and they touched her at her core. 'I love you more than anything.'

'Alex,' she said, her voice breaking.

'Come back.' His breath brushed against her lips. 'I need you with me. I'll fix what needs fixing. I'll do whatever you say.'

'No, that's the problem.' She speared her fingers into his hair. 'We can't control one another. This has to be an equal partnership. We can be each other's protectors, but we can't close ourselves off from the world – no matter how much we'd both like that.'

'But we still have a chance?'

'Oh, Alex. Of course we do.' She rose up from the cushions onto her haunches. 'I told you I loved you. I meant that with every fibre of my being.'

Their mouths came together in a hungry, desperate lock.

Elena felt stripped to her bone. Her emotions were laid bare, but she didn't care. She'd missed him so much it hurt.

They clutched at each other, both wanting to touch but not wanting to let go. He tried pressing her into the sofa, but she came back at him with a fury. He always took the lead. She wanted to show him she was just as strong, that she could withstand whatever they had to face.

She climbed on top of him, and he rolled back into the cushions. The pencil skirt of her suit gave her little freedom to move, but it also heightened her urgency. She kissed him hungrily, sliding her tongue across his and nipping his bottom lip with her teeth.

She started unbuttoning his shirt, wanting to see his chiselled body. She needed to touch him, skin to skin.

'Elena,' he groaned as she spread the dress shirt wide and ran her hands down his chest.

He was hot and hard, almost too defined. He'd been pushing himself again, punishing himself in the gym. She splayed her hands wide across his six-pack and kissed all over his chest, trying to make it better. She could feel the vibrancy of his body. Feeling reckless, she stroked her tongue over his pounding heart.

His air sucked in. 'Don't leave me again.'

She continued on her downward path. His flesh was intoxicating. So warm and velvety. She traced the lines of the muscles of his corrugated abdomen, and his hands fisted in her hair. The sharp tug felt sexy, domineering even, but he was the one submitting to her.

She ran her fingernail along the line of his dress pants, bumping against one hipbone and then the other. His body rocked at the sensation.

'I'm right here,' she crooned.

She'd known she was hurting him when she left, but it had to be done.

Just like she had to make up for it now. Heat rushed through her. She knew what would make him feel better. After all, he'd done it for her – and had left her boneless and mindless.

'Your turn,' she whispered, catching the end of his

belt. He went still when she scooted down his body and knelt on the floor.

His chest heaved, the white shirt rising and falling as he watched her. His eyelids grew heavy as she pulled the belt through the buckle. She nestled more comfortably between his legs, and he spread them wider to pull her in. The position put her up close and personal with the growing bulge behind his zipper, the one she was toying with now.

'You don't have to,' he said, his voice like gravel.

Oh, yes, she did. 'I want to.'

She wanted to see him again, touch him and taste. She loved this part of him and how it could make her feel. She wanted him to experience the same bliss.

She caught the tab of his zipper, and her knuckles brushed against him. His hips bucked like a bronco ready to come out of the gate. He wasn't going to just lie there and take it. Her mouth began to water and the throbbing between her own legs heightened.

Slowly, she pulled the zipper down, careful not to catch him.

Glancing up through her lashes, she found him looking at her, eyes hooded and stark. Hunger burned from him, but he lay ready and waiting for her to take him.

She caught the band of his boxers and pulled them down. He obliged her, lifting his hips to let her do what she would. His gaze never left her face as she stripped him bare. The act was so intimate, so powerful. The material fell from her sensitised fingertips and made it no further than his thighs. They were thick and bunching, but that wasn't the part of him that captured all of her attention.

His erection was freed. Raring.

He was harder than she'd ever seen him, and, from her position on the floor in front of him, bigger. The pang at her core intensified and she felt dampness in her panties. Her body craved him like it craved air and water. Nourishment.

Reaching out, she ran her thumb along his staff from base to tip. His air hissed through his teeth and his erection strained upwards. His hips, though, ground into the cushions.

Power and security ran through Elena in equal measure.

Notorious and intimidating as he was, he was hers.

Settling in close, she pressed her lips to his bulbous tip.

'Christ,' he swore, his fists clenching at his hips.

As hard as he was, his flesh was unbelievably soft. She wrapped her hand around him and felt pulsations under her palm. She cupped her other hand underneath him and, finally, dropped her head.

His groan echoed through the room.

It encouraged her to continue. She wanted to show him her love and her desire. They could make this work if they joined forces as a team.

They had to take chances. Experience life and all its dips and thrills.

She took him inside her mouth and her tongue glided over him. His groan had turned into a steady sound and his hips began to twitch. She sucked him harder, taking him in deep and then pulling back. The sensation was exquisite for her, but torturous for him. She caressed his chest and felt his heart thudding like a racehorse's.

The stud wanted to be turned loose.

Closing her eyes, she took off the reins. Her hands worked him, rubbing and gently squeezing. Dropping her head, she began an insistent suction.

He jerked, pressing deeper into her mouth. She was surprised, but she relaxed her throat and took him. Reaching over his head, Alex caught at the cushions. His muscles flexed as his hips rolled.

'Look at you,' he growled. 'All professional and businesslike in that suit.'

What she was doing wasn't very businesslike at all.

His head rolled back and the ligaments in his throat pulled tight. 'So damn hot.'

He lost control then, and Elena loved it. She loved that she could do that to him, push one of the world's most feared business leaders over the edge, knowing that she'd catch him.

They moved together, his hips thrusting upwards and her head bobbing down. He took her mouth with authority, and she sucked him in deep. He was getting harder, impossibly thicker. She could feel the energy snapping all around them. He was trembling against her lips.

His hand cupped the back of her head, and the clip that held her hair loosened. The strands spilled forward, draping over his lap. They caressed his belly and his hips, and he let out a shout.

His body arched, locking in a chiselled pose. Warmth hit Elena's tongue and she lapped it up. The connection was hot and wet. Intimate and naughty. And so private it made her ache.

She needed this. She needed them. Together.

He finally sagged back onto the cushions. His eyes were narrow slits that glittered bright. He was still for a dangerous moment, and she saw the wolf lurking.

She let out an excited squeak when he pounced.

\* \* \*

Alex wanted more. He wanted all of her.

He followed her to the floor and manoeuvred her so that she was kneeling with her back to him. There was a rending sound as he yanked up the skinny black skirt.

'Ah,' she gasped.

'Katrina can fix it,' he growled.

He pulled the skirt all the way up to her waist, but stopped when he realised what he'd uncovered. He spread his hand wide over her bottom. The material didn't cover all of her curves, and it was snug tight. 'The leather?'

She moaned, and her bottom wiggled into his palm. 'I wanted to feel strong and confident.'

He slid his fingers under her panties and traced her curves to her hip. 'I see how these would do the trick.'

She squealed when he tugged the leather outwards and let it snap back into place. Reaching around her, he unbuttoned her jacket. Her hands were already there. Together, they worked it off. The expensive garment flew across the room, leaving her in only a sexy bra.

He cupped his hands over her breasts, lifted them even higher. It was a pretty picture, with his necklace settling deep within her cleavage. The paw print was like another touch of his upon her, one she accepted eagerly.

He used his weight to bend her over the sofa. The necklace dangled, but the bra held her breasts tightly.

It could stay.

'I need you,' he murmured into her ear.

'But you just ...'

He was already hard again. She'd been gone from his life for too long. He'd thought he'd learned about the intricacies of time during his stay at Otisville. He'd thought he'd understood how it could expand and contract, but he'd entered a time warp when she'd walked out his door. Seconds had turned to minutes. Minutes became hours. And days?

There had been too many.

Her skirt was hooked around her waist. He left it, too, going straight for the panties. He yanked them down. Her body jerked and her curves jiggled.

He stripped her and assumed the position behind her.

She liked it this way. He remembered how her body had clung to his, outside on the balcony of the manor.

Using his thumbs, he spread her delicate lips. She was pink and swollen, already wet and waiting for him. What she'd done had excited her, too.

He aligned himself and thrust.

She let out a cry of surprise that quickly slid into a moan of pleasure. He held himself deep, letting her become accustomed to the feel of him again, but she didn't need time. Her knees worked wider and her back curled. She pressed into him, and he groaned.

She was a tiny thing, but there was no doubt any more who had the upper hand.

He grasped her hips and began to rock. 'I love you,' he whispered.

He picked up the pace, thrusting harder. Her hands clawed at the cushions and latched onto a pillow.

'I love you,' she moaned right back.

She was so tight, so greedy, his control slipped another notch. There was no way he could last. She had him on a hair trigger already.

He felt himself tightening and he reached underneath

her. Jamming his hand between her body and the sofa, he approached her from the front. His fingers slipped through her wetness until he found the nub that brought her so much satisfaction.

He rubbed his fingers over it, and her body bowed. She gripped him tighter, and Alex felt himself starting to come. He pinched that delicate bud between his thumb and forefinger, and she shot to the front. Her body was clenching from head to toe as he spurted into her, and their combined pleasure heightened each other's.

Alex sagged over her, rent but replete. He'd already gone one round in the gym this morning. After going a second round with her, he'd be doing well if he could crawl to the bed.

In fact, he just might curl up on the sofa with her here.

The idea that he could do so made him happier than he could say.

'OK?' he whispered into her hair.

'Mmm. That was an even better graduation present.'

He turned her in his arms. They sat together, naked and dishevelled on the floor of his penthouse. The coffee table had gotten bumped aside, and his notebooks were spilled everywhere. The computer bag was balancing precariously on the edge.

Grunting, he leaned forward and pushed it so it was more secure.

She snuggled against him. 'It's OK. My boyfriend can fix those.'

He combed out the tangles in her hair. 'Boyfriend' sounded kind of silly for what he was to her, but he kind of liked it, too. It sounded innocent, like a fresh start.

He hugged her against his chest. 'Damn, Siren. We did it up good that time.'

'I missed you.'

He hooked her hair behind her ear. He'd missed her more. He had the deepest urge to take her away, to bundle her up and escape the world. It was an impulse he knew he couldn't follow any more.

'Where did you go?' he asked. 'I was worried about you.'

A curious look crossed her face. 'I was at the lake house.'

His neck whipped around so fast, he nearly got a crick. 'You went back to Bedford? James said he took you to the airport.'

She bit her lip and her flushed cheeks turned a little pinker. 'I took the helicopter. James picked me up.'

A laugh escaped him. It just bubbled up from out of nowhere. His people were more loyal to her than they were to him.

Then again, he'd ordered them to be.

'I hope that was OK,' she said.

He ran his hand down her back. It was more than

OK. She was half-dressed, tousled and sexier than ever. She could have anything she wanted when she looked at him that way. 'It's fine. Why do I get the feeling Leonard had some part in this?'

She traced circles on his chest. 'He and Marta have heard my presentation so many times they probably have it memorised.'

Alex shook his head. He trailed his fingers down to the necklace she still wore. She'd never really left him. She'd been at Wolfe Manor the entire time. She'd been busy making it a home.

'Did I ever say congratulations on your achievement, Dr Bardot?'

She smiled. 'I don't remember. It's been kind of a busy day.'

He gave her a fast kiss. 'Get ready for more, baby. I'm going to throw you the biggest graduation party ever.'

# Chapter Seventeen

The night of Elena's graduation party, Wolfe Manor sparkled like a jewel. The gates had been opened and visitors were welcomed from far and wide. White lights glimmered in the trees that lined the drive all the way from the main road to the house. It was lit up, too, with violet sashes adorning the necks of the wolf statues that guarded the front door.

The press had been allowed inside the gates to film the comings and goings of celebrities and power players. Their positions were strictly monitored and one who had tried to explore further had already been escorted from the premises by security. A chosen few from respected news organisations like *Time,Fortune* and *Entertainm ent Weekly* had been allowed access beyond the doors.

Caroline Woodward, unfortunately, had not been on the guest list.

Unbeknownst to Elena, the fourth floor of the manor housed a ballroom. The festivities were being held in the massive open space with gorgeous hardwood floors and French doors that opened onto the top-floor veranda. Women in gowns looked like princesses as they climbed the never-ending staircase out front. Friends and acquaintances mingled on the landings in between. Security had the rest of the house blocked off, and all doors, for once, were closed.

The sheer size of it all was still rather stunning. Anyone who was anyone had fought for an invitation. Wolfe Manor hadn't been open to the public in decades, and the party was the event of the season.

Elena stood at the head of the room in a casual receiving position. She'd greeted friends and strangers alike, and she was happy about that. She wanted Alex to get back to his old life.

The one he'd had before everything had come tumbling down around him ...

She gave him a soft wave, and he was finally able to escape his discussion with a congressman.

He kissed her temple.

'Are you having a good time?'

'The best.'

The event was being catered by Jean-Georges, some-what to the dismay of Marta. Instead, the cook had been given the honour of making the cake. It was stacked four tiers high and frosted in NYU's school colours. Matching purple-frosted cupcakes filled the rest of the table. Her mother had provided those.

Music was provided by a DJ, although several stars of the music industry were in attendance. Many of Alex's colleagues and upper-crust friends were starting to come out of society's tightly grained woodwork. The two of them had their supporters and their enemies. The press had split two ways. Half thought that the new software Wolfe Pack had in development was genius. The perfect way to salvage their reputations and make the best of a bad situation. As Elena had guessed, though, the other half thought it was a ploy, a way to make money hand over Ponzi fist.

That still irritated them, but she and Alex were finding ways to cope better with the bad attitudes. They could put up with a lot now that they were together.

She smiled when Dr Walters came up to shake her hand.

'Congratulations again.'

'Thank you, Professor.'

He shook his head and his wire-rimmed glasses wobbled on his skinny nose. 'When your young man here called me in to consult at Wolfe Pack, I really didn't have much to offer him. Little did I know that you had the answer. You'd shared bits and pieces of your work, but I didn't have the opportunity to see the full picture until your presentation.'

Alex looped an arm around her waist. 'It was a surprise to both of us, Professor.'

'A welcome one. This is setting some in the economics field on their ears.'

Elena bit her cheek. She was running into naysayers there, too. One thing was certain. People always had their opinions and they were willing to voice them. Loudly.

'Well, I'm happy to join the debate.' She gestured to the table full of cake. 'Please, enjoy yourself.'

She looked about the room. That was what she was enjoying most about the party. Dignitaries were mixed with Wolfe Pack developers. A group of her classmates was gathered around a Yankee pitcher, and a television actor was getting cosy with Jorge over in a dark corner.

'I had no idea this was up here,' she admitted. 'A ballroom.'

She thought they only existed in old stories.

Alex took a drink of his champagne. 'It hasn't been used in years, not since my parents were alive.'

She smoothed his lapel. 'Thank you for opening it up again for me.'

'I can't think of a better reason.'

He looked so sexy and mysterious in the tuxedo, she could hardly keep her hands off him. She'd already failed once in that regard, ripping it off him about an hour before guests were scheduled to arrive. A blush heated her cheeks, and she hooked her hair over her ear.

A big part of her couldn't wait to get him alone again. As much as she'd encouraged him to rejoin the world, she wasn't accustomed to having so many people around. She'd never been comfortable with the limelight, but it was a role she was going to have to get used to. If he had to attend society parties again, she was going to be at his side.

'Ms Bardot, hello.'

Elena spotted a familiar face. 'Dr Hoff, I'm so glad you made it.'

It was the veterinarian from the zoo. She looked fantastic all dressed up, with her hair in an up-do. The woman held out a present. 'I know these are supposed to go in the gift room, but I wanted to give it to you myself. It's from everyone at the Grey Wolf exhibit.'

'Oh, that's sweet.' Elena set her empty champagne glass on a passing waiter's tray. A few people near her turned at the sound of ripping paper. The gift was flat and rectangular. Elena could tell it was a picture, and she hoped it was of Siren. When she opened the box, tears dampened in her eyes. 'I love it.'

The veterinarian helped gather the torn pieces of paper so she could get a better look. The photograph was of more than just the wolf pup. It was a picture taken on the day the wolf exhibit had been dedicated – before things had gone so dreadfully wrong. There she was with Alex and the little black wolf pup. The shy little thing was snuggled up tight in her arms, but its head was tilted back to enjoy the scratching Alex was giving its ears. The photo was simple and sweet, and Elena cherished it.

'Thank you,' she said, giving the woman an impulsive hug.

'Thank you for inviting me.' The pretty blonde's face was animated as she looked around the room. 'I've never been to a fancy shindig like this.'

Elena laughed. 'Hockey players are on your left. Movie stars are to your right.'

The woman wiggled her eyebrows. 'Decisions, decisions.'

Like a phantom, Leonard appeared to take the framed photograph. 'How wonderful. Where would you like me to put it?'

The butler was attending as a guest, but he couldn't seem to help pitching in where he saw a need.

'Above the fireplace,' Alex decided.

'Excellent choice, sir. I'll make sure it's hung tonight.'

The partying and dancing continued late into the wee hours. Elena spent time with her mother, who was leaving in the morning. She danced with Alex and opened gifts. Most of all, she just celebrated the big turning points in her life.

There were so many of them.

Finally, she had to catch her breath. Alex found her some time later alone on the balcony.

'What am I going to do about you?' The nip in the air was biting, but the night was crystal clear. He took off his tuxedo and wrapped it around her shoulders. 'What does it take for you to put on a wrap?'

She tugged the jacket closer. It was still warm from his body heat. 'I could go find the hoodie.'

He chuckled and stood behind her. He settled his chin on her shoulder and braced his hands against the balcony railing. 'Don't give me ideas.'

She was wearing the daring little black dress he'd bought for her. It was a bold choice, but she knew she looked good in it. With the secret black lace lingerie she wore underneath, she felt good, too.

'What are you looking at?' he asked.

The view from up on high was spectacular. The fourth-floor balcony looked right down into the lake. With no wind, the water was like glass, reflecting the stars overhead. They were shining like a million bright pinpoints of light.

'It reminds me of the evening you came home, only then it was the sun reflecting off the water.'

He rubbed his chin against her shoulder. 'I remember, but I was too busy checking out the sexy little brunette gyrating on my dock.'

She smiled. She'd taken to doing her yoga in the gym. It was too cold to do it outside any more.

'What else is going on inside that head of yours?' he asked.

She shook her head. She didn't want to spoil the night. It had been close to perfect. 'Nothing.'

He pressed his face into her hair. 'I know you better than that, Siren.'

She sighed. 'Seeing all these wealthy people partying and enjoying themselves ... It makes me wonder ...'

'Wonder what?'

'Don't be angry.'

He leaned over further to look into her face. 'What's bothering you, Elena?'

She tilted her head back against his shoulder and looked at the sky. 'Is your grandfather out there somewhere, going to parties and throwing money around? Is he in a chalet on a mountaintop with a sherry in his hand?'

Alex blew out a long breath. 'Don't get yourself worked up over what-ifs.'

'I can't help it. After all you went through, after all *we* went through, it's just not fair.'

'Life's not fair, baby.'

'I just want to see justice served.' For the Ponzi scheme ... but maybe more for what Alex had gone through as a child ...

'It has been.'

Three words. Soft and clear.

Her heart dipped right into her stomach, and she went very still. 'Alex?'

He tensed. 'Damn it.'

He hadn't meant to let that slip.

Questions started flying through Elena's head at dizzying speed. There'd been so many harsh rumours. So many suppositions and lies. Most of them had been refuted.

366

Most ...

Except for the one Caroline Woodward had thrown at her that had hurt the most.

Her arms tightened around her waist. 'What are you saying?' she whispered.

A rough sound left his throat. Time passed, stretching out until the chill went through the jacket all the way to her bones. When he pressed his mouth against her ear, she felt like she was about to shatter.

'He's not enjoying any riches. He's dead.'

Her mind just stopped. 'You?'

'No. Not me.'

Her blood started moving again. The weight lifted off her chest, but her legs felt even more wobbly. She leaned back against him. Secure once again, her brain began clicking.

'Suicide?'

'No.'

'Then who?'

His hand left the marble railing and his arm wrapped around her waist.

It was then that she knew. There had been three people purportedly involved in the Ponzi scheme: Bartholomew Wolfe, Alex and ... her father.

The truth was like a punch in the gut, and she folded in half. Alex kept her on her feet, his body warm around hers and his face pressed into her hair.

'It wasn't intentional,' he said, loud enough for her ears only. 'It was an accident. My grandfather and your dad argued. It was when their scheme was starting to fall apart. You have to understand. My grandfather was an odious man. Rotten to his core. He'd already begun covering his trail so all evidence pointed at your father. Randolph felt trapped.'

'What did he do?' She could barely get the question out, but she had to know. 'Where did this happen?'

'Here, out front of the house. They fought and Randolph pushed the old man. My grandfather fell and hit his head on a rock. He didn't get back up.'

Off in the distance, a howl cut through the air. The sound was eerie and prophetic.

Alex held her tighter. 'It's a coyote.'

Others joined in, and the calls were long and mournful.

Elena couldn't bear to hear them. 'You were there? You saw it happen?'

'No.'

'Then how do you know? Who told you this?'

'Leonard.'

Her air choked off in her throat. She remembered her tense discussion with the butler in Bartholomew's room.

'He was there. He saw the whole thing.'

'But why didn't they call an ambulance or the authorities?'

'I wish they had,' Alex sighed. 'But apparently

368

Leonard's loyalty to your father outweighed that to my grandfather. Randolph convinced him he couldn't stand up to murder charges, that my grandfather had already framed him.'

Elena rubbed her hand over her face. It was all so terrible. 'Where's the body?' she whispered.

He nodded off in the distance. 'The family plot is at the northern end of the property. They buried him there.'

She shook her head, aghast. She'd known her father was selfish, but she hadn't known how deep it went. 'And my father just walked away?'

'No, baby.'

Again, it took a moment for it all to sink in.

'He went home and hanged himself,' she breathed.

Alex wrapped himself around her. 'In one day, everything turned sideways and the only person who was left to tell the story was Leonard. I couldn't say anything. That sweet old man is the reason I'm here. He's always protected me.'

Elena swallowed hard and a tear fell from her eyes. 'I know what your grandfather did to you,' she choked out. 'I ... I saw the closet doors.'

Alex went stiff behind her.

'You had to protect Leonard,' she whispered.

'Technically, it made me complicit,' Alex admitted. 'That's why I didn't put up a bigger fight against the insider-trading charges. But I've done my time.'

Off in the distance, the coyote howled again, making her tremble.

She folded her hand on top of his on her stomach. 'But the cost?'

'I prefer to look at the reward.'

She turned around and buried her face against his chest. He wrapped his arms around her and rubbed his cheek against her hair. 'You're the best thing that's ever happened to me, Elena. We might have started out in disgrace, but we're going to make this Bardot–Wolfe partnership work.'

'It makes me hurt to think of what you went through.'

'With the way it all turned out, I wouldn't change a thing.' He took a shuddering breath, and his voice went rough. 'I didn't want you to know. I tried to spare you this.'

Her hands bit into his back. 'Nobody can ever find out. We mustn't tell a soul, but the questions are going to continue.'

'I figure, in time, I'll have Bartholomew declared legally dead. The courts will have to sort it all out.'

She brushed the tears from her cheeks. 'How many skeletons can two families have?'

'Shhh, that's a question better left unasked.'

Another lonely howl cut through the night air. The sound made a shiver go down Elena's spine. It wasn't a wolf – she knew this wasn't their territory – but the timing was sinister.

'What if it's in our genes?' she whispered. 'What if it's just the way things are?'

'Then we'll have to start scandals of a different kind.'

She was shocked when he pressed a hard erection against her belly, and she looked quickly towards the ballroom.

He took the opportunity to nuzzle against her neck. 'In fact, with you in that dress, I've got ideas already.'

'Alex!'

His lips covered hers in a hot kiss. 'Forget the rest. Just remember I love you.'

She gave in and kissed him back. 'I love you, too.'

That was all that mattered, scandalous or not.

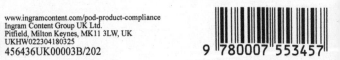